The
INTERIOR
ROOM

KERANA ANGELOVA

Accents Publishing and Publishing House SIGNS

Lexington, Kentucky • Burgas, Bulgaria • 2016

This book has been translated with financial support
from the National Culture Fund in Bulgaria.

Printed in the United States of America
© Accents Publishing
© Translator: Christopher Buxton
© Cover Artist: Nevena Angelova

ISBN: 978-1-936628-46-9
First Edition
Library of Congress Control Number: 2016962143
Accents Publishing is an independent press for brilliant voices. For a
catalog of current and upcoming titles, please visit us on the Web at
www.accents-publishing.com

The
INTERIOR ROOM

KERANA ANGELOVA

Translator's note:

This is a literary and not a literal translation of Kerana Angelova's masterpiece, set in the isolated and magical mountain area in South East Bulgaria, known as Stranzha. The world that the author projects is specific, timeless and out of time; the narrative moves between the present and versions of the past; voices speak directly to the reader and they mingle; characters are caught in dramatic dilemmas, their options are limited by their archetypical dimensions. Their conflicts play out against a pervasive but threatened natural environment.

The translator has chosen to remain faithful to the author's punctuation and free movement between past, present and future tenses. These reflect entirely the author's view of existence.

Inevitably some nuances of language cannot be translated. The name of one of the leading characters is Nebesna, which means literally: of the sky or heavenly. The Bulgarian word for log is also the word used for a human corpse. Malebi is a blancmange style sweet. The martenitza that adorns the sacrificial kid consists of red and white threads knotted together into a familiar shape. It symbolizes health and beauty and on the first of March they're pinned to the clothes of friends and family, as well as tied to animals and fruit trees. The festival of Kukeri involves men dressed in bizarre animal costumes, driving evil from their villages. On this day too, dogs are swung from ropes. Stranzha is famous too for its fire-walking.

～ *PROLOGUE* ～

IN WHICH ALL THE HEROES IN THIS NOVEL SPEAK TO THE READER FOR THE FIRST TIME ABOUT THEMSELVES, THEIR LIVES, THEIR DREAMS, THEIR DISASTERS, THEIR BRIGHT DAWNS AND THEIR DARK ABYSSES.

When I look at the golden edge of the dawn, I know that I am eternal. This conviction is as unshakable as the rock of the Great Papiya peak. I am young and my life lies ahead, so that I've lost the measure of life. Just the same with death. The most important thing I've learnt over time is, that we are alive and dead simultaneously from the moment of our birth. But this goes without saying. The graveyard at the eastern end of the village is paling out. The crosses are signals. Arms stretched out. Petrified wings. Under them lies someone who has embraced. Another someone who has dreamt of being a bird. Dusty snakes slither through the grass, their tongues darting like lightning. Larks sing in the corpse's ear, enraptured by life, telling its story. And below white skulls with black cavities, darkness crawls in the bone whistles. And instead of air to breathe – earth, baked, solid, heavy. Eh this is what I could stand least about death as a whole, it'll be tight for me in there, tight and heavy. Even so, I'm ready to accept it if I get the answer to one question, if they reply honestly and openly. What is beyond, so I know. Let's send one of the living there, who can see with their own eyes, then return after that and tell. Ignoramus, it's as if I'm sleeping on top of a poplar, as if I'm walking on the edge of an abyss and some all-powerful being is watching me from his hiding place, but he doesn't even offer me a finger. Eh that's my impression and I don't know whether to trust it entirely.

And life is small, but it's sufficient for me forever. I don't want much from it, all in all I want nothing. What comes, God, what comes: bright dawn, white fog, cold, heat…I'll still manage, don't you doubt it. Even so if I'm allowed to wish for something, it's love – that goes without saying. However, lifting my strong eyes towards the night sky, I'm horrified: so many stars, so much radiance, cold and proud, so many colours, I'm rocked by vertigo. What are we, against all this? Star dust. We're star mud. Who'll sit down and care about our pathetic lives, I don't know anyone like that, who cares for the little folk down here below. They say that God the merciful cares. Because he created us, for this reason, he carries the responsibility. Well but what if it's the other way round? What if he's created us to teach ourselves how to take on responsibility on our own? I suspect him of just such a business. He's shoved us out of the nest like swallow chicks, fly if you can, meaning, whether or not, save yourselves, in whatever way you please… We're life in life, fate in fate, a girl once told me and in her half blindness her look was heavenly. Then, I didn't understand what the point was, what she wanted to tell me, now I know: we're humans, we're on our own, we're seeking support. Here and now we're seeking it, we seldom think about afterwards. And that which we call afterwards, what is it. It is after but also before.

That is my feeling, however, I lack the words to define it. I see myself one moment flying between the stars like a stray feather, the sky is dark blue to black and desolation wafts from every direction. Stars and between them emptiness. And I'm wearing my dress as red as a poppy. When I got here, I don't remember, surely in a dream. However, I'm not dreaming, some kind of internal voice is telling me. Something else is happening to me, something similar to a dream, but much greater. Huge and empty is what is in it. If this emptiness around us is infinite, as everyone says, in different words, but the implication is one and the same, if this is it, it's horrifying. It gives me the shivers. If I'm to get back, I'll have to be very careful. I'm greedy for life, and that's harmful like every craving. Cautious, rational, danger-free living is what I'll choose from today onwards. Cold wafts from the other side of life, especially at night. That's why I've always waited for the morning impatiently, I'm the earliest riser of all over the whole mountain. Let's hope that this time too I can return on the morrow.

It's only when I look at the olden edge of the dawn, that I feel I am eternal. All my fears disappear like the night shadows of the trees. Questions have no need of answer and answers have no need of questions. Beneath my ribs jubilation surges. Dust from the sun has stuck to my nails and shines. Amidst the green foliage of the apple tree, under which I'm standing, apples glow. The yellow sunflower still sleeps with bowed head, in its broken pot, but once the dawn breaks, it'll stretch its thin neck and lift its face to the light. The only thing I think, when at last the dawn makes its slow royal way over the mountain ridge is that for this life, I am ready to give my life.

I've never had the feeling, like Antula, that I am eternal. Neither have I looked for any kind of meaning in life. I'm centuries old, but I don't remember looking for it. I just existed and that was enough for me. The world is made up like this and there's nothing to be done about it. Not one thought can change life's exit, isn't that so. Not even the weightiest. My thoughts have fallen silent. There's no worry. No questions. On the contrary. Day after night, night after day I hope to forget life. So I forget the one eyed lighthouse and my service on the shore as lighthouse keeper. So I forget the wrecks of ships and boats. And my women with their gilded round tummies. Women with icy fingers, with hair like straw or with cinnamon powder on their locks. Just forget them. Forget the split rifle butt. Hanging over the marine abyss, let me be turned into a deep sea fish. To fall, to fall, to fall through the void. Maybe even reach the bottom. To bury my head in the sand. To begin dreaming my fishy sandy dreams. Gradually to turn into a sea monster. In any case, I'm covered all over with sharp scales. In any case my eyes are empty. Unmoving in their sockets, full of salt crystals. In such eyes the world is not reflected. Such eyes don't remember. Isn't it so.

I am half blind, but in contrast to old man Ilya – I mean to say in contrast to Ilya – I maintain that my eyes remember everything that they've seen. The pear tree blossom like a cloud, eyes in the dark, like lit candles, bees like sunny scales, images on icons like real living faces… Myself I see as how I remember from the time when my sight was strong, there was such a time for a little while. Sometimes at night I lift my eyes to the sky and with my clapped out pupils I still manage to make out the stars. They palely twinkle and my soul is calmed by the glow I feel. I don't ask myself like Antula, what's out there, because somehow I know that. I know the desolation and I know the pain of desolation. And I know that which is in the pain. Its sting. I can't share it with anyone, it's as if I'm sworn not to reveal a world secret. That's why the secret is a secret, so it remains undisclosed. And only sometimes my sight begins to strengthen a hundredfold. It's just for a second. My half blindness pulls back: the sky is dark blue to black, the stars shine through, fearfully enlarged and bright, and between them, sleeves fanning out, a woman flies askew seeking her heavenly path. Her dress is purple-red and it throbs in warning. I know the woman is looking for the dawn, she's expecting to see the golden edge of the dawn. After her, the skirts of her dress sweep the sky and so resemble a solitary comet. Afterwards she suddenly disappears. The stars once more mist over and my exhausted eyelids cover my wasted vision. The longing for the invisible in me is a sickness, which I cure with solitude. I am alone, surrounded by life's secrets. In the inner room of my house solitude is lit up by an undetectable presence. It's as if someone is observing me surreptitiously and is ready every moment, when I am in need, to offer a supporting hand. Otherwise my life is marked by silence and half-darkness. The light that I imagine is so much stronger. And my half-dreamt, half-real worlds come alive with two gold eyes on their darkening horizon.

The woman with the silver tongue appears before me again. She opens her mouth wide and then I see: it's been torn out at the root. Her orifice is a sad hole. Her tongue lies in her lap, in the folds of her wine-red robe and it glistens like a curved brooch. A child with pitch black curls plays with the silver object.

Suddenly I remember that I've torn it out with my own hands and thrown it over my shoulder. Horror overcomes me. I show my hands to the woman so she sees how dried up they are, how crooked my fingers are, as though they're old roots, and they can't move. How ugly and guilty my hands are. That's when they took to shrivelling up, on that unforgettable day, when I did it for the last time, having climbed on top of the temple. When I tore out the tongue. Now I show these hands and blood drips from my heart. The child stares at them, his eyes at this moment are white and tender, as though he's looking inside, like my blind daughter. My hands begin to shake. The woman smiles. She takes the tongue from her lap, and places it in her mouth. Again she gapes and I see: a miracle, her tongue has come alive and flexible, it's moving.

The woman starts talking to me and as she utters words, they ring. Do not worry, Mavrud, nothing has happened. Didn't you see with your own eyes that nothing bad has happened. I kiss your weary hands, I will pardon them for human justice…And suddenly my hands warm up, fill with blood. They come alive. Incredulous I cross myself three times. And again her words ring out. Go now in strength and health and remember the ringing of my tongue. Remember it on the road, remember it on the mountain, woodsman and remember it in the inner room of your house. Let the meaning of the biblical parables return to you.

And I walk that hour towards my home, across the mountain, I come back after hundreds of days' exile and solitude and I feel as though the times have shifted and at last the time has come for the universal human truth.

The universal human truth? Does any truth exist beyond everything universal? As I think, I see that there is one thing over which folk on the earth ponder much more than everything else in this life. Their belief and unbelief in the existence of God, the creator of the visible and the invisible – maybe these are the things, which are the most universal, that's what I think, Cripple, Mavrud's son-in-law and, with God's approval, husband to his half blind but far-sighted daughter. If you deny God's existence, you don't make Him less powerful for all the rest, isn't that right? Still believing in Him renders every discussion of the question redundant, the faith of a person makes God unavoidable and available, and factual, I think. In an important sense, you get something at first sight untenable: to believe in God, means to create Him, just like He has created humanity. Eh, doesn't this suggest that a mutual creativity exists between humanity and its Father. I chose to believe in these things and that makes me free, but I am sure that whoever has chosen not to believe, has also gained freedom. Every choice is an opportunity to value freedom and reach it. This is what the universal human truth is for me and neither more nor less, it is called God of our human choice. From there the road onwards towards knowledge opens up – I believe in it and am ready to follow it, wherever it leads me. I strongly hope that it's in the Light, really, I strongly believe and hope.

My fur is prickly with the cold. My ears are sharpened. My eyes are piercing. I possess intuition, which is real knowledge. I stay in my own time and peek through a crack towards other times. In one of them they will imagine me. It's as though they'll call me by name. I'll squeeze myself through the time crack then and I'll stand in front of a tall locked door. It'll be biting winter, the wind will spin in spirals and my whimpering will be a baby's, thin and pitiful. A sad lonely infinity around and me in its midst. And then the door will open and two thin hands will take hold of me....

Numbing, hopeless rain pours down. The world slips away. The ground is saturated. The two of us, Vassilaki and Bethlehem, old incompatible humans, sit under the eaves of the shelter and look out for hours through the murky curtain of rain. We look and look, as though we'll discover something unseen. As though we'll meet people from the past or the future, or a wonder will spring up before our eyes and we'll be returned into two kids and we'll be amazed by life's first sweet path.

And we're a pair too, only that one of us will be present only for a little while in this book. We're the youngest of everyone who have introduced themselves so far, but what does it mean to be younger or older in this relative world. We were born in our time more than forty years ago in the shallow salty sea one after the other – just like white little dolphins. There's just ten minutes difference between us and it's not significant, as it's implied – the difference between folk isn't in the time between them. The difference drifts from the surroundings, locked up in their skull boxes. Anastas and I in fate's plan inhabit one and the same space: we grow easily in our thoughts, guessing, recognizing, anticipating each other. We are inseparable, however huge the distances are now between us, making those ten minutes meaningless. The natal cord between our two souls still intact and stretches painfully from time to time from one soul to the other. And then we know that we are both halves of one world, which we create, as we live, second by second.

When we were children, sometimes our eyes took on an unmeasured strength. It's hereditary – when the sunlight is especially bright, when it becomes blindingly white, it's as though we're in the heart of a lightning strike, in that second as though an X-ray eye pierces each other's body. That's when we see each other, we pierce each other: in the rib cage to the left a throbbing red heart like a big fruit, quivers, beats, contracts and releases its juices…That's when we began to quietly count every time our blood pulses coincided, not one beat was shorter or longer than the beat of the other heart.

Ten minutes younger, I, Anastasia, always felt protected by a big strong brother. Now I am really incurably alone on the shore and I seek firm ground. I sometimes grab hold of my hair, turning red from the blonde dye, and I tug, and I console myself now and at every time it's necessary, that I feel how the umbilical cord stretches out from the other side of the ocean, through four hundred and twenty minutes of time difference through all its twenty five thousand seconds. Through waters, dry land, continents, countries, climates, folk who live in them, just like a telephone wire it reaches a high frequency rescuing sound, so unexpected, that my hair stands on end, it spikes up over my head like yellow grass and I am shaking all over. I swing like a clock pendulum and begin too measure my internal time in the opposite direction to clock hands.

We come from different times but everyone is their every predecessor and successor. Every one of us.

~ *PART 1* ~

And how much the killing resembled work
....
Oh my Captain, it shouldn't have been…
Didn't we know, we're shooting at friends

Hristo Fotev

The Chinese mushroom was swelling and shrinking like a jellyfish. Miniature tentacles dropped from its stomach and then hid themselves again, bubbles erupted in the liquid surrounding it, the mushroom was breathing as if alive in a blue ringed plate. The old crone, Russa bent from time to time over the plate, strained her short sighted eyes, so as to see more clearly, and then pulled her head back as far as possible, as she was simultaneously long sighted and whatever she'd seen close to and at a distance, clearly didn't please her. She shook her head and spat surreptitiously into her bosom: it seemed to her that the mushroom jellyfish had bright blue eyes, tiny as pins, which suddenly jumped up, blew up like a frog and bore into hers. She rubbed her eyes, murmured angrily.

She approached the iconostasis and crossed herself. The candle flame swayed, as though someone invisible had blown at it. Russa murmured again and stroked the glassed tender hand of the Virgin. Under the glass, the paper, on which the icon had been photographed, had crumpled up from one end, black and smoky, because it had been burnt in a fire in 1930 as it was transported from Edirne, Thrace. The face of the Mother of God shone, like an elongated rain drop, her gaze bent downwards – in her lap she held her curly headed son and she was looking heavenwards over his head.

As soon as she had reverently touched the icy hand of the Mother of God, Russa calmed down. She approached the mother's bed, touched her hand and although she was frightened by the temperature which had reddened the young woman's skin, she mumbled soothingly, her s's and th's turning into f's.. Nuffink to be fcared of, you'll haff the baby today already. To add conviction, Russa grinned from ear to ear and her one and only front tooth shone in her mouth like a pearl in a huge oyster, scraped black. The mother-to-be paid her no attention, sunk in her fever as though in a swamp which she had no desire at all to leave. Her head was muzzy in gentle smooth slime – the air-born roots of the transparent marsh plants curled around her body, gently crawled around her neck, tightened with loving care so that her vision grew darker and more blessed because of her restricted access to oxygen. Marioo-Fino, clenf your teef, thiff biffneff iff ftill far off. Just call me Maria, the woman ordered through her teeth, Fina is the name from my other life.

Russa went to the bottom of the bed, where on a wooden chair to the side sat Maria's half blind mother. She bowed her head down over hers and mumbled in her ear, spit flew in every direction. When the muffroom openff up and fftretcheff, that'ff when ffe'll giff birff, now it' fftill early, there's fftill anoffer day to ffuffer. Good, God, holy Moffer off God! Thiff muffroom is fftill called God'ff flower, thatff itff name and it ffows ekffactly when the moffer'ff womb will open and ffrough its door the young born will come out.

Maria's mother wrung her hands, without uttering a sound. She looked like a big black crow. She silently chased something away from herself and her daughter's bed. Russa went again to the iconostasis and she writhed and in her deep prostrations, the thin pleat on her back jumped and twisted round like a frightened lizard. The mother-to-be suddenly uttered a strange sound, after that she turned over in the bed. She managed it very strangely, the two women froze in surprise; she suddenly threw herself up in the air and her bubbling body curved into an exquisite arc like a real white dolphin, which tries to dance in a dream. And again the same sound. From a dolphin that's dreaming. Unconsciously she'd freed herself from the swamp, she'd risen out of the sweet poison of its depths, she'd untangled herself from the snares of plants and their predatory roots at its bottom and now had escaped to the limitless smooth sea with no coast lines – similar to that which beat its waves and roared outside a hundred metres from her bed. But her sea was so much more real than that, so much more homelike and kind, amidst its caresses, you could happily curl into a stunning arc and she did it a few more times. After that she relaxed on her back and remained motionless, with her eyes closed, just her stomach was heaving in a storm.

And yet another day passed in this way. The woman just jerked a white torso like a dolphin drugged by fever, her shirt was sprinkled with drops of blood and they sparkled like forest strawberries on a snow field. At dusk, Russa looked at the blue earthenware plate and cried out to heaven: It's opened, the muffroom haff opened, the child will be born. Maria will giff birff. Maria really did part her thighs and barely bore the first spasm and gave an order through clenched teeth, it took them time to catch on. : fill Mattei's boat half way…fill it with water… Because apart from anything else, the long wait had made them lose all sense of anything in this world, the two women didn't object or ask why Maria wanted a boat full of water. They scooped water from the well with a bucket to fill it and mixed it with hot water from the pail which was boiling the whole time over a huge black stove outside under the awning. They filled Mattei's boat which showed up white in the falling dark by the thorn hedge, like a beached dolphin, and they fell silent.

Now bring a few buckets of sea water and pour it in.

And they did that. And for a little while they crossed their hands at Maria's bed and they looked into her closed eyes: through her tapering blue eyelids they could see how feverishly the eyes rotated in their sockets. With a monstrous strength she'd born all the spasms, while she waited for a little sea to be splashed into the boat. Help me to go there, she ordered, they hardly managed to get her out of the bed, shuffle her to the boat and stand her up. Maria slipped off her shirt, it slid over her shoulders and fell at her feet. They held her on both sides, lifted her, without looking at each other, shook their heads and only in their heads they crossed themselves, only in their imagination.

The mother-to-be carefully got her legs over and splashed into the water. She sat at the bottom of the boat and only her head could be seen. And she yelled, speaking out her pain. Maria sang it like a song without words. The water bubbled, pink foam appeared on the surface like delicate lace. Bubbles rose and something slippery, moving and white swirled through the water, began splashing there, whipped itself up and finally launched into a tall arc. The two old women could swear that they saw this with their own eyes: the snow white little dolphin twisted and dived again and Maria was swimming in the boat, at last she lifted her hands above the wa-ter – she was holding the naked body of a little boy. It was delicate and clean, his skin, washed from the gunk and the blood, shining like gold in the last rays of the setting sun. Old Russa took him and wrapped him in the sheet, which they'd prepared beforehand, and as she squeezed him to her breast, she watched in amazement as suddenly Maria thrashed about again and how again the song of her pain wound out. The water boiled and again something slip-pery, mobile and white twisted and arced up high, and another golden body glowed in the air. Maria caught it there straight away. She handed the little girl to her mother, she then rested in the water and for a long time did not move. They didn't dare call to her, or look after her, they left her to lie and come to herself.

When Maria got out of the boat and they dressed her and left her to lie in clean sheets, and left her two children one on each side, the village midwife Russa began to get her things together.

16

She looked one more time surreptitiously at the new mother's bed. It was dusk, but above the bed, light shone. Before putting the divine flower back in its special vinegar jar, the old woman peered at the blue earthenware plate: there the mushroom had lost its puff, looked dead with its stretched slimy body, exhausted too by Maria's long delivery.

The hill is blood red with poppies. They smell bitter, sometimes their smooth petals fly out towards the sea, another time in the opposite direction towards the forest close by. Anastasia is picking poppies. Anastas watches how she picks. Anastasia is as slender as a poppy stem, dressed in a scarlet dress with a green knitted jacket and she resembles a poppy from head to toe. She's lost in the meadow, she merges into it, she's swallowed. Anastas's hair is parted neatly with a wet comb, it's not yet dry and it shines in the sun. He sometimes puts his hands in his pockets and hisses through his teeth like a man, his spit plops on the grass like a frog. He is a whole ten minutes older than the girl. Anastas and Anastasia, Maria's little white dolphins. Twins born in Mattei's boat, in the sea of his boat. In the Maria's sea of her birth. The father is far away and unknown, he's just left his name – it's only a word. They read it and the two of them spell it out for ten years now. They spell out their father out loud, they consciously elongate and read out the two words over the ribs of the old boat M a t t e i   D o l p h i n . That was his nickname, his signal in this world was just so. He left through time, outside time, through the limitless sea into some new space – a few months after the moonlit night, in which the glowing little tails of thousands of shining stars moved through the milky way of Maria's womb …living seeds, elongated and frisky as tadpoles inside the fog and the warmth of the Milky way. Agile, determined, lively, life creators, of the future, beginning and continuation of the thousands of years of human times: the present catches the future and overtakes it and turns again into a more future time in Maria's womb, in her glowing fruited womb.

The morning after that night Mattei the Dolphin got up and wanted to wake up Maria. He felt pity for her sweet sleep, for the thin shining saliva running out of her half open mouth, for her bare arms swept over her head, but most of all for her glowing belly, which quivered on the bed. He left the yard, stood on the hill, looked at the sea. The waves were as gentle as women, today the fishermen's task would be easy. He went down to the port, walked on the sand, threw stones into the water. He sat on his favourite rock and gazed at the sea. The sun had not yet swum up, but a pink line lit up the horizon. And exactly from there, out from the line – some white eruptions, little spouts of foam. Two paths from there to here: they line up, lengthen, they become two paths of joy, of stormy trust, of friendship. Two snow white dedicated paths.

Mattei smiled and waved his hand. At last he cleared his throat, cleaned the roof of his mouth with his tongue and put his hands round his mouth. He trumpeted out his call and then squeaked. They answered him, like every time. They laughed. The dolphins were now close by, twenty metres from the shore. They played before his eyes, uncoiling their agile bodies into the air, their skin glistening in the first rays of the sun. It was the same pair, male and female: for several months up till now they'd turned up and greeted him with joy. The male was heavy but exceptionally agile, the female had a dark purple mark under her eye like a huge mole. With every meeting with the couple, Mattei discovered that the female's tummy had grown yet rounder, so that he finally realised: the female was pregnant. And now her tummy had grown even bigger than the previous time. The dolphins danced, and then uttered some tender words. This time they weren't aimed at Mattei, but exchanged between themselves and he was surprised. When other fishermen came down on the beach below, the dolphins turned away and swam further in, while they trumpeted their calls to each other. That's what happened every time. Mattei watched them, until they reached the horizon and behind their backs just white narrow wakes were left in which the water frothed and boiled.

Hey Dolphin, how are your sea-relatives, there was no malice in the men's teasing. He didn't answer. They climbed into their fishing boats, they called them rockets for short, entered the depths and the catch was really rich: garfish bluefish goby, big, shining living pieces of silver, which flowed from the nets into the baskets. Wealth, wealth, the fishermen gloated, all of them clenching Arda filter-less cigarettes in their teeth, thumbing their beards with pride and joy. Have your fun, but you have no idea what I've got up my sleeve for you lot, Captain Manolaki announced for the first time, a Greek from Akhtopol, broad, moustached, bearded. If you knew what a stew is boiling up, you'd not sleep tonight! Everyone will be driving a Moskvich car into their yard come autumn, I stand guarantee for my words and I sign off on them. And Manolaki drew his ministry signature in the air, everyone saw how his hand swept an enormous M with a lengthy tail. In the late afternoon he sent two or three men to set nets right out to sea. The fishing boat got as far as the horizon, from the shore you could see how the men bustled about, tiny as herring gulls, how they bent over the rails and waved at each other. Mattei watched them from the window of his house and fear formed a ball under his left side ribs.

Show me how the dolphins sing, Anastasia lifts her head. She's stuck an enormous poppy behind her ear and she smiles brightly. Sing to me like a dolphin, Anastas. Anastas grows serious. He clears his throat, clears the roof of his mouth with his tongue. He listens to himself a long time. A thin keening sound, squeaking from deep down inside. Dolphin language is special: cheeping, short and long sounds like the Morse code: like electric impulses in the throat, like the trilling of strange birds: lower, higher, it's as if they fuse into separate words. Up till now the boy could only observe them, he hasn't yet learnt to decipher this language. Anastasia claps her hands, jumps up, tears the poppy bunch and spills the petals. And why can't I do it, isn't Mattei the Dolphin my father as well? Why don't I speak dolphin? Silly, so what if our father is Mattei the Dolphin, he was a human. He was called that because he loved dolphins. If you want to know, I don't understand dolphin, I just look at them. But still at some time I'll learn it, I promise you. But me, the little girl continues to insist, I mean, can I do nothing in this world, Anastas?… Don't you worry, you'll be granted something else to learn, as you want it so strongly. Anastas puts his hand on Anastasia's shoulder, she angrily pushes it off and his arm falls. Didn't Grannie tell you, that we…that Mum…that we were born like dolphins? In a small sea, made especially for us, in our Dad Mattei's boat. Anastas is amazed, his Grannie has forgotten to tell him the story of their birth, and his mother Maria doesn't like talking, just keeps quiet and watches the sea. If that's the case, the boy voiced his doubt, if it's as you say, there's no way I'll not learn dolphin. I am sure, just like we two are twins, Anastas and Anastasia, so it's certain that I'll learn dolphin language… And me too, I'll learn something that you can't, it's absolutely certain Anastas! I don't know exactly what, but it'll be better than your dolphin, the little girl stamps her foot, and then she bends down and begins again to gather poppies. The boy sits to one side and listens far into the sea.

Mattei the Dolphin was sitting on the cliff and listening far into the sea. It was very late in the afternoon, the dolphins rarely came at this time, but now the man really hoped to they would feel his sorrow, gained from who knows where, to hear his summoning plea. He cupped his hands to his mouth and the rounded squeaking vibrated over the water's calm surface. And they came.

He saw from afar how they swam quickly, as if life or death: In the moonlight, their backs shone, they arced, or stood straight up on their tails, they cleaved the moon road. At the beginning their speech this time resembled baby goo-gooing, but after that it turned throatier… It wasn't like it was before. It was more clipped, deeper, the sound frequencies were higher. The dolphins didn't clap, and they didn't dance, they didn't convey wild joy. For the first time, since they'd got to know Mattei, they were thoughtful. The man felt this and also strained himself. And so in a second it seemed to him that he recognised words. He couldn't believe his ears. The noises which continued to emerge from deep inside the animals, were turned into an echo in his brain. They throbbed strangely, like magnetic tremors, they flashed like thin forked lightning. His head swelled like a huge electric light bulb, in which glowing filaments quiver and tinkle, flickering in short and longer impulses. In the end they formed thoughts, as though articulated out loud: Help, if you can, if you can, help! And without realising it, the man cried out, he screamed in his normal human voice: What's up, tell me what I have to do, tell me… The Dolphins fell silent, after that they repeated: If you can… They turned around and plunged out to sea, right along the moon road. Wrapped up in himself, Mattei climbed up the beach.

The next morning Manolaki divided his people. In one group Mattei and two others were to fish near Maslen Point; with the other boats Manolaki and the majority of the fishermen would go further out, over the horizon. For turbot – this was Manolaki's limited explanation. We'll hunt bottom feeding fish this time. At their parting he wished him good luck, as he avoided looking into Mattei's eyes. And they set to work. And at the end of the day what sort of soap can you get from dolphin fat, I can't imagine. The fisherman who along with Mattei, was dragging the net into the boat, said this and spat his Arda fag end into the sea. As if there aren't enough pigs on this earth for soap so now we're going to kill dolphins…I mean soap from fish is going to stink, phew! Unless they perfume it… Mattei dropped his end of the net on the floor, fish poured out in all directions, slapping their tails with glaring wild eyes. What soap, what fat, he grabbed the man by the jacket and shook him hard. Hey take it easy man, the other pulled back, it's not me who's thought this up… It's state business, orders from on high, to hunt dolphins for their fat. That's why Manolaki is out there, they even prepared the nets last night.

Mattei didn't remember how they brought in the catch and how they got back to the shore, nor how he waited for Manolaki's group. He only saw that the baskets were empty and spotted the sour expression on the Greek's face and understood that they'd had no luck that day. And the rest were in a poor mood. The way things are going, forget about the Moskvich, I won't be able to buy a buggy for my son next year. See, you don't make promises in advance, snapped one of Manolaki's band and the Greek tried to calm him down. Eh what do you want the first time, dolphins aren't stupid beasts – we've got to wait a bit more to catch them… Mattei threw himself forward and fixed his hands round Manolaki's throat, you're a beast, you are, in no time you'll start killing folk this way. So you melt them down into soap. That's why you'll be the first to be thrown into the pot… you're such a fat-guts, we'll make a whole basket of soap out of you, Captain Manolaki! The others got involved and tore him off the fat man's throat and Mattei lurched off to clamber over the beach, blinded by hatred and fear. When one evening Manolaki's crew came back with the first dolphins, Mattei grabbed the Captain's sleeve. They thought he was going to assault him again and they stood alert, but in his rancour he just spat out short words: I'm leaving, going private. I don't work with murderers!

And Mattei turned his back on everyone and with his head held high he climbed up the beach and went home. He lay on the bed, burrowing his head into Maria's swelling warm tummy and stayed there a long time.

Look what a little egg I found, Anastasia holds it in her hand, opens it up before Anastas's face and he warns her to be careful, not to break it, that's a lark's egg. You can tell it's a larks egg by the spots, look how they're grey or olive in colour, they look like a quail's, but a quail's egg is light brown with dark brown marks and spots.

Put it back now where you found it... The young girl reluctantly obeys, goes to the nearby bush, pushes her bare hand in and leaves the egg in the nest, which the lark has made from bindweed, dodder and yarrow. She comes back, sits by Anastas and burrows her head in her knees. She doesn't speak a long time, such a long time, that he's concerned, he nudges her: What's the big deal, didn't you put it back... You don't know, Anastas, what a bad thing I did this day...and the other day...and the other day. I want to die, I want to die, Anastasia begins to thrash around, she jumps up and rushes straight through the poppies down the hill towards the sea. Anastas runs after her.

By the very edge of the water, the girl crosses her legs, falls and scrabbles with her fingers. She throws sand, dry veils of grit arc over her head and fall behind her back. Anastas squats down by her head. At this moment they hear from the sea's depth a trumpeted call, two bright haired heads rise from the sand, Anastas and Anastasia, head by head, smile by smile: Dolphins, that's the dolphins! Anastas cups his hands round his mouth and answers in shortened rounded shrieks.

In shortened rounded shrieks Mattei called them but with no success. His dolphins had gone somewhere else. To other shores perhaps, to foreign, faraway and safe seas. He went home, put on his wedding suit of grey gabardine and combed his long tangled hair with a wet comb. He stroked Maria's tummy and set off to the town on foot. The woman stood to watch her husband's back till it shrank in the distance into a grey dot. He returned late in the afternoon. He was like a rain-cloud – there were whaling fleets, they were fishing bonito and every other kind of fish, so how were dolphins different, what was so special with them... I told them that they could talk, that they were something like humans in the water. They laughed and sent me away. You're not seeing mermaids, Mattei, sea women with bare tits and seaweed hair, it's not them you're talking with, so you think you're hearing dolphin talk, one of them shouted after me, giggling like a sissy. Matteo, he shouted, with a mermaid you can only get oral, there's no other way, make sure your wife doesn't find out or you'll get a bad name…. Maria laid her hand on his shoulder, and stroked it with the tips of her fingers. And sighed.

The little girl sighs. She's standing in front of the mirror and she's gazing at herself with frightened eyes. Her eyes have increased in size, clear as dewdrops, which drip from the eaves this day after the great summer rain dawn downpour. Her mouth quivers, even though she's pursed her plump lips tight and now they are fixed into a thin pale line. She stands transfixed by her mirror face, and then she opened her mouth wide. She peered into the moist pink cavity, the roof of her mouth is swollen, her tonsils are juicy, with reddened arcs. She can't see any deeper, however much she tries to pull her mouth open. Her mouth splits at the corners and at last she closes it. She feels the exhaustion of her face muscles and rubs them. She searches out her throat with her fingers and freezes. She feels the pulsations, then quivering, the spasm of the thing that she has been trying to control in there. Her vocal cords swell and shrink as though alive. They swell up, grow bigger and her eyes, they'll be scared out of their sockets. Anastasia jumps up, knocks over the chair, rushes outside, Anastas, help, help, Anastas, through the poppy field, down the steep incline, through the wet sand, towards the shore where her brother sits on top of a black rock and looks out to sea… She runs, she waves her hands, she trips and falls and gets up…

After the downpour, the sea is wild, the waves crash thunderously and the noise they raise is indescribable, so that for the moment the boy can't understand what his sister is screaming. With bulging eyes and mouth open wide, she runs towards him, her hair streaming, waving her hands, trembling and squirming. Anastas gets down on the sand, grabs her elbow and leads her up. On the hill the roar of the waves doesn't deafen them. They sit amidst the poppies. Anastasia opens her mouth wide and points her finger inside. You're sick, your tonsils are swollen, says the boy. The little girl makes an even more impatient sign, to contradict his supposition. It's not that, it's not that, it's something else. The horror in her eyes is so real that Anastas impulsively hugs her and begins to stroke her to calm her down: It's nothing, it's nothing, it's nothing.

It's something, says his sister, suddenly come to herself. It is something, Anastas. My throat is full of skylarks.

…At dusk, the skylarks were still singing up on the hill and the dew on the grass tips resembled Maria's tears, when she sometimes cried for joy. Maria's tears, the dew, the rain, which spread its grey nets over little house, the surrounding sea, which rose and fell in its bitter salt breathing, the sky above them like the dome of a huge blue parachute… all this is great and there's so much freedom in it, as though destiny itself has fingered this place, this sky and this sea, and this woman: Here, Mattei, here you're free to live your life as you think you have to live it. You have complete freedom to live the life of your choosing. I am your way, but you are free but you're free to carve out the paths that lead to it.

And Mattei the Dolphin, descended by one of his paths. The sea met him with necklaces of thick froth, with the smell of sea-weeds and mussel shells thrown up during the night, overgrown thick with sea grass and sandy tussocks, He untied the boat, pushed it into the sea. He hauled himself in and rowed towards the place. He would wait there, he wanted to see with his own eyes. And to stop them. To explain to them calmly and patiently that this could not be right. This could not be right. On the horizon the sun was just rising. A school of dolphins jumped up into the very heart of the dawn: a score of big animals, male and female, flew off and there was so much freedom in their jumping, in their diving, in their splashing of tails, and the exquisite arcs of their smooth wet pol-ished bodies. His pair however were not amongst the school. Mat-tei dropped his oars, stopped to watch their dance and he sighed and his face darkened: they were like children, they believed in the sea and its blue depths, in the turquoise water, and in the dawns and sunsets, in Mattei, in Maria, in the future children and in all the folk on this shore. The man knew that this was how it was and how it should be. He went further out and the dolphins met him with a choir of squeaking song.

When the launches approached, the man stood up in the boat. He waited for them standing upright. The fisherman looked at him, but when the launches got really close, they simultaneously shifted their eyes from his face. They set to stretching the spiked nets – they went about in a circle, a very broad circle, very wide. They set the metal nets and circled the dolphins from afar, they dropped them and circled and the dolphins continued to jump in the dawn: the length of their arcing bodies glowed, they splashed with their tails and powerful spurts and blinding fountains of water erupted from them. They talked and sang animatedly, because freedom demands singing only. That's what they'd learnt in the deep water – freedom is great, blue, sparkling and the dolphins are her children. But the nets circled and sank into the rocking water, they swung beautiful-ly, simultaneously rapacious and tender.

Mattei stood upright in his boat and watched. The circle of bobbing nets around the dolphins closed. The animals remained in the middle of the enclosed sea, the water beneath them boiled from their dance of wild joy. Now they'd tighten the nets, but how would they draw them out, there were so many dolphins, five fish-ermen could not manage it and Mattei sighed in relief. They'd try and they'd release them. There was no other way. He looked at the animals, trying to make out whether his dolphins were not there. And while he was staring, rifles and ordinary carbines began pop-ping, gun-smoke drifted towards the boat, Mother of God, ripped out of Mattei, what are they doing, what are they doing, are you crazy, have you gone mad, stop at once, you crazy fucking mothers, stop, I tell you! The fishermen fretted on deck. With hooks fastened to a primitive winch, they began to catch the dead animals and haul them up. The water was dyed in blood, like dawn, like sunset, like a sky gone mad, like something that Mattei had not seen up till now, or that he thought he could see. The dolphins turned up their stomachs, some still slapped their tails, one was unharmed and crashed powerfully into the nets. Mattei did not wait to see what would happen later, he sat back in the boat, turned and rowed at full speed towards the shore. He rowed like a mad man and bitter tears ran from his eyes and mixed with the spray of sea water, which flew up from the oars.

Bitter tears are flowing from Anastasia's eyes, they're furrowing her cheeks and drying into white paths of salt. My throat is full of skylarks, she repeats. Anastas shakes his head, nudges her laughing, come on now, come on, what are you thinking up, you want to act a play for me. Feel it, she says, just feel it. He doesn't want to feel, Anastasia grabs his hand in hers and puts it to her throat. The boy feels how something is throbbing, it's swelling and shrinking and moving… It's from your crying, you'll break your muscles, do you see, when you don't shut up. Anastasia doesn't listen to him. Those are the skylarks, that day, and the day before and the day before that I gulped skylark eggs. I pricked them with a blackberry thorn and I drank them. Anastas, didn't Grannie say that quails' eggs are good for the blood, so kids grow up strong and clever and I thought that they were quails, but you said they were skylark eggs… their spots were grey and now I realise that the little birds have hatched in me. In the warmth of my throat, it's full of skylarks, don't you feel them?

Anastas is scared. He summons the strength to scold Anastasia but he's thwarted by fear and he has to pull himself together. He nudges her harder, it wasn't a skylark's egg, it was a quail's. I lied to you, Anastasia…As he is searching for words, the boy freezes appalled on the spot. The girl stands up, grabs her throat in her hand and her eyes become slits. Her face is pale from effort, her eyelids cloak her eyes and her face is a horrifying sight, it suddenly becomes alien and adult, from the horror experienced and the expected wonder. It ages in years, in centuries – as though an invisible spider has woven a net of wrinkles above her, and spread it over her smooth forehead and it's folded in waves. That's how Anastasia will suffer every time when there's a reason, and often when there is none. She'll turn older from atavistic fears, of pain, of love, so immense, that that they'll surpass her own measure of human feeling. And also from insult, from measureless longing, from everything beyond her slight awareness of the cosmic energies, which put folk in a spin, and render them simultaneously weak and strong, crushing them with age one second, and with youth the next – because of the vortices of all the magnetic, electric, radiating, ultraviolet, infrared and every other kind of alpha, beta, gamma rays, which pierce human brains with bright red, blinding yellow, blue, violet, until their skulls light up like torches. And there somewhere in all this colour whirlwind of her personal cosmos, as though enclosed just in itself in the skull case for seconds, her thought will flutter as with skylark wings and will try to fly outside, and it will manage in such a natural and simple way, it's as if there was no such thing there in her skull, as though it's filled only with a huge, blue, proud incomprehensible sky – the sort that folk's eyes recognise in moments of special awareness of belonging. And now the little girl squeezes her throat with her fingers and understands with some super-intuition, that she is alone, truly small and fragile, she is much more than everything seems to be.

They stood a long time like this, the pair of them: the brother transfixed by his sister's face, the sister transfixed by herself. And in the end a miracle happened – Anastasia's wrinkled skin stretched out, her cheeks glowed pink, her eyes sparkled, their irises lit up the colour of spring grass and over them her eyelids fluttered like dragonfly wings. The mouth that had been wizened by spasms, relaxed and a strange melody, at first shaky but very tender, spread over the girl. Through her and around her. It emerged from her every pore, through her skin, through the fontanelle which stretched and thinned, and her hair moved over her crown, parting like living grass and revealing a pulsating island of stretched skin. It beamed in this spot on her golden skull. Where did this melody originate, from so deep. Anastas could not work it out. As though an invisible skylark had joined strength with tremulous joy, and it was unwinding its bright trill. And then the little girl lifted her hand and pointed to her throat, and Anastas understood: this strange skylark song came from Anastasia's throat, but not just from there. It flowed through her open skull, bursting through the bleached wheat of Anastasia's hair, the melody billowed, golden and tender and throbbed in trembling short waves. And from the girl's little pulsating navel, there flowed a bright trilling, from the tips of her fingers came a curtain of light, from the pores of her delicate skin… like a golden radiance from inside outwards. From the inside outwards.

Mattei the Dolphin wrote many letters, five ink cartridges were used up in writing to the state. No answer. As he scratched diligently away with a squeaking old fashioned pen, one and the same picture appeared before his eyes. The bloody sea, the wire nets, the sunset and it bloody too, the dolphins with their heavy stomachs turned upwards and the only one alive amongst them, who was thrashing powerfully, in the fishermen's netted prison. And he changed this picture for another, also dark and cloudy: human brains like jellied mushrooms oozing out of the skulls split in half by shell fragments, writhing limbs separated from bodies, the bodies are dead but the arms and legs are still alive… Rolls of guts quiver amidst open stomachs or hang on the thorns and bushes round about, blood and excrement is dripping, and over the corpses the war blusters and bangs and pours death from the skies – heavy iron machines belch fire, their mother is crazy human invention, creating these planes, tanks, rocket launchers, rockets, automatics from the biggest to the smallest, down to the cylindrical heavy cartridges full of their tiny fruit, the cold round hazel nuts of death. With all this the human mind has rebelled against nature itself, against what's most valuable – against her creatures and against its own self, and this is its greatest madness. It's war, I've been at war and I confirm it, killing dolphins is war, Mattei wrote with a crooked pen and ink drops spattered and sank into the paper like blue blood. Only that the enemy is armed, the dolphins have no weapons, to be our equals. This is a massacre, genocide. This is fascism, greater than any other fascism on this earth, wrote Mattei. His pathos was the most natural human feeling at this moment and he didn't feel any shame, even though usually he didn't like raising his voice.

At last he stopped, nibbled his wooden pen, read through what he'd written and made careful corrections. He crossed out *Their mother is human invention* and wrote above it, *Their father*. He put down the pen, looked at the sleeping Maria and began silently to transmit his innermost thought. He just looked her in the face, in the eyes between her brows and the woman caught this thought in her dream. She tried to give him a sign, that she understood him, and she moved the fingers of her hand and he just smiled enough, isn't that so, Maria, God has given us so much freedom, we are in it, it embraces us from all around, doesn't it, the air is freedom, the sea and the sky, the dolphins and the birds, we just have to make our choice, to be like them – not to be more, not king over nature, choose freedom to be equal with everything else around. This also is freedom, the greatest as far as I'm concerned. And what's more Maria, freedom is so many things, and that's why I think freedom is the same as being alone against everyone, when you know you're right.

Mattei sent one of the letters to Manolaki, he pushed it through the door-slit in his fisherman's hut. The very same day the captain came and sat by Mattei on the hill meadow and looked at the sea as well. They'd looked at the sea all their lives, there wasn't anything else to look at in this place. Manolaki slowly opened a packet of Arda filter-less cigarettes, stuck it unlit in his lips and spoke: It's a job, like any other, Mattei, don't get so het up. The State has ordered that we do it, so that means we've got no choice. How did I make a choice, Manolaki, my choice to not have anything to do with this. If I have to, I'll stop having anything to do with the state too, a state like this doesn't interest me, when it doesn't read its citizens' letters… What kind of citizen are you, Mattei, you're a fisherman, same as though you're a soldier on the sea, don't you get it. When your country commands, you go in and do your stuff, like her soldier…If she tells you to kill dolphins, that means, we kill them and that's it. And stop writing letters here and there, so nothing happens to you. I'm giving you a friendly warning.

Mattei waved his hand. He didn't want to look at Manolaki in the eyes, he didn't want to talk with him anymore. He just said quietly and fiercely as if to himself: you live next to the sea and you cannot be free to say no… It's not given to everyone to live next to the sea, Manolaki.

Anastasia runs down the hill with arms outstretched, she can't stop through inertia and with legs folded she falls into the water. A gentle wave splashes her and she laughs, rubs her wet face and turns to face Anastas. The two of them set off on the sand, they dig in their bare feet and they leave long furrows, as if they're ploughing some golden crumbly field. The boy gives voice to his dolphin words and tries to catch their meaning. Anastasia, so as not to be left behind, pumps up her throat. Gentle wings fly around, the little one blows on them with her plump lips and they are worn smooth. That's from my skylarks, Anastas. Anastas stops for a moment, stays on the spot and a sudden thought cuts his forehead like a herring gull's wing. Do you know, Anastasia, that only a few years ago, the dolphins moved around in whole schools and were not at all scared by folk, coming right up close to the shore and that's how our father learnt dolphin language. I don't know how it's possible, dolphins emit high frequency sounds. These sounds meet barriers ahead, before dolphins get to them, so they protect them from crashing, because the noise comes back in fractions of a second. This is called echo-sounding. But our father really mastered dolphin, understood what the sea animals said to him. This is what I call sharing. In the end they began killing them and turned their blubber into soap, put it in their oil lamps, for night time lighting and used it for various other things, and their meat was the cheapest, they sold it for pennies in the market. That's why so few of these animals are left and the dolphins don't trust everyone… The boy was quoting from his favourite zoological textbook, in a rush, without looking at his sister. She stops, amazed, her skylark song stops. You're lying. You're lying Anastas. Anastas doesn't say anything more, he carries on ahead, but now he doesn't carelessly furrow the sand with his feet. He walks a long time, lost in thought. When he turns he sees that Anastasia has stopped a long way back. She's standing on the spot, holding her head in her hands and rocking it.

He goes back quietly, the little girl doesn't want to remove her hands from her eyes. I don't want to look, I don't want to. He carefully holds her below the elbows, pulls down her hands, bares her eyes. Lord, Anastasia's eyes, impulsively he covers them with his palm. He holds his hand over her eyes and feels how her eyeballs move in their sockets. At some point she pulls his hand away from her face herself. Her eyes are again the eyes of a little girl and they gleam unbearably: they should have been green from her birth, but they're blue as well from so much gazing at the sky and sea. She pulls her brother by his sleeve, come on let's play at freedom and she laughs. And Anastas laughs. And they begin playing freedom, that's what their game is called. They stretch out their arms and begin to rotate them round and round, at full strength faster and faster, the water spray soaks them and they laugh, the air, the sea the sky merge into a vertiginous glowing blue ring and they spin this way till Anastasia feels sick and she falls to the ground and begins to throw up straight into the sea, over its white loose lace – it seems to her, that she is suspended over the whole moving, powerfully breathing world of water and deep secrets, because freedom's become too much for her.

Out of the blue their mother Maria Fina arrives. She grabs them, drags them up. Her look is like a knife and her voice is like a hard edged stone, rolling from the one to the other and back again. Come here to Mum, my son and daughter, who's said that I've allowed you to play at freedom like in the theatre. It's enough that your father played at freedom. Up above the beach she forces them to sit and dumps them among the poppies. Who's told you that freedom exists. What is freedom, tell me as you're so open, how you understand it with your shallow skylark brains. What's freedom, I'm asking you. The sea, says Anastas. The sky says Anastasia. The dolphins, says the boy. The skylarks, answers the girl. They answer their mother in one voice and their mother laughs spitefully. She stretches out her hands and sinks her strong fingers into their fontanelles. She bashes them one against the other, turns their heads simultaneously to the left, towards the forest, towards the graveyard at its edge. And then she wrenched them back to look into her razor sharp eyes. When you have no free will to choose your death, when you're not free to choose its time or to put off death for ever, there is no freedom. It doesn't exist. Am I clear. As long as man hasn't the free will to choose his death, he isn't free. He's not free by design, by birth, by another's will. Am I clear. If someone gives us the right to die, only if we allow it, if someone allows man alone to choose life and death in this world, I myself will teach you about freedom. That's when Anastas calls out: This means that we'll never choose it. The mother comes to her senses, hugs their heads, and holds them to her bosom: I forbid you to think of these things. I forbid it.

Anastasia looks at her with wide eyes. Anastas rocks, stunned for a moment. His face is white as a sail: Why then… why then did you give birth to us as dolphins? And Anastasia pulls herself together, narrows her eyes, very carefully so they are not wounded by her mother's sharp gaze: my father chose his death on his own didn't he? Her eyes are tight, but she's looking at her mother straight in her face. Maria takes such a deep breath, that the air swells her lungs and she almost suffocates, because she doesn't think of releasing it. And Maria finally says with a whistling sigh: Your father Mattei the Dolphin did not choose death, is that clear. He had no time to choose whatever. Nor did he need to. Because the choice was in him. And it wasn't death.

Anastasia has stuck sellotape over her mouth. A transparent sticky tape over her curled lips right up to below her forehead. She didn't realise that she wasn't going to stop it this way – the song's remained in her and grown alarmingly inside instead of outside. Whatever that is in you, it seems like freedom, whatever Mum says. It seems like it and it's dangerous like this, it can scatter you like smithereens, whispers Anastas in her ear and she signs to him crazily with her eyes which begin to roll in their sockets. Unstick it, unstick the sellotape, Anastas. Anastas unsticks it, and then leaves a blue seashell in his sister's hand and she fixes it to her ear, and begins to listen to the sea from its mother-of-pearl depths.

Mattei was lying down and with his ear like a seashell, he was listening to the gurgling, sighing and quavering in Maria's tummy. I think they're two, you'll bear me two little dolphins, won't you Maria. Maria rummaged with her fingers, making partings in his thick hair and promised pensively: If you say so I'll bear you dolphins, Mattei. Just don't abandon me, just be with me, Mattei, I'll bear them for you. And at last Mattei got up and set out and turned back a few times. He took off in the early morning and never returned again.

His dolphins were in the bay. As he was coming down the path, he heard them and he was filled with a wild joy. He shouted, without realising it. In his human language he yelled: So you're alive, you're still alive! The male and female dolphins clapped with their tails and piped their welcome, and Mattei put his hands round his mouth. Squeaks emerged from his throat, as though he understood dolphin words suddenly on his own. In some impossible way, he thought that they were full of content. Maria Fina will bear me little dolphins, little dolphins are what Maria Fina will give birth to, Mattei proclaimed, and more than one thought quivered inside the words. As he gave the news about Maria, he warned the she-dolphin as well: Take care of your dolphin babies, watch out for the dolphin hunters! You're pregnant, look out for yourself… The Dolphins danced a little, the she-dolphin had grown very heavy and got tired and the animals released their arcing bodies more slowly than before, and swam out to sea.

They were fifty metres away when the launch puttered up. Mattei hadn't noticed them, he'd been lost on conversation or the men had taken pains for him not to notice them, that's why he saw the fishing boat only when its engine rumbled. They didn't even greet him, they all turned their backs at the same time. Mattei stood, and then untied his boat, pushed it into the water, jumped in and grabbed the oars. He rowed quickly, the launch was quite far ahead, from where he was. Mattei saw what a wide foaming wake it left and realised that Manolaki had increased his speed. They've seen that I'm following them and speeded up, the motherfucker.

His palms were bloody from the grip, this hadn't happened to him till now. For a second he dipped his arms up to the elbows in salt water, then grabbed the oars again. The distance reduced between him and Manolaki. He rowed with his heart in his throat, his neck muscles were close to snapping and when he lined his boat next to the belly of the launch, he saw that he'd come irretrievably late.

The male had turned belly up, his body still rocking on the surface of the water. The last bubbles of his breathing frothed about his body, the sea was dyed in blood. The she-dolphin was thrashing, the violet spot under her eye looked like a flower dissolved into wild horror. All around it seethed and boiled, the animal banged into the nets, tried to escape under the water, but got tangled in the mesh below. The nets were metal spiked, and she rose to the surface again, uttering mad noises – of horror, of pleading, and of wild panic. Stop, screamed Mattei, she's pregnant, stop, I'm talking to you. I won't allow it!

The men above were lifting their rifles, and they didn't hear, they didn't want to hear what the fisherman was shouting from his boat. Manolaki was first to fire but he missed. The she dolphin sang some crazy song. The noises ricocheted through the frothing ball of blood, water, seaweed and jellyfish. The gun barrels glinted in the sun, the first rays sparkled joyfully on the muzzles. At the same time, seconds before the shots, Mattei got up on the edge of a board, his body curved into an arc and he dived into the bubbling bloody sea with the dolphin.

Class mammal, order Cetaecians, family Dolphins. Common Dolphin, Delphinus delphis. Its body is a spindly shape. Its mouth is lengthened into a beak. Its upper jaw has 39-53 teeth. Its length 160 – 219 cm. Its back is dark, its flanks are grey with white markings…Its stomach is white. In the Black Sea it is encountered across the whole area. It forms large schools of 100-200, sometimes 2500-3000 even up to 5000 individuals in one square mile.

Anastas stops reading from his Zoology 8th class textbook, squeezed his palms over his ears and tries to mute the chirping, the squeaking, the piping – he tries to mute the whole dolphin choir of high frequency sounds but does not succeed. They sound in his ears and they are not now ordinary ears: through their conch like funnels enters the sound of waves, an unbearable undulating sea swells up and in its foaming waters, a whole school of dolphins is jumping and arcing. Their white bellies shine like snow drifts. The dolphins are talking, piping cutely, the adults sometimes exchanging tender words, and a thousand little dolphins goo-goo from the interior, they cuddle on to the bellies of their parents and they try to take full part in the celebration of squeaking joy, in the frenetic excitement of the dolphin fiesta, which the school has set up. Anastas narrows his eyes, to see better: the sea froths and boils, an unprecedented sight, indescribable, his father Mattei's dolphins are there. The she-dolphin with the violet spot under her eye is looking after several dolphin babies, she strokes their bellies with her sharp beak and tickles them, she helps them launch a higher arc, all the more exquisite. The male dolphin encourages them from the side with a trumpeting sound. Anastas thinks amazed: weren't they supposed to have killed them, those guys from the launch, with rifles, didn't they kill my father Mattei as well, by accident, they said, they didn't want to kill a human, only dolphins, didn't cloudy bloody seas flow from here to the end of the earth, because the waters of the seas and the oceans gather together, and all together they're an amniotic fluid, it's an undulating womb of all earthly life, and they killed straight into the womb…Didn't all this happen. Why did it happen, Anastas poses himself this question, but he has no time to seek an answer – at the same time something amazing happened and he gives in to everything, that is. With his body, capping the zoology textbook and frozen immobile over it, with the insides of that body, which is supposedly full at that moment with its separate organs but is somehow emptied of them – they're all incorporeal and hollow and filled with radiance, it's a hollow golden tunnel, and its end cannot be seen, and only what is happening at this second, fills him up to his impossible infinities.

And the chanting of the dolphins falls silent. All the five thousand dolphins fall silent and the sea grows calm, it withdraws through the shining tunnel of Anastas's body. It pulls back further out from its shores and at that moment in the moonlit night a voice is raised which can be seen from everywhere like a thin thread pulsating in blue. It emerges through the one miniature ear opening of an enormous grey-white dolphin, lying over the water at the centre of the bay's dolphin population. The voice pulsates, it rises crystal clear, as though emerging from the soul of some angel voiced heavenly being. The bay resounds like a church. Anastas is by now not sure whether this isn't really some angel...and at this moment he wakes up.

As he has been lying on his zoology textbook, he continues to listen to the song, and to dissolve into its golden bliss, his very self thinning out before his eyes. He sees from the side-lines how he's turning into a thin sparkling thread, tied somewhere at the other end of the space, which he's circling while listening to the singing. And now he continues to circle, tied to the end of the thread – with an ease, that hasn't suspected existed, he flies through all the solar systems, through all the galaxies, past their suns and stars... through the whole cosmos of this impossible dolphin angel song. He forgets that he's simply been lying thus over the textbook and is lying thus right up to when he hears a woman's voice announcing to the dear listeners that they've all been listening to an a capella performance of the Ivan Kukuzel Choir.

Anastas lifts his head and his cloudy eyes stare a long time at the radio transmitter on the wall, then he gathers his strength and sets to reading the lesson from the 8th class zoology textbook. He reads out loud and listens to the words' echo. *The number of the common dolphins in the Black Sea in 1965 compared with 1961 has dropped tenfold. The reason was the intense hunting with guns and steel nets. In 1966 a convention was ratified on the halting of dolphin hunting. This convention is renewed periodically. It is supposed that today in the Black Sea there live scarcely...*

Maria Fina made them sit round the table. She smoothed the torn edges of the plastic table cloth, she traced with a finger her garden of pink roses, without thorns, blue chrysanthemums and white carnations, faded by the hot bottoms of plates and sunlight, which came through the window in the afternoon and continuously shone on the table. After that cupped her hands and they resembled a boat according to Anastasia and a dolphin according to Anastas, but according to their Grannie these were the hands of a restless woman, who tried to give courage from one hand to the

38

other and back again, that's why she'd knitted her fingers in this way and their soft finger pads. No-one said anything out loud, the three of them looked at her hands, and somehow didn't dare look Maria in the eye, because today their look was as sharp as a knife, it happened like this sometimes and they knew, that when she looked like this, she had something fatally important to announce. While she was seeking how to start, Maria suddenly said in three words what she had to say to them, I'm getting married.

Her fingers separated, she put her hands on the table and stayed like that. She was waiting for their questions, but no-one asked anything at all.

In the evening she presented the man. They'd met him, as he was exercising on the beach after continuously driving his pickup, he used to turn up with it for the logging, afterwards distributing the wood to the coastal villages. Five years ago he'd seen Maria as she was weaving a fishing net, sitting in the yard in the shade of the fig tree, he'd seen her arms naked to the shoulders with their bulging agile muscles and caramel tan, he had met her gaze from under knitted brows, and he'd remembered her: the contrast between this weighty dark look and her fleeting white toothed smile, light and pearly, appearing the moment, she'd seen him duck behind the fence like a frightened boy, hiding his intrusive presence. He'd remembered this strange woman and her even more terrifying children, who were inseparable like most twins. As they loaded his truck in the logging camp in the mountain behind the village, he walked on the shore and saw the boy and girl running headlong, circling round each other with arms outstretched a long time and half fainting from exhaustion after that, lying on the sand and remaining motionless, until the air above their faces shimmered in some strange coloured haze. He'd seen Maria scolding them, bang their heads together, and point out the graveyard, surely because their father was lying there, commemorated in perpetuity, the fisherman Mattei the Dolphin, whom he'd heard the locals talk about.

He waited two or three hours for them to load the logs into his truck and the whole time the truck driver stayed on the shore and gazed furtively at net-maker's house with the hope of spotting her, or sat on some rock and pensively watched the youngsters' giddy games. One afternoon when the sun poured out its heat and Maria was again sitting in the yard under the fig tree, and her sinewy hands thrust the shuttle through the holes and the net was flung over her lap and her legs, the driver stood behind the fence, cleared his throat and called out a Good-day; he somehow survived her heavy stare, in the hopes of a bright smile, but this time her lips didn't relax, and on the contrary pursed into an unpleasant expression and the woman shrugged and angrily retorted with what was so good about it? The man tapped his feet on the spot, after that suddenly opened the gate and entered. Maria looked at him, dropping the shuttle on her lap. Close to, her eyes were suddenly blue, over one the eyelids fluttered like the wings of a big butterfly, the other didn't move. The woman felt his stare and explained: when I was little, they hit me in the left eye with a stick, from then on I don't see well through it. It's not obvious, observed the man. The net swung and its shadow made a carpet of delicate empty squares over the baked earth, which somehow pulsed in the heat between them. I want to buy nets, said the man, he took out a large handkerchief and wiped his brow and neck with it. Why, you're not a fisherman are you, Maria snapped, at last she removed her gaze from his face and continued to weave. I want to buy for a friend in Sozopol, he ordered some, when…when I told him about…the nets you weave.

The driver bought all the nets, which Maria had woven, one by one, every time, when through five summers, he came to load up wood; he had many fishermen friends on the coast and they'd all liked the first net he'd bought, he'd shown it off and they'd really approved.

Now the man sat at one end of the table and sweated in discomfort, and Maria didn't even try to help him. He took out a large orange handkerchief and wiped the sweat off his forehead. He carefully folded the handkerchief in one of his pockets, from the other he took out a handful of sweets, green and blue, and left them on the table. He rummaged in his pocket once again and put a marzipan in front of Anastasia and Anastas, I looked for "Cow" chocolate, but they didn't sell it in the general store, but these have gone soft in the heat so…His fingers were brown with the melted marzipan, he took out his handkerchief and set to wiping them. They watched him, no-one said anything and the grandmother, who at last caught on to the man's discomfort, suddenly tutted, that her lemonade was warm and she'd wondered what to treat the guest with, and as she got up from the table, she nudged her daughter Maria in the back. Maria got up and suggested a walk by the sea to the man.

Anastasia is in front, Anastas follows her and ploughs his feet in the hot sand. They walk a long way and reach a rocky shore. Anastasia stops, looking at the cliffs. It's here somewhere, the gap is narrow, we'll have to suck in our tummies to get through. Anastas also looks and somehow doesn't believe that what his sister had told him about the unknown place could be true. Here it is, the girl points out the secret entrance. The crack is very long from the top of the cliff to the ground, but it's really so narrow, that it's beyond belief for them to squeeze through. I've done it but I was two years younger; I was on my own and got terribly scared, I haven't shared this fear with you up to now, Anastasia says and takes a deep breath and holds it, then with an effort she squeezes herself and slips in there. Anastas tries to do the same, but he's bigger and doesn't succeed. He takes off his jacket, the girl urges him on from inside and her voice is muffled. The boy strips naked and this time he manages to squeeze into the crack, he rasps his shoulders and back and murmurs unhappily, you and your fantasies, not to be believed, but still I get caught up in them. He's met with semi-dark, in which blinding yellow spots are dancing in front of his eyes, because of the sudden change from light to dark. When at last he sees, he blinks strongly:

it's a cave hugely vaulted, their voices ring and their steps are like the steps of giants, the crunch of stones under their feet provoke a noise like a landslide. Here look, Anastasia points and Anastas sees, the whole inner space is filled with loose silvery lace, huge finely woven cobwebs, which wave their concentric circles, as if an invisible wind is blowing them out and in. In the middle of each web sits an enormous grey-brown spider, each as long as at least a foot; Impossible, the boy whispers, spiders are three centimetres at the most, the girl puts a warning finger to her lips. Anastas tries to count them, but gets mixed up, at any rate the spiders are more than a hundred, over their backs the big cross like marks stand out from afar, and they look like an army of crusaders from past times, who hang repellently and threateningly under the vault of the cave and from lack of anything else to do, have taken on practising the weaving profession. Their jaws to the front of their skull are so sharp and savage, that the boy begins to tremble. He knows that through them the spiders inject their poison into their victims' bodies. Some of the crusaders are weaving at the moment, their eight legs nimbly move and their webs get bigger, others watch for the deluded flies and hurl themselves upon them, kill them with their sharp poison, they pour digestive juices into them, after that they wrap their victims in the web and leave them. They carry on watching; at some point they return to the wrapped up fly and suck out its mushed up inside, with the help of their muscular suction. I want to tell you, that in its suction-stomach the food is used up a long time in portions, Anastasia continues to inform him in a whisper, she's taken the trouble to read all of this in the same zoological textbook and announces competently that this is called external digestion.

Anastas doesn't hear her words, he's fixed his eyes on the nearest web. He can't believe his eyes. The owner of the web, which because of its proximity, appears in a magnified length as if it's been afflicted with gigantism, has caught in its delicate lasso a strange creature. It looks like a dragon fly with transparent sky-blue wings, but just like the spiders in this cave it has gigantic proportions, longer than a foot. Its wings are a filigree cut across by thin exquisite lines, more light blue, almost silver, framed by a firm dark blue strip, which according to the rules of contrast strengthens the blue. Anastas however is shocked not so much by the beauty of these improbably enormous and at the same time defenceless delicate wings, as by the creature's eyes. Through the empty rectangles of the cobweb the head is seen, shaped like the head of a miniature girl, with a smooth cream face with high cheekbones and in the midst of this face – unbelievable bright purple eyes with long fluffy lashes; the eyes looked out with all the horror that any earthly creature is capable of feeling. Wonderful, horrified, almost human eyes, which forces a sharp hoarse cry out of Anastas. And Anastasia has seen the blue wings which flutter in the web, and is amazed how they can't get free of the web, so big are the wings, and the woven web is so thin. But the creature inside makes no effort to regain its freedom, it seems hypnotised by the stare of the spider, which hangs close by: a fixed stare, rounded, also furred in some strange way, no less poisonous than the inner juices of its brown predatory body, a hypnotically loving, cruel look, which has overcome the sparking blue creature in the web with terror, but also with some kind of tolerable sweetness. Anastas has already found a long stick, he'll tear the cobweb he whispers and he pokes it with the tip. He's extremely surprised: this isn't the usual delicate spider's lace that sticks to your face when you walk through it, without you noticing it; this cobweb is hard almost like mesh. I'll go for a knife, go out and wait for me outside the cave, Anastas orders, he grabs Anastasia by the hand and leads her to the crack. They suck in their stomachs, they become flat as boards they squeeze in and get out. The blinding daylight greets them, they shut their eyes, rub them, dazed they set out on the sand. The vision remains before their eyes of the innards of the hidden cave, and in its kind of secret workshop, the spiders silently and industriously weave their webs and the boy Anastas suspects that their purpose is not just to hunt their naïve victims, their purpose is a lot more savage, but the boy cannot decide what this could be, he just suspects it.

He returns in a little while with a knife with a long handle, he enters the cave with Anastasia again. The blue creature has become more sparkling in its mortal glory, which it feels along with horror. The boy lashes with the knife, the cobweb rings, it shakes, but it doesn't tear. He slashes a second time, this time the web gives way, a large hole appears and through it the creature somehow slips out. Confused, it begins to flutter its wings, then it flies wildly upwards, it returns again close to its prison, it circles it fluttering. The spider moves two legs, readies itself to jump over its prey, but the latter suddenly aims its vertical flight at the bright light which streams from the crack, it seems that it's escaped at last from the hypnotic love bond between executioner and victim.

And the twins hurry to escape through the crack, outside they shut their eyes again, and by the time their eyes get used to the bright day, the blue wings have flown almost a kilometre away. From here they seem to have shrunk, down to the actual size of the dragon flies they knew, and if it weren't for the cascades of blue sparks, which flow from under the wings, the boy and the girl could say that this was an ordinary dragonfly, which is flying towards the nearby mouth of the Veleka and flutters carefree.

…Maria Fina has taken off her black scarf. For the first time in fifteen years, her hair is free, wild and impervious to the wind, the sun, and the salt sea spray. One solitary silver thread hangs by her left temple and shines like a metal splinter. Her plump lips are pursed and the woman has not talked since they've walked on the beach. A thin wrinkle between her brows like a hint of heavenly lightning, which once seemed to have cut her high stretched forehead; darkening blue eyes and thick lids, spread out like a fan, the look from beneath them is strong, sharp and distant; a healthy, sunburnt neck, bronzed shoulders, and milky white skin, which was sometimes vis-

44

ible under the broad straps of a dark blue cotton dress. The driver looks furtively at her often. He's quiet too, he's said everything that can be said in a serious conversation between man and woman who think of living together. They've been walking a long time, they're far from the village, they've reached the mouth of the river and beyond, now they're returning. It's growing dark and the evening star begins to pulsate solitary in the sky. Without saying a word the woman, folds at the knees and sits in the cool sand. She sits and listens. The man sits too without reservation. They stay like this until the moon's path begins to rock the waters. I much prefer your second name, I'd like you to be called Fina. Don't even mention it, the woman snaps. The man stretches, leaves his hand on her rounded shoulder. It's like marble, cool, smooth and it doesn't move. The man slips down the strap, the white skin glows underneath. He leans and touches it with his lips. It has the taste of fig juice. His hand slips down the other shoulder strap, and then the whole dress falls right down over the shoulders, some seams split, burst. Maria's breasts appear white, he touches them and feels their weight, two dark moons around the nipples, a dimple like a star on one side. The man buries his face into the woman's bitter hair, his hands begin to roam her body, yet more feverishly, down her straight back, the hollow of her stomach, under her arms where the fig juice smells thickest and most thrilling. He looks into her face and for a second is amazed, because she's half closed her eyelids and hidden her gaze, he's suddenly felt helpless and somehow pitiable. The driver quickly moves his eyes away from there. Now things are easier for him. With insistent movements he tries to lay Maria into the hollows their bodies have made. For a moment he feels stiff resistance, but the woman quickly relaxes, The man takes her indifference for compliance and throws himself upon her body as if it were a tree whose fruit he has to harvest, before it's too late. His hands squash her breasts, he squeezes fig juice, he pushes down under, he pinches the round hard hemispheres, he tries in the end to part her thighs, but something is happening, something which the man in his hot arousal cannot understand; Maria's thighs, it's impossible, Maria's thighs cannot be separated one from the other, it's as though they're absent, it's really impossible, to the waist Maria is a woman, wonderful, marble, but below there's something missing, however much he searches with his hand, he can't find the warm spring of the womanly deep, it's completely missing, the slopes of her thighs are missing, the opening and the easing moisture, even though his fingers are entangled in the sharp undergrowth that surrounds the secret of womanly openings; more and more desperately he bumps his hardness into Maria's body, seeking the entrance to her womb, and as he fails, he seeks relief in the hollow of her damp stomach, he thrusts there and while he pours out the wet from his pulsating sore member, the man feels some kind of tail slapping out towards his legs, it sprays a veil of sand over their naked bodies, sand pours, fish scales glitter, their tiny stars glint and cover the lower half of Maria's body; whether this is moon-silver, cut into slivers on the sand, the man cannot understand, another thought crosses his mind and he moves back startled, he puts his hand over his eyes, he stays like this a long time. In that time the woman wipes off the stickiness from her stomach, gets up, and without saying a word, goes into the sea, by the moon path, from where she hears the quiet trumpeting of a solitary dolphin.

The man stands on the beach and waits for her to come out, to brush off the glittering droplets from her body and to set off with slow wide steps: her thighs spring, her thighs are tall, muscular, Maria is a woman, again she's a woman with a healthy, strong taut body and nothing is missing, nor is there anything unusual…

…Oh Maria-Fina says Mattei the dolphin. He thrust his fingers into the thick forest of her hair. He got lost in it. His nostrils filled the smell of dry tobacco leaves, mint, spearmint, scorched lemon balm, of everything Maria's hair could smell of. His hand stayed there a long time, then it descended by the steep throat, pressed the pulsating vein, listened to the throb of the blood, it slipped into the hollow in front and anticipated all the hollows that he'd be reaching on the long road of Maria's body. In the oval of her armpit the heady scent of fig juice filled his nostrils, thin snaky hairs tickled his lips and he continued impatiently downwards, over the peaks of her hard breasts, through the cleavage between them to the stomach stretched taut as a string, which pulsated frantically in the shady circle of the navel. A new soft lowland there, like a silver foxglove, full of moisture, his hot tongue sank, felt the hardness of the muscles, gathered the moisture. O Maria, Mattei repeated, before putting his face in the boat of her two thighs. O Maria. Call me Fina, when you make love, call me by my other name, it's the name of my love, the woman begged. Fina, said the man and the name tickled his lips like a fine haired butterfly. Fina cried out lingeringly, her body vibrated even in the smallest muscle. Her lips dried up, and quivered without being able to stop. The man put his finger on them, after that he spoke abruptly into the shell of her ear, if another man touches this body at some time, I curse you to turn into a mermaid, Fina, I curse you…And he laughed.

Maria- Fina opened her thighs, crossed her ankles over his back and Mattei fell into the dark precipitous abyss of her rocking body.

Maria's mother sends them to the mouth of the river. She sits in the lorry's cabin beside her daughter, in silence. In her continual half blindness, she catches only the light of the August day and the blue of the sea, the darker and lighter patches of the woods; tussocks of scorched grass and lonely trees by the roadside blur as they flash by. She senses the world more with her nostrils: she recognizes at least ten summer smells, mixed up into a common bouquet of plants, which only grow on this coast and nowhere else. The figgy smell under Maria Fina's arms wafts thicker and heavy, the old woman realises that her daughter is troubled, that the unknown scares her, however hard her character has become; behind in the empty trailer Anastas and Anastasia are sitting, she recognises their tension from their silence.

Immediately after the bridge over the Veleka, the man stops the lorry. He helps the grandmother to alight, he kisses her hand in farewell. Later we'll bring you back to the town, he tells her, as soon as I build the house on the side, we'll take you in as well. It's as if she hasn't heard. I'll go to my village, me, in the house of my father Mavrud, I'll go there in a month or two's time, when autumn sets in, she tells her daughter, suddenly excited, it's clear, she's taken the decision at this very moment. Through the last years she's lived with them, they thought it was impossible for her to leave. Don't worry about me, don't you know that I see the world in my own way. And when I get back to my house in the mountain, I'll be completely OK. And isn't your friend Bethlehem there, Maria, and her Vassilaki, she's like my own daughter, they won't abandon me, those two… I'll come then with the pickup and drive you, the driver tells her full of respect, she smiles, I can go on my own, it's nothing, that I can't see, by the old narrow gauge if I set out on it, it'll lead me, into the mountain. Some six kilometres into Stranzha, what's the big deal. Maria doesn't speak a word in reply. The old woman suddenly snaps at Anastasia; and don't you forget, Anastasia that you've got a second name, your double name is from the names of both your grannies, don't forget that because it's important. I don't want my second name, it scares me, Anastasia answers, what are these double names, which you've given us, folk get muddled as to what to call us. Your Grandfather was a catholic, he insisted, when he adopted my Fina, your mother, he wanted to call her Maria, he christened her after the Virgin. For the saint preserve her from new evil, because of what happened to her earlier…I think that having more names is an opportunity; for example to hide yourself from life, when you have to, with your other name…But it's difficult, Anastasia insisted, without looking into her grandmother's words, you just define your life with one name, and then they force you to define it with another. It's as though you become a new person, isn't that so, Grannie. I don't want to be here one person, there another. Leave me to be called Anastasia and that's it. The old woman strokes her shoulder hurriedly. In one person, there are many people hiding, girl. But you might be right, what do I know. In that case I don't insist. The pair of you are fifteen, it's really a young age for you to have the courage to change your life because of one name. Maybe I'm mistaken in what I'm saying, maybe a new name won't change the person who'll bear it. Maybe folk are right to say that a person makes the name and not the contrary. I don't know. But your second name isn't new and if at any time you feel the need to use it, you'll have another opportunity; apart from that, I'll be happy that you're not distancing yourself from my spirit.

After that the old woman pulled the man by the sleeve, leading him to one side. She wants to tell him how her daughter Maria-Fina was once a quick spoken bright child, her hair was sunny and looked like corncobs, and her words were good- natured and shy; she often was happy for no apparent reason, then she preferred to be called Fina and everyone called her just that; they frequently pronounced her name, as though they suspected that just the name made her happy. And when that one thing happened, and her one eye burnt out the light, the other shone twice as bright. Light, it seems finds people, who reflect it best, and fills them to the top, up to their hair tips, to the bottom of their eyes…Because if there aren't such persons, how will the others realize that people are from light…This is what the old woman wants to tell him, but doesn't find the words to describe the clear circle of golden glitter, which lights up her inner blindness with the memory of her one-time child, Fina. And so she quickly exclaims: that was the name of her grandmother Fina, great-grandmother of the twins, Mavrud's wife, and her own mother, but it's also the name of her soul. Lad, remember this business and use it very carefully, very carefully say the name Fina. She herself, from the time that stuff happened with her husband Mattei, insists on only being Maria, but you try, try to bring back her holy name. Names are important in our life, as you think about it… Eh off with you now. I'm returning to my father Mavrud's house, there on the same street with Bethlehem and Vassilaki, people close to my life, close to me, as if I'm going back to my own daughter.

Anastas and Anastasia, standing straight in the trailer, catching on to the ropes, watch how their grandmother grows smaller. She stands and doesn't move, the wind blows her black scarf. At first sight the old woman is like all other old women. At some point, she turns and walks back with the upright, careful wooden step of a person who hardly moves. Anastas says thoughtfully, I didn't even remember you had a second name. Double names have always confused me, I prefer you to be Anastasia and nothing else.

~ PART 2 ~

In Which in One Place it Rains,
and in Another Place Quite Close By,
the Sun Shines. There Where It's Damp,
Saturated by the Rain, the World is
Intoxicatingly Transformed, and in the Sunny
Place by the Green Bench, Dusky Things
Come to Pass, as a Result of Which One Woman,
Fallen into a Trance, Feels Light Years
from her Being.

It rained intoxicatingly and with no hope of respite. The world was entranced. The earth was saturated, storms blew up, it smelled of cattle manure and rotten straw. When the rain stopped and the floods receded, they saw two mushrooms sprouting under the old walnut tree, one red, one white. They unfurled before their eyes. Look at this wonder now. They're sucking on one and the same earth, but the white one – edible, the red one – poisonous. It's the way it is from itself alone, the poison comes from within itself. The old man Vassilaki voices his wonder at length. The old woman Bethlehem, shrunken and dried up, holds her swelling stomach and asks timidly: pick the white one, Grandad, so we can cook a mushroom stew, I feel like eating everything these days.

The old man puffs, gestures, shakes his head. He bends down and tears the stem from its roots. He carries the mushroom in his two hands. The two of them sit down on the little bench, they lean

51

their backs against the patched cottage wall. Huge rain drops fall from the roof and drip at their feet like shining grape pips.

It's getting closer, Vassilaki, my time is approaching. The old man stares into Bethlehem's eyes that are sick with yearning. Why do you need this great name, when you are this…nobody. What unseen thing did they want to happen in this life of yours. Bethlehem, that they named you after a star. If the name makes the person, by now your light would have shone, showing the way for every lost and lonely soul, and me especially. And you sit and crackle like some twig, and nothing else, nothing your whole life, just this tummy of yours… Let's see when this crazy thought hit you…in the winter of that same year, when the blind mother of your friend Fina returned to her father Mavrud's house forever…I reckon that's exactly when it happened in 76. Eh reckon it out let's see, a whole thirty years have passed by. We already passed the year 2000, a new time, a new century, a new thousand years, they're calling it a millennium on the TV, and you…

The old woman doesn't move but somewhere inside her a little bone cracks, pretty much like a twig, so gentle and fragile the sound. The old man carries on talking, mostly to himself, because Bethlehem clearly is absent. Take it from me, Bethlehem, a person comes into this world so something happens to them. But in our life with you, from when we popped up, we don't remember anything like this, with any meaning or effect on the world. If only you'd born a child at least. Bethlehem sighs. Supposedly she's not present, still she mutters: that's not settled! She strokes her stomach, just about. The old man waves his arm half-heartedly. A whole life, Bethlehem, with this pitiful tummy of yours…

Impenetrable rain pours again, the two of them stay under the shelter. Thunder rattles, lightning flashes rip the sky's pinned up skin, embers of the latest flash pour into the river nearby, skim and burn out in the water. Look Bethlehem, look! God's power doesn't know its own strength! They sit, blinded and deafened. At some

52

point the old man loses his numbness, goes pale, he doesn't believe his eyes: Look woman, the lightning strikes are writing letters with their fiery whips. They be letters of fire, look up, look up Bethlehem! The old woman puts her hands to her brow. The old man leaves the shelter, he wanders stunned through the downpour, he comes back again. Lightning flashes again, sometimes simultaneously. Heavenly electricity turns the houses, the trees, the pair of them on the bench into a ghostly blue. Bethlehem keeps her hand on her stomach, she sighs. But she herself doesn't manage to hear her sigh. Where are the stars now on this stormy night, in which the sky shakes, have all of them fallen and won't shine…

Mummy Antula, Mummy Antula, a star's fallen from the sky. Could it not be mine. Star of Bethlehem?

At the same time as dusk falls, the Seaside Park in Burgas is dry, shadowy and dense. The mossy shade creates another world. In it time stops: slows down, crawls between the trees, finally nestles in the grass. It turns into no-time.

The woman who was sitting on the greenest and loneliest bench, senses this and surrenders to the feeling. A frog jumps, a mosquito whines, the silence hums. The woman barely shuts her eyes. It seems to her that a fox is passing down the path. Its scarlet tail brushes the asphalt and shoots out sparks, its foxy green eyes light up from the sunset. Psh, the woman tells it. Go into the wood, go back to the wood. The whole fox turns copper in the sunset's rays. It's crept silently by the shore. And it could be a dog, homeless and with sad eyes, surely it's swimming in the sea by now, foam dashing itself to rags on its slippery body, waves billowing and the ginger bitch snorting. Perhaps it's a wolf, secretive and golden eyed. Holy Mother it's not that wolf. But no, it was a fox, she's sure of it; it shrinks in the watery depth.

With an effort the woman lifts her seized up eyelids, her facial muscles stretched out. The sea must have thrown out the fox on to the shore, it must have shaken out the water, water droplets flying out like a rainbow; replaced the sand with her tail, and finally disappeared, as though melted into the wind. The imagined world turns off. It becomes dark and empty. The park empties of people, leaving just her, the woman on the bench, in her orange dress, with her orange fabric sandals, on her bare feet, with her hair turned orange by the sunset, with her miniature tattoo on her milk white shoulder, a black rose bud, a Dutch rose with velvet leaves, with its deep hidden interior, like a girl's vagina, like the heart of a poem read in one's youth, a black rose on a milk white shoulder, the emblem of her being, separated light years away from the green bench and the woman.

One time my mother, Nastasia the Greek put a copper pail under every drain pipe and collected rainwater, we washed our heads with it, do you remember, Bethlehem? In the other houses too the women put out pails to catch the rainwater and the drain pipes rang out in different voices. Do you remember, the whole village of drain pipes. Now there aren't any such pails. I do think however that even for the drain pipes to not ring, there is still some point to the rain,; if only to clear the animal dung off the street, it's still useful, isn't it. And to fill the river, so it doesn't dry up in the heat… What do you say, say something woman, open your mouth at long last. I'm now wondering what to say, raving rainy-bloke random stuff at this age, my mouth's getting blisters from talking, because I'm talking on your behalf as well, and you keep mum, keep mum as if to spite me …

Every summer I came from the town to Grandma's and on the very next day I'd bolt. Right at lunch time, in the heat, on a solitary walk under the fire of the protuberances, over the meadow between the village and the mountain. Anastas stayed in Burgas, he preferred to share in the proximity of the big water and its deep secrets and although the dolphins had decreased by thousands through the killing and took care not to approach the shore, he would sit for hours on some rock and hail them with appealing dolphin squeaking; I got closer and closer to the mountain. I would walk with a white scarf over my black hair and a never to be changed scarlet dress, nothing suited the summer better than a flared cherry-red cotton dress – I'd walk and deliberately stretch out my suffering like a brainwashed masochist. From the salt taste of the heat, my skin peeled and cracked, my lips split and swelled like an African's, and my eyes burnt as if stung by a jellyfish and numberless scalding odious tentacles crawled over my body. Over the meadow a heat haze shimmered and my eyes lost focus, my bare feet sunk in the deep dust, burning like firewalkers' coals, while my sandals dangled fastened to my middle finger by their laces.

On the way back, instead of taking the direct route, I took off on paths you could scarcely make out, stretched out like snakes in the baking sun. Sometimes a thorn drove itself into my heel, and so I'd sit Turkish style on a tuft of grass, I'd gather my saliva with an effort, unstick my lips and spit over the heel, black from dirt. I'd scratch with the tip of my nail until I'd cleaned a pale patch of skin around the thorn. With another sharper thorn, I'd begin to jab it like a needle and with long effort the golden tip emerged. I left it to germinate. Sometimes I'd try to remember that skylark song of my childhood, but nothing came out, just my throat swelled and throbbed from the strain. For quite some time I'd observe the ants emerging dazed from the cracks in the scorched earth and crawling in all directions, without stopping to drag seeds or bristles. I broke off a sharp blade of grass, chewed a little on its stalk or pushed it through the gap between my two front teeth. At some point I'd get up and set off. Here and there in the fields grew walnut trees with many branches, but I'd deliberately avoid their deep shade. A temporary refuge could be a mistake, a self-deceit, a weak hearted relaxation of the senses. The route was more of an inner feeling. That's why I heeded my inner being and carried on walking. Sometimes I'd stop and turn both directions, having lost the sense of whether I was going somewhere or was returning. The path itself could be a fraud, an illusion, but it was still better than no path at all. And I'd walk and form the indistinct suspicion that this could be the most important pathway in my life, as I'm so attached to it; I didn't know how it was possible but I really believed that in some blinding moment in the future it could uncover the secret of my creation from the seed in my mother's womb to the seed in the earth's womb, into which at some time I'd return. Well Lao Tzu had said it, in the end, the path is inside ourselves. In other words us folk are a pathway…

However much it stretched out, the path still finished, always somewhat unexpectedly. First of all, you'd hear the noise of rapids. There was so much life in it that I was amazed when I heard it. The water greeted me roughly. And so I'd consciously slow my steps. To drag it out as long as I could. To put it off just a little bit more, even though this was in fact the final point of my planned thoughtless walk. To make it longer. I walked the last metres with the speed of a tortoise. I took in a breath and held it, and entered the cool of the bank like a temple. The willows sprinkled me kindly with moisture. I stayed quite a time not breathing, with my face turned upwards. After that I wiped my features with the back of my hand, as though I was wiping my own tears. Gradually I came to my senses. In the end I would slide down the clay bank and put my feet in the river. God, I thank you for giving us thirst. I took a scoop in my hands, leaning my face down over them, but I didn't drink. My parched lips stayed a breath away from the water, a kiss away, a prayer. I let it run out between my fingers. Only then did I fold at my knees and they sank to the sandy bottom. My dress spread out on the surface like a red parachute. Thus the water reached my neck. I lowered my head and began to drink with my lips right in the water. The water splashed, poured over my face, it was drowning me. I took a moment to breathe, I closed my eyes against the scorching fire of the sky and submerged my face again. Thirst quenched at last, I straightened, and buried my toes in the sandy bottom. Grit was caught up, muddying for a moment the green watery mirror which flowed past me. Seen in her, I left myself in the magic: along with the water I began to move as well. Both banks flew backwards and the willows and the neighbouring village cottages and the sky with its sun sparks also flew by. And there was a whirlpool inside me, making me faint as though in flight. The river was also a pathway. Rooted to its bottom, unmoving amidst its green water, I was travelling.

I was a river and I flowed.

You wouldn't believe that it was me. If someday I get the urge to do something similar again, I'll surely want to try something completely different, what it would be like to travel to the bottom, I'd want to find out what it would be like to travel below the bottom, because Virginia Woolf didn't come back from there to tell us and there's no other way to find out. God preserve me from the urge to find it out in a real river. Painful experience is more attractive than that which hands you happiness on a plate…

Bethlehem, speak one word at least, girl. You haven't forgotten human speech have you? My mother Nastasia used to say that when she delivered babies from their mothers' wombs she'd tell their fortunes in her head like some kind of soothsayer. That was the custom. And as she was your midwife too, I wonder if she'd realised that you'd come into the world just for me and she decided to do me the favour to rescue me from women's idle chatter. She decided that you shut up, and look out with these two eyes here, that's what doomed you. Open your mouth, tell me what letter you saw the heavenly whip draw in the sky. Tell me at long last, Bethlehem.

A. I saw A.

In the Seaside park it's became as dusky as a dream.

The whole park is some kind of verdant cool, tranquil dream, in which twilight things occur: faraway muffled voices of unseen folk, wandering the paths, quiet dark blue processions of ants crawling on the tree trunks, linden pollen which drifts in the air, until its dense dry smell numbs the nostrils; also the orange woman on the green bench, caught in the web of this dream, and when she goes, and when she sits on a green bench and when she falls silent, and when she laughs or cries, someone dreams of me, someone dreams a long deep dream of me.

That's when I heard the little voice. It was timid and not from here, after it, a woman called out, her voice was rounded as a river stone with green moss at one end.

Grannie, Chrissie is bad, do you know how bad Chrissie is.

Wasn't she your friend…

But now she isn't, because she's bad.

Now I'll open up this croissant for you to eat and we'll go.

But, Chrissie did something bad. Are you listening Grannie?

OK OK!

No I'm telling you, that it's bad!

Watch out, you'll stain your blouse, you're forever dropping chocolate on your clothes

Don't say forever, don't say forever, we don't live like that.

Come on we're leaving.

No no, listen about Chrissie, about Chrissie!

What about Chrissie? Your friend Christina from the nursery?

She did something bad, Chrissie is bad.

Come off it, isn't she…

Grannie, Chrissie killed a pregnant snail!

There aren't pregnant snails.

There are. I saw, inside the big snail there was a little snail, I saw it under the shell, I'm not lying! And Chrissie killed it! Oh Grannie!

Stop it now, eat…

She smashed them and even laughed. And made them a hard grave, a very hard grave and it was narrow, I saw!

Suddenly they come out from the shadows and set out down the path by the green bench. The little girl is straw-blonde and thin-legged. One foot limping and the heel of her sandal is twisted. She's wearing spectacles like magnifying glasses, and when she turns back, the woman on the bench sees the child's eyes: blue, sky blue eyes, eyes from heaven, eyes from the sky – unnaturally enlarged by the lenses, somehow taking over her whole face. The woman on the bench, shuts her eyes in worry, a painful memory pops up. These eyes resemble other eyes, she doesn't remember where she's seen them.

I saw everything, it's no lie!

She says this to her Grannie, but looks at the woman on the bench.

She's seen everything. Someone has killed in front of her eyes, horrifically enlarged through the lenses of her glasses. With her very own all seeing heavenly eyes, she's seen pregnancy, murder, death, a grave.

She knows by now.

The woman on the bench notices how the curls, spread out over the thin shoulders, glow gentle and gold as straw. She notices the crooked heel of the sandal and above it the thin ankle with the scrunched ribbed sock, and the sharp shoulder blades on the back like folded wings and the shadow of the words spoken a second earlier – the shadow of the harsh revelation of childish words over their heads, getting larger and hiding the memory of the recent sun.

The little girl turns again, the gaze from her unnatural eyes meets the gaze from the woman in orange.

They stayed like this, their eyes lock together…and the woman saw the loneliness in the child's left pupil shining like a golden ball, but there was no way to help, she wasn't able to move, as though the childish otherworldly gaze had nailed her forever to the green bench: she sat there like a giant dried up butterfly in her orange dress and her orange hair – a horrid memory of the once black curls – with smeared red lipstick, crushed by the loneliness of the child, crushed by the loneliness of eternity that approached from all sides and reverted into hers alone. And because she had no strength to bear so much loneliness and she didn't know what to do with it, nor how to put her cruel freedom to use, the woman simply screwed up her eyes. She screwed them up with all her might and the little girl's gaze penetrated even the thick skin of her eyelids. And still through her eyes shut tight, the woman managed to see how the girl opened her wings, enormous over her narrow shoulders, shining as though embroidered with amazingly fine threads of exceptionally thin silk, a macramé of aquamarine, hemmed with darker blue and at this moment the sun made its last appearance, from behind the clouds and lit up the creamy little face with its high cheek bones and a cascade of blinding sparks scattered beneath the child's wings.

An unbearable tick twitched her lower lip, the cigarette came unstuck from the corner of her mouth and fell on her lap and only then did she move her hand. With the nail of her index finger she pushed the glowing ash which had already burnt the material of her dress, it fell into the dry grass and in a little while it smoked. The woman came to her senses, jumped and began to stamp on the grass.

When she stopped and looked around, she saw that the child and the old woman had gone.

You say, the letter A. It looked to me like an L. We can't do anything except to go round the neighbours tomorrow and ask what they saw in the sky, it still could be telling us something. From a high place, I mean…

The child had gone, gone was the child.

I observe life, memorize it, after that I write it on a piece of paper. I dress it with words, I transform it like that peasant woman who dolled herself up in a velvet stole like a young bride. Because I feel the transformation I look into the words and I listen to them. At some point I forget why I contemplated them with such concentration and I go to the other extreme. I begin to fall in love with them narcissistically. I luxuriate. As though my words are gold, hardly any silver. As though the world will be entranced with excitement or the earth will reverse its spin. But then I get a grip anew. However much we take care, however much we are responsible for their use words change reality to a great extent. Look even at that moment after the girl with glasses has disappeared from my view, through half open eyelids I try to see far away, behind the blue ridges of the mountains opposite. Here on the shore in the Seaside Park, it continues dusky and dry, and hot, but behind one of the ridges it's raining. It's simply raining. Raining. However straight away a sentence pops up in my head and it's pretty illogical, glitteringly cool rain is falling, it pours out like molten glass, such a sentence lights me up. Could molten glass be cold, does rain stay the same if we pretty it up with words. Not at all. It's just raining there. It's raining and I'm sure it's horrible and soaking in the mountain. That house could have sprung a leak. Old Vassilaki and Bethlehem could have been swept away in a flood. There is no molten glass gleamingly moist. In the village it smells of mould and mud and cow dung and washed up animal corpses. Well yes, and of washed nettles, I mean to say, just nettles and grass and a river that's burst its banks. It's nothing and amounts to nothing, a dark flow of water pours out of the sky, but just mention the word rain and something happens to me. The very word excites me. It reminds me that behind the visible and attainable something else exists, invisible and unattainable. It exists in things, but also in the words with which we name them. If there was a way without manual intervention for thoughts to go directly from the brain to a white sheet of paper and words to write themselves, surely nothing of the original energy of the word would be lost, but sadly the path from the brain's spark burns out in a matter of seconds, it's light years away from the tip of the pen.

Write, write, write. Writing's a chronic disease.

Old man Hewlett Packard warms up slowly and this is his only failing. Otherwise he's an eternal genius. No sentimentality. No detours. Precise programme. Perfect control. Hewlett Packard. The foreigner in her life and on top of that so dedicated, just as he had to be. He'd surpassed himself, the guy who'd invented the computer. He'd created a little faultless God. The most self-centred of all Gods. Thus spoke Hewlett Packard, let there be no Gods apart from me.

She realised herself that she was overdoing it, to the cost of her health. Her messy orange hair, the perpetual cigarette in the ash tray, ready ground Nova Brazilia coffee, the hottest coffee which she always drank cold…the translator award, letters to Anastas, always busier, always further away, half-hearted attempts at chat, peeks through some of the holes in web door to the big village, to her endless amazement it doesn't sleep at any moment, even late into the night, so many people without faces, without eyes, have turned to words and so feverishly search for what they need and seek it so far away that they've stopped noticing what's under their noses. As always a person moves away from themselves, stretches out, goes far away, anticipates, lies in wait, supposes, foresees, and this pre-ordains that things happen in a strange way, as though they've overtaken themselves in advance. And maybe really close by there's nothing which deserves attention. Maybe what's interesting is always at the other end of the world, otherwise, why does such an inexplicable sleeplessness cover the world.

The television in the corner shut up a long time ago. She doesn't switch it on. She stopped it after a cookery programme seven or eight years ago. She'd just gathered the courage to struggle with that monster Joyce. Pumped up but at the same time somewhat shy, she took the fateful decision to seek out as many Bulgarian words, each neurotically overtaking the other, as to be worthy of expressing Joyce, words too so staggered, hurling themselves to all corners of the Joyce universe, still so aimless and beautiful in their ingenious craziness. Joyce's yearning prose, stream of consciousness, sudden deconstructions, verbal whirlpools, total disintegration, from which a blinding thought is reborn from the fire like a phoenix. She didn't even seek a publisher, didn't plan anything in advance. This was her personal task. But first to complete the task. They'd brought her the book from abroad and Joyce's giddy Irish-English associative flow grabbed her, took away her breath. On that same day, with the cookery programme. The presenter donned his intricate chef's hat, smacked his chops with no restraint and explained his new recipe. She listened and froze on the spot. We gut the turtledove and fill the cavity with stuffing, tamp it, sew it up tight with thread, after that we open out the legs, fold the wings into the body and we knot it fast with string, so the turtledove keeps its aerodynamic form. You roast it in a medium oven.

…Mummy Fina, Mummy Fina, the dove in the yard is all filled up with cooing!

That same evening she decided. Keep away from chefs. Their bloody fancy aprons and bonnets like bell towers. She snapped the off switch and the screen blanked out, in that moment the room began to fill with new time, which she called Joyce. In some way time resembled a river which was trying to flow backwards from the sea to the source. It would be interesting for her to sink into the waters and try to reach the river bed.

Vassilaki walks in high spirits from street to street, from house to house, flying over the slippery mud and cursing quietly out of habit. The rain has stopped, the sun has broken through. Did you see the heavenly letters, do you remember the divine letters, but no-one could remember, just one unknown old woman, shorter even than his Bethlehem, a real doll, whom the village children, however few remained, could easily make fun of, as far as she let them, just a white haired doll with gentle eyes and vacant look, with a face turned old as though an invisible rapist has sadistically carved into it, she smiles brightly ahead, I saw it and read it, it was a whole word but I can't remember it. Who are you, asked Vassilaki, the old woman failed to answer him and sighed lightly: as far as I remember there were two letters, but they meant as much as any human words.

Returning old Vassilaki sets each and every one the task to rack their brains, which apart from being small have dried up like goat pellets, to exercise their brains so as to get their memory working. Because it could be a word from heaven, of special importance for the village or the whole thing could have been the mysterious signature of God himself; even though our eyes are too weak to see his face at least his signature can appear to us: look therefore my people, as I've set my signature there are no lies or trickery, I confirm my existence which means, people that you too exist and it's not just you thinking it.

Fragments of a second and the old genius Hewlett could not manage anything. It turned out that the old genius Mr Packard is an ordinary mortal. Delete. Deleted. Fuck you, she was initially furious, bloody American spy! Always from time to time she pressed the wrong button by mistake, she rethinks a second later, someone has pulled our finger against our will and pressed the key for a split second. We don't even press, we just touch for a split hair of a second. Delete. This is what happens to her when she hasn't learnt to archive as she works. Every carelessness is punished. And farewell Joyce, farewell Dublin, farewell Dubliners, farewell Ulysses, farewell my fate, farewell five years of my life, my pestilential life, ha-ha.

Really a lightning thought occurred to her, that in such a situation folk have no reason to live any longer. Her self-centred God had destroyed her life's work in one breath, the meaning of her life, with one touch of her little finger he'd erased the whole horrifyingly huge translation. From one side the situation would come to appear tragi-comic in time but at this moment she could only feel the pathos of loss.

It was a frosty evening. She set out through Burgas and lost herself in Dublin. She walked the streets emptied of folk and like a dramatic actress, driven out of her wits by mighty experience, she began muttering different Joyce phrases.

Burgas was readying itself to sleep and all doors were locked, only in the town's Art Gallery, situated in the building of the former synagogue something was happening. Inside it was lit up, a waterfall of piano notes flowed out into the crystal night. People's backs were seen, immobile, resting in chairs. She stopped, read the poster, stuck to the door. HERE IS EVERYWHERE, the blue letters announced the pre-Christmas exhibition and evening piano concert. The music floated and perhaps because of her excitement, she saw how the sounds leaked through the windows and through the walls of the synagogue, through the roof and rose up high sparkling and lonely-otherworldly into the winter night. Here is everywhere, she repeated the strange sentence from the headline as she passed by and the music continued to rise above her head and shine out like a comet tail from clear cosmic energy. Everywhere is here, she changed the word order and felt the slight change without fully understanding. Everywhere is everywhere. I am everywhere... her painful exaltation threatened to turn into its opposite. Joyce's translators had managed brilliantly that was a fact. The Dubliners had struck lucky with them. She hadn't succeeded with ULYSSES or ULYSSES had not succeeded with her. With some it worked. With some it didn't. And well if she hadn't wanted it to happen, that delete key, she'd been subconsciously primed to press it, to save herself from all the inaccuracies, fears and complexes.

She got back frozen and decided to switch on the television. To be so good as to return the world to her home. To sit opposite it and stare into it without a thought in her head.

And it was no coincidence that she switched it on at exactly that moment. After five years of cobwebs and dust, silence and emptiness, turned into a desert, the old box filled again with light, artificially enlivened by the strengthening red, yellow, blue and green colours. A woman's face filled the screen. Hair, light to reddish-gold, spirited features, eyes sparkling with intelligence. In fact she knew who it was. A famous translator. For the first time in Bulgaria...How many years did you need to translate Ulysses? The woman gave an answer. Dear God. Dear God.

She was sitting without a thought in her head. After that she pulled herself together. Everything fell into place. Fate was giving her a sign, as for the moment she sat shocked and half dead with the thought that she was an ordinary nobody with her orange dishevelled hair and her Dutch rose tattooed on her shoulder, with her cold hot coffee, with her neuroses which rhymed banally with roses, she should get away and continue somewhere else. She reflected and felt suddenly calm. Just at that moment she was surprised at the ease with which she achieved it. What a silly sparmannia, she told herself. There are things that don't depend on delete, is it down to me to tell you. There are such things, they can fill you over the brim and it's not necessary for you to be an ocean, you can be a river which flows towards its source. Even a little village laundry pool. I love little rivers, water flowing from somewhere, tugging at pale fish, withered grass and twigs, donkey droppings, reflections of sun and moon and all such other stuff. Sparmannia, sparmannia, how could you not understand…

Her melodrama had calmed down through this little or nothing word, mysteriously filled with secrets and future. She came across it some time ago in a home improvement magazine, abandoned in a trolley bus and she was very impressed when she read that there was a house linden plant which reached two metres in height and they were really beautiful plants, but with no scent. Their botanical name was sparmannia.

Do you know Bethlehem, when I found the pail, how different the drain pipe sounds.

Wet through to her bones, she walks through the forest through impenetrable rain. The downpour caught her on the way. She set out in daylight from the regional town, the seven kilometres didn't scare her. But now she regrets her thoughtlessness, but she's already half way. Half way on your intentions can get confused, to carry on or to go back, it's pretty much one and the same thing. Nevertheless she carries on, more from inertia.

The lightning turns the surrounding mountains blue, blue with a quivering light, thunderclaps split the sky. It's terrifying, lonely and wild like prehistoric times. Sudden headlights appear, from these she realises how far she is from the road. She starts shouting and waving, tries to run, but falls in the muddy grass. She gets up and watches the zigzags of the headlights. Standing there it seems her that the car is flying towards her, but realises this is an illusion, the bends here are so sharp.

Suddenly an enormous bird with open wings launches itself into the headlights' cone. The eagle's wings are powerful but cannot gain height, the eagle looks old or injured. The driver tries to turn the car, the horn parps a warning. The woman suddenly realises, the bird doesn't want to pull back, it's deliberately flying towards the car. With all its strength it hurls its body against the windscreen, the car catapults it up high. Everything happens in seconds and it seems to her that she's been watching a whole eternity. After this nothing else can be seen, the car headlights have turned and disappeared into the dark. The eagle suicide, she has seen it kill itself. Shocked she starts up again.

It rumbles, it flashes again and like on an enormous video screen it lit up the nearby houses of the imminent village, its trees in the gardens, the church bell tower, the willows on the river. At last she finds herself, almost unconscious from fear at the beginning of the storm itself and its suicidal indifference to its strength. She begins to shout from delayed shock, from relief and from disbelief that it has happened, that the world is whole and unharmed, lurking in the dark of the surrealistic night. Her cry drowns in the gloomy depths of a dark damp abyss.

Only now she reckons that she's been tossed by the storm for hours through the forest, rendered senseless by the buffeting wind, aiming at something whose appearance she's forgotten. Now she recognizes it in the widow of the squat cottage at the beginning of the village like a bright point. It flickers sometimes, almost blows out, but its continuously burning eye again winks. Her skirt flaps and twines around her slippery thighs, her hair hangs in strands over her face, in the dark the eyes becomes brighter, she almost rushes the last few steps towards it with her knees buckling with exhaustion and in front of the cottage door she falls face down in the mud. She tries to lift her head towards the shaking sky, there some lightning strikes thrash their tails. She has a momentary vision that the lightning is writing letters in the sky and she gets up to read them but her strength deserts her and she slides down again on the porch. Behind her eyelids an enormous gold letter is left to glow.

Did you see Bethlehem, the sky! I don't see very well and my brain grows weak, that's why I didn't memorize them. I sort of read them when we were outside and in a second they rubbed themselves out. Do you remember those letters? Maybe they have a discovery to reveal to us, what do you think?

Bethlehem sits and stays silent. Something is happening with Bethlehem. Her frail body trembles, her twiggy bones whistle emptily. Her ash grey pony tail thrashes and jumps on her back. The old woman tries to stand up, supporting her protruding stomach with her hands. O-o-o I can't stand any more, Grandpa, I haven't got the strength, she smiles palely, my time has come, my time has come o-o, didn't I tell you it hurts, my tummy hurts, life hurts.

The rain pours down the window pane like a stream of molten lead. It's hurting, the empty hole within me is hurting, Vassilaki. She begins to tug her blouse, her fingers are unexpectedly strong and the material tears and splits and her cotton skirt with little blue flowers bursts and splits; her tummy distended from emptiness and about to burst, begins to shoot out chicken feathers to raise a thick white cloud to the ceiling. Bethlehem strains and forces the fluff from the depths of her tummy, aren't I here, in this sick life to carry on…look now it's starting…look now I'm giving birth. Vassilaki stands in shock and watches how the little old woman strains the insides of her womb and expels the emptiness and pain in her life, he watches and has no means of helping with another's pain. I'm giving birth now Vassilaki, it's really hurting, my tummy hurts, Vassilaki, the world is hurting me, the rain is hurting me, the night is hurting me-e-e. Vassilaki I'm giving birth.

Bethlehem finally falls silent. The disembowelled pillow cover hangs in rags. All the fluff lies across the floor, a whole foot of chicken feathers. Just a little fluff flies over the candle, the heat raises it, it falls a centimetre then rises again. Bethlehem sits amid the feathery carpet and lets her head droop over her naked dried up breasts. The old man can't take his eyes away from their prematurely aged nipples. His Adam's apple moves, his mouth quivers. Those are Bethlehem's golden apples, where is the stretched smooth skin, now they're shrivelled and pathetic, he hasn't seen them in years, when did they become like that? Life, life, close your eyes so you don't see, the lump is in his throat is like a sharp flint.

At that moment, there's a knock at the door. Through the noise of the rain, through the thunder and heavenly elements it seems that someone has taken the path to their house and this was a real miracle on this doomed night and in this sick narrow life. This somebody opens the door and stands rocking on the threshold.

The wet dress sticks to her thighs like a second skin, a puddle is forming at her feet but the woman doesn't move, leaning against the door frame, the whirlwind strikes, the candle flame quivers, almost blows out and regains its strength. Vassilaki timidly invites her in, come in come in so we see who you are.

An eagle …killed itself in front of my eyes… just a minute ago.

Bethlehem looks caught in a spell, with half open mouth. And most unexpectedly, without looking at the old man she calls out in a confidently joyous voice, who is it, *who is it*, are you still asking! Well who could it be Vassilaki, don't you know? I'll tell you that life was hurting me. Let her know that her turning up at this moment on exactly this day is no accident. I wasn't expecting her exactly, but she's been sent for me and I recognized her. She and I are many people, we are everyone before us, all our ancestors. Bethlehem's words turned into a gabble: we're a confused tangled up ball we have to find its beginning so that each of us can know their own self Vassilaki I'll tell her everything I know, I'd bring out this messed up life of ours in my tummy, to stop life hurting me, good and bad, to stop hurting the sky and the earth and not hurt me because I gave birth and my tummy was empty and she is here.

The woman dries herself by the fire. Her dress steams, her hair smokes. Bethlehem sits amid the feathers and rocks. The old man watches both, he stands motionless in the dark corner and opens his mouth several times, before being able to speak: an eagle you say, you've seen an eagle-suicide. How did it kill itself? You didn't imagine it did you? Eagles don't kill themselves!

IN WHICH THE WOMAN WITH THE ROSE TATTOO ON HER SHOULDER REMEMBERS WHAT SHE KNOWS ABOUT THE INNER ROOM, ALSO ABOUT THE SOLITUDE IN THAT ROOM AS A CHOICE AND AS A WAY TO STRENGTHEN INNER ACTIVITY, AND VASSILAKI AND BETHLEHEM WILL CONTINUE WITH THEIR MEMORIES SO THAT EVERYONE CAN UNTANGLE THE BALL OF THEIR SHARED LIFE AND STRETCH THE THREAD LIKE A PATH THROUGH TIME

The inner room of the old house. The sooty stone masonry fireplace. The small window in the west wall. Semi-dark inside, both winter and summer, dove coloured eyes behind the glass. Solitude as a choice, like an internal strenuous activity, to the maximum, to complete isolation, to freedom, harsh, self-harming and unyielding, freedom inside. In the secret room in the big house, in freedom's cell...From that place I think to share with the old folk the life of those closest to me, passed on into timelessness or into different times, The stories which excite my imagination, and also the memories of Vassilaki and Bethlehem begin at the start of the twentieth Century immediately after the refugee wave in 1913.

My old folk tremble with excitement. They wait to hear what I know and remember from the tales of my mother, Maria-Fina, after that they'll carry on, because Bethlehem is right, the ball is tangled and we have to find the beginning, so as to unravel our shared life and to stretch out its thread like a path, like an umbilical cord which will tug our souls, just like it was stretched between me and Anastas through times and spaces, when clearly we are both absent from each other's lives. As I sit in the little room and look through the window at the curtain of rain I think what a silly sparmannia I've been without my own scent, but the time came and I believe no delete can rub out what I've begun.

Because he hoped to teach himself to read somehow by himself, when he leafed through the family bible and scrabbled through it with filmy eyes and crippled thought, in spite of having inherited weak eyesight from birth, so that this was a pointless exercise, Mavrud didn't give up on his desire to learn the letters. He scrabbled through the thick book, its pages thinning out, he scraped dust off his fingers, but before his eyes the same fog hung. This lasted years. And one day before he set to build his own house at the bottom of his father's yard, as he carefully turned the pages as delicate as butterfly wings, Mavrud realized that the white cataracts on his eyes had fallen. He saw them with his sharpened sight at the very moment in which they slapped down on the open book like two white sultanas.

He rubbed his eyes. Tiny letters danced in his vision, jumping like fleas. He squeezed his eyes in disbelief and froze. That's how his wife found him, grey eyed Fina my great-grandma. She touched him so gently on the shoulder with the tips of her fingers, so as not to scare him, because she thought he'd fallen asleep in this uncomfortably wooden pose. When he unstuck his eyelids and slowly lifted his eyes towards her, she put her hand over her mouth in surprise. His eyes had the colour of spring green and she'd only known their ash grey veil. He looked her over thirstily and for the first time saw how unusual she was, with her cream-brown complexion with a light mother-of-pearl glow, with high cheek bones on her swarthy face, framed by smooth raven-black hair, straight as a broom. And how unexpected her eyes were, drawn gracefully towards her forehead, dove-grey in colour, very quiet and distant. For the first time he saw how distant his wife's eyes were.

In the end Mavrud put the bible on the shelf in the big lounge alongside a toothless saw, a pruning knife and a pottery bowl with a blue peacock painted on its inside bottom.

So many times he looked into the ancient book, so many times a gentle warm tremor unfurled beneath his ribs. His brother's son, a pupil in his work detail, showed him the letters, taught him to read out the syllables and one day he took down the book once again. He wiped off the dust with his sleeve, sat down by the window, elbows on his knees. He stayed there for hours. His sight was young and clear as a hawk's. His eyes caught the first line, as though he was unwinding a ball. "In the beginning God created the heaven…"

Years went by and a few more months until he reached St John's last Amen. Only then did he leave the book again on the top of the shelf and set to building a house.

To the surprise of his nearest and dearest, Mavrud began talking in proverbs. One day he took to teaching his neighbour Jora who had a cleft palate. Jora, he said to her. The tongue is a tiny organ but it utters big stuff, look at a small fire and how much forest burns. This is from Isiah, did you understand Jora? Jora stood with mouth wide open with her pink and not especially small tongue hanging out as a sign of genuine amazement, because Mavrud had been a reserved and deferential man, but since the cataracts had fallen from his eyes all at once he was speaking wondrous stuff. She wasn't even angry with him but worked her tongue all the harder once her astonishment had passed.

Mavrud talked this way to his family and they too could neither be angry with him nor even answer him because the meaning of his words slipped away from them. More to the point, they seemed to find many so meanings in any one of his statements, that they couldn't differentiate one from another and this hurt them. In the middle of the Christmas meal he turned to his brother Niko, looked him straight in the eye and declared: Don't look at the wine, how it's turning red, how it's lighting up sparks in the glass, how smoothly it pours; afterwards it will bite you like a snake and sting like a cobra. Your eyes will feast on other women, your heart will whisper corruption and you'll be like one asleep at sea and dreaming at the top of the main mast. He stopped. Everyone stared at him motionless. Niko's wife covered her mouth with her hand, her eyes shot daggers from Niko to Mavrud and back. Niko didn't know what to say, he squeezed the glass of ruby wine and without realizing, rolled it in his hand, the ruby drops flew and rolled down the outside of the glass. He pulled himself together, however and muttered darkly, what have I got to do with a main mast? And straight away Mavrud answered with a new proverb: Don't answer a fool according to his foolishness, so you don't become the same. Then Niko could do nothing but jump up and grab him by his jacket because the meaning had become clearer than clear. And it was just as well that out in the yard the carollers were singing, otherwise no-one could tell what might have come of Mavrud's passion for speaking in proverbs.

After several months of hard work the refugee Mavrud had now built the inner facing walls of his house, but one day something occurred to him and he said, I'm knocking it down. They were amazed, trying to convince him that this was not necessary, the foundations are sound, the bricks are well baked, sunny and strong and the walls are good for a hundred years. But he paid no attention. I left out the most important thing, the most important thing left out. It was drawn up so clearly, but there now, I didn't realise in time.

And he demolished the building. Amidst piles of rubbish, beside the ruins of the house that was not to be, he waved abstractedly with his hands and drew a plan of the new, the perfect building in the air. And it would be perfect because Mavrud was not going to forget the most important thing.

And again set to stirring the clay for the bricks down by the river. They poured it into heavy moulds, turned out the soft bricks into the sun and they began to slowly bake, taking strength from the light, creases from the wind, scent from the surrounding grass, nightglow from the stars, murmur of the river and most of all the motivating power of their owner at any time during the day. A pigeon feather had stuck on one of the bricks and its print remained, on another a butterfly had landed and her deathly dust nestled into the clay forever, and grass had left its mark and falling willow leaves, and ants, and dandelion fluff. On one dewy June morning, they found one down in the brick room, it was unclear when and how it had fallen there; it was completely intact, so Mavrud knelt to put it in its place, but at once he saw a strange mark. Everyone gathered together, brought their heads closer over the brick and gave their comments. A forester was passing by, he bent down as well and said it was from a deer, a stag had come around, probably drinking from the river.

By now Mavrud talked only in proverbs and this when he reckoned it was absolutely necessary to speak. Throughout the rest of the time he stayed silent and looked into Fina's dove grey irises or dreamt in real terms about his future house and his future children in it, or he simply left his mind to rest from the many thoughts, which multiplied there non-stop, so that from the beginning it seemed to him that they buzzed like a hive of bees, and this was not especially pleasant because for ages his thoughts had been clumsy and heavy, and there was no-one to prod him into waking from his lethargy. He now thought of so many different things at once that he could not but wonder where these thoughts had been to this moment. Whether other folk lived like this, whether he'd simply been isolated from them. He began examining folk, mostly their eyes. He began to see unsuspected things. Through Fina's dove-grey eyes he sometimes sensed boundless distances, somehow motionless deserts, another time he made out rivers of green water, which flowed through deserts and watered them, and raised grass to the very heavens, so that drops from their leaves fell as big as tears and so filled Fina's eyes. Another time a grey fog flowed out as if from a deep well and veiled them, that's when it seemed to Mavrud for a second, that he had lost his sight again. Sometimes Fina's irises shone so blue, that he blinked opposite her and shut his eyes tight and he felt a strong desire at such a moment to uncover the secret, which bubbled up from the depths of her soul and appeared at the surface so changeably just for a second, and then disappeared without trace. Before really looking, Mavrud had known the heat of her body above all, the pearly smoothness of her skin, the smell of lemon balm, which suffused her hair, her low slow voice and that was all. With filmy eyes, he'd circle around her featureless face, her body as thin as a tree branch, her cloud of hair and admitted timidly that Fina could be beautiful in some way, just as others described her, but as he couldn't see the invisible, he accepted it, that this was the woman for him, because in spite of the handicap he'd had from birth, Mavrud was a handsome man, that's what everyone said. Now with his clear eyesight he penetrated. He sought. He compared. And more and more reached the conclusion that Fina was not the woman for him. He was shocked by his discovery. The only thing which reassured him, was the other discovery that Fina was not the woman for any man.

Bethlehem and Vassilaki listen, without interrupting me, although perhaps they know these things themselves. Bethlehem looks at me, mouth open and her lips are moving, as though they're soundlessly repeating the words, which I speak. She repeats them one by one, and this makes her look a little crazed, as though she and I are some synchronised duo, in which she's a little old lady shaken with excitement with an enthusiastic look which she doesn't divert from my face, a tremulous parody artist who second after second loses her reason from the exaltation of her feelings; or a prompter, who soundlessly articulates, pale from the effort, because she suspects that the most important thing at the moment is for not

76

a single mistaken word to be spoken. And I continue, encouraged to speak, having barely closed my eyes, because this way it's easier for me to see, and I really see, I see everything, as it was, look here.

On the day the builder climbed on to the roof and hammered in a post with a white towel flag, and in a loud voice intoned a blessing on the house and the good health of its husband and wife and a whole lot of other good things.

Mavrud also climbed on the roof. He stood next to the builder, whispered something, the other drew back, and the owner of the house grabbed the post, gave a rasping cough and shouted out as loudly as his voice allowed: "For everything there's a season, everything has a season under heaven. A time to be born and a time to die-ie… A time to laugh and a time to cry-y!…A time to find and a time to loo-oose! A time to destroy and a time to build!" From Ecclesiastes! He fell silent a while and then added unexpectedly to himself: "A time to see darkly and a time to see clearly anew!"

His voice stopped and he fell silent. He was silent a long time. He didn't hurry to descend, he didn't speak, forgot about the people below. At length the builder, feeling awkward, touched his shoulder. The man came to his senses, coughed again and began to speak normally, loud enough for his nearest and dearest to hear in the yard. He explained why he'd demolished the first building and started a new one, so the mistake had been rectified in this way, most importantly to have a house. Matthew the Evangelist opened my eyes, I looked a second time when the cataracts fell from my eyes. I'm telling you the truth. Listen all of you that your eyes be opened. The Gospel of St Matthew chapter 6: "But thou when thou pray enter into thy closet, and when thou has shut thy door, pray to Father which is in secret; and thy Father who sees in secret shall reward thee openly." That's why I started over again, I built a house in which there'd be an inner room, a room of secrets, a room for secrecy, a room of the hidden, of solitude, and protection from strangers' eyes. A room for everyone, but just for one. Here that's what I did for times eternal, so folk from me and after me have an inner room.

He descends from the roof, makes a sign to his folk to wait, he is the first to enter the house. On his own. He holds up ten minutes, after that he returns and opens the door wide.

Not out of spite, nor as a provocation but because of the little barred window the rest begin to call the room a cell. Mavrud had made an additional request on the insistence of his folk that at least some daylight reach into the room. The room is situated exactly in the centre of the house, surrounded on every side by narrow corridors and the other rooms lead off the corridors. One of these has no door, so that through its big window light can come in, cross the corridor, and enter the inner room, and sneak through the little window and scatter the dark. Why do I need outer light, Mavrud tries to explain, isn't this precisely the purpose of an inner room, that no outer light should enter it. They try to argue with him, it's not that, you don't get the Biblical meaning of the inner room as you should, he gets angry, he retorts to his brother Niko who understands least of all: "If the light that is in you is dark, how dark will it be?" Take to learning Matthew, brother, maybe you'll get to see! In the inner room you need no outer light, how otherwise will it be inner! They stop arguing with him, but amongst themselves they continue to call the room a cell. Isolated from the whole house in its lonely centre, the cell is wholly empty in the beginning, just on the eastern wall facing the little window, Mavrud has fixed an iconostasis with ten icons. And it's strange the faces painted on the icons appear to be looking outwards through the window.

In the beginning, Mavrud sequesters himself often in the cell. Sometimes he talks to the heavens, sometimes to the earth, sometimes with God, other times with himself. One time he comes out of there with a cheery face, another time his eyes have darkened like autumn grass. Because talking to God turns out an easy and clear exercise, but talking to just yourself turns out unexpectedly difficult.

When he talks with God it's easy because there are two of them, that's when Mavrud senses a presence. Of course God departs when suddenly the questions stop answering themselves. That's when the time comes for exhausting endless questions that have no answer. That's how the days pass and just in winter when at last the month has come for Fina to give birth, something happens to Mavrud. Suddenly he stops entering the inner room. They see him sometimes stopping in the middle of the yard to lift his head towards heaven, to shake it a little, and his lips murmuring something inaudible the whole time; another time he stops in one of the corridors, leans his shoulders against the wall looks at his feet and the expression on his face changes as though the wings of a bird have passed over it. It happens to him in the forest, where he's started work as a wood-cutter: he sometimes stops, grips the axe's handle, after a short time lifts it, fixes his eyes on a one point. He's understood that he cannot escape the questions, wherever he happens to be and sometimes answers find him in the most unexpected places, not particularly in the inner room. Many times, however long he stays in the inner room, no answer comes. The man is puzzled.

…When Fina's birth pains started, Mavrud bustled, fixed up a bed frame, in the same room under the iconostasis. Slung a new mattress over it, full of hay, spread a clean striped sheet over it, brought the expectant mother to lie on it and rushed off to the village midwife, the Greek woman Nastasia. He didn't even think of telling his folks. He quickly returned with the woman, but to their shock and horror Fina lay bloody as though slaughtered, and sticking to her breasts was the slimy little body of the new-born. She looked at them guiltily with her dove-grey eyes, their whites were pink with so many broken capillaries, she smiled and with an effort nodded towards the shears, which lay on the pillow. I snipped it out myself, I had to help it.

They tried to stop the bleeding with alum, with ash, with fresh sheep's cheese, with whatever came to them. Fina became ever paler, by the evening her skin was taut and lemon-hued, that grey fog seeped from her eyes, veiling her entirely; Mavrud thought that he'd begun to lose his sight again. But what did this mean now, when he was losing Fina. He remembered the thoughts he'd entertained at one time, that Fina was not the woman for him, nor for any other man and all at once he felt guilty for everything that was happening. For Fina's pain, for the fears of her mother, who had rushed around, and for the disordered, meaningless words, which he'd begun to utter, like a medium fallen into a trance, for the rain, which poured its despair down the window panes, for his previous idiocy in thinking of Fina in that way, for the grey river of her look, which was already flowing in the opposite direction, for her blood, which had the colour of a black rose…He leant over his wife's hand, her fingers were thin and frosty like icicles, and he began to pray silently, stay, come back, stay…

All this time the two women rushed about the room, overwhelmed initially by horror, later afflicted by some kind of fear induced indifference: with measured movements, back and forth, they pulled up the night shirt, washed the thighs with a wet rag, pulled the shirt down again, wiped the forehead with a vinegar soaked towel, lifted up the shirt; rags dipped in the children's potties, from Mavrud's nephews, woken up in the night, fresh cheese, a sudden single groan, a wet towel like a snake, wait not like this, rags soaked in an infusion of sumac, dried tobacco leaves, shredded over the wound, hang in there, Fina, don't even think of it, don't go anywhere.

…When the women collapsed from exhaustion, right on the floor and propped their heads to the wall and fell into a deep painless sleep at that very second, Mavrud realized what had happened, Fina was looking at him clear eyed and there was no trace of absence, the deserts were not there, the fog had lifted, her irises were clear as though newly washed, just the broken capillaries seeped around them and from the corner of one eye a bloody tear had formed. I'm not crying, it's come out of me. I'm here, don't worry, where is the child?

80

Only now Mavrud came down to earth. He rushed about the house, to see what had happened to the little one. She was in the arms of Niko's wife in one of the nearby rooms. He lent timidly over, amidst the white swaddling clothes he saw the swarthy face with the unwashed whitish gunge sticking to it here and there, with one eye closed and the other wide open, from which seeped grey fog, he took her in his arms and took her to Fina. He stayed rooted to the spot, looking at both of them, and at last spoke in a deep voice, not his own: thank you for being alive!

Fina just glanced at the little one: let's call her Nebesna? Mavrud swallowed and didn't answer – only then did he realize that that day when he was rushing about in a panic, he'd forgotten to pray to God.

This happened the day after Fina and the baby were moved from the inner room to another specially prepared for them. Mavrud went back to get something forgotten and stopped in the doorway.

His wife is sitting straight on the floor in the inner room. The child in her lap. Relaxed in sleep, quivering from time to time. Her face as pale as flour. From her half open mouth saliva glistens like a snail's trail. Long shadowy eyelashes form tender curves under her eyes. The woman is leaning her head towards her right shoulder. Meditating. Some odd light sorrow puffs the features of her face. From time to time the woman dips three fingers, thumb, index and middle, into a deep finger bowl, which has been left on the floor on her left. The bowl is full of apple vinegar, it smells strong. Its outside is painted with golden snakes, each wound around the other, the biggest of which has pointed its long thin tongue in such a way as to appear to be drinking the contents of the bowl. The woman strokes the child's forehead with her moistened fingers and sighs three times.

In the semi dark of the bare room, someone is sitting opposite the woman. Back hunched, stretched out on the wooden chair. At first he's invisible, just a shadow. Later light rays seep through the window showing his bare feet. Huge feet, cracked by long walking. Each with six toes. The end of a dirty cloak, similar to a tunic, curls on the floor. The man and the woman are in one room, but in two different worlds, removed one from the other by a whole sky's distance, that's what Mavrud feels.

And he senses himself in a very strange way, just like a presence in the room, fallen into some strange weightlessness. He sees how beads of sweat, as big as raindrops, glisten in the child's tarry curls. The woman again dips her fingers in the bowl, rubs the moisture of the apple vinegar into the hair roots. The child cries. She looks ill. The woman unbuttons the top of her wine red robe, tries to put her nipple into the little one's mouth. She spits it out. The woman carefully lays the child's head over one of her knees. She takes the bowl and splashes the contents over the man's foot. She opens up her top, takes out her white swollen breast. She lightly massages it. She squeezes the nipple and a spurt of bluish milk rings in the bowl. She recovers her breast. At this moment the biggest of the snakes, painted on the bowl, moves. It comes to life. It lifts its little chiselled head, shoots out its tongue like a spark, and into the bowl fall two drops of shining poison. The woman dips the small finger from one of her hands inside and stirs. After that she licks her finger. She lifts the bowl and brings it to the child's mouth. The child drinks. She begins to drink more thirstily. A thin whitish drop runs down her chin, the last one. The child rests her head into the woman's elbow. The colour of her face changes. It becomes peach-like at first, then grows pink. Her eyelashes stop their restless quivering, the shadow below her eyes becomes gentler. Her chest rises steadily. The woman sighs three times from relief. Milk and poison. A little death in life, two drops. The yeast of living.

…Mavrud tried to breathe with relief, but because he was living through it all like an invisible presence, it wasn't possible to do it. Plaits of straw scattered down the back, a crooked heel, an ankle with bunched ribbed sock. Silent eyes, stranger than strange, sometimes Mavrud was reluctant to look at them. Questions that are answers at the same time, not for this age, as if out of this world, even Mavrud had difficulty in understanding them, though he was pretty advanced in this subject.

It was a summer morning, the little one was looking about in no direction. By now she was four years old and her eyes were exactly like Fina's. She kept them wide open and very seldom blinked. Mavrud looked into them to see the sky with the white clouds, with sparks of sunrise, with spots of blue from sudden rain, which pours from a cloud in a second. The world was reflected in the eyes of his daughter, unlike the eyes of any other human being, at least Mavrud had not seen anything like it. *Do you remember? I was a drop?* As always the first moment, he could not understand, he began to seek the exact meaning. There was no exact meaning, as always. At dusk the same day, again: *Sad?* Mavrud followed her gaze, saw a troubling sunset, saw at the same time a suffusion of peace. Which of the two, he asked himself. What is *sad?* In one of the child's eyes the sunset appeared, in the other peace.

…One day Mavrud finds her in the inner room, on her own, curled with crossed legs on the bare floor and rocking rhythmically and looking straight at the iconostasis. She senses her father's presence without turning and asks and answers at the same time: My eyes? Eyes no? There *are* eyes, there are eyes, don't you see how big they are, even…they even look out through the window outside. The man feels embarrassed. The child repeats without stopping: no eyes.

She was growing imperceptibly and she resembled Fina more and more, but at one point Mavrud realised with heartache that Nebesna could not see into the distance. And also could not see things close up. As the years passed her horizons contracted, distances shortened, because her sight was becoming more and more veiled by the thick currant cataracts, the same as Mavrud used to have from birth. Just that hers were internal, invisible, the surface of her eyes were clear as spring water and continued to reflect the world around. When one day the little one said: *cloud* but in her eyes Mavrud only saw reflected a blossoming pear tree a step away, he became seriously concerned. He set to taking her to doctors, but no-one gave any hope. It wasn't just a cataract, it was something else, and up to now there was no way to cure it. Nebesna was ten years old when she completely stopped seeing things in all their details. She saw a snake as if it was a string, a person as if it was a shadow, a needle like a thorn…

The world appeared in her eyes but they did not recognize the world. It just approximated it and Nebesna tried to not forget what she had seen up till now, but little by little, without even noticing it, she began to create another world, just hers, a mixture of the visible and invisible, and because she wasn't old enough, to have known the material world in all its details up to this moment and for it to feed her imagination in her new situation, Nebesna began to get to know things with the tips of her fingers.

Inside Mavrud froze with horror when he saw this for the first time, but he kept control over himself and called out in a measured tone: Oh Nebesna, what are you up to? That's what folk do who are blind from birth and you're not like them. He said it because he still fed hopes that his daughter would laugh at his fears. She'd kept her habit of talking in statements, which consisted of one word, two or three at the most and now she answered with a half question and forced him to think a long time on what he heard.

And the blind see?

A number of days passed, only then did Mavrud decide to seek an explanation. How can the blind see, my girl. There followed, with no delay, a surprisingly long question-answer: inside, outside, behind, in front, with fingers, with ears, with voice, with memory, with dreaming, with thinking it out…Mavrud didn't ask anything more, he entered the cell and he stayed there a long time. Fina didn't talk with her daughter on this subject. In fact they almost didn't talk at all with words. She would just sit down next to her and gaze continuously at what they could see.

In the summer the little one liked to bury her nose in a rose and take in its scent until the petals drooped and lost their aroma. I'll go through the rose, she said then and Fina tried to understand this statement. She didn't manage and fell silent. They were mostly silent, shoulder to shoulder. Sometimes Nebesna recounted with minimal words what she saw inside: river, willow, sun, fish, white, blue, scarlet, bright coloured, you and me, happiness, the world dissolving, sky, big, big…To Fina's surprise they often came to see one and the same thing, each in their own way. Gradually she gained her daughter's trust and one day Nebesna spoke at unusual length, a complete sentence, she recited it like a white haired old lady, separating words one after the other with a pause between them. I think that if you haven't been blind from birth, but it befalls you, blindness is something like Light's inner room.

As he was sleeping one night, Mavrud jumped in his dream. He sat trembling in bed. The usual nightmare. Most often he dreamt of the war in which he along with rest of the village had taken part. It had disturbed his naturally sensitive character to such an extent that he continued to dream about it until the end of his life. But now he'd had a dream that dug out of his subconscious what had happened with Nebesna before. The man had forgotten it, had not paid attention to it in time, and now when it swam out of the cellars of his sleep, he was torn apart. The event was unnaturally focused in some details, others on the other hand were magnified as if under a microscope, and did not relate entirely to reality, but the man tremulously tried to regain his dream. He squeezed his eyelids shut and this was really effective: in a feverish half-awake condition he continued to see and extend his dream, because he realized that perhaps the vision, in which previous events were magnified, could give him the answer to the one question. It had tortured him a long time and was most of all linked to the young one's blindness.

It is St George's Day, it rains warm rain, stops and rains again. The earth smells of life. A white kid revolves around Mavrud's legs, eating its last grass. The knife has been sharpened, sun sparkles on its edge. In just a moment the kid's head lies on the grass. Mavrud has put the knife between his teeth and with a clenched fist has masterfully stripped the skin from the body, which now hangs on a hook under the pear tree. The thin white skin is warm and soft, like silk, it separates easily. The stomach is delicate to the touch. The guts can be seen and the rest of the offal. The flesh is fresh, pale pink with a skein of fat. The water, which Mavrud ladles out from the pail to wash the kid with, smokes and the steam surrounds his face; that's why maybe he did not see the most important thing, but now he does see it as his brain helpfully magnifies it and the man jumps in his dream: a child's head like a huge dandelion, rises from the grass, the eyes are as blue as the blue sky on this bright May day, the vision has become enormous, it's impossible for him to grasp it…The man tosses and buries his head in the pillow, but the dream continues to enlarge the child's eyes and he follows their direction: the kid's head in the grass is as if sculpted, beautiful as a child's with milk blue eyes turned towards the sky and with a tongue clenched between its teeth; in one corner of the mouth a grass stalk sticks out. But what is the most shocking and what Mavrud cannot bear, and he feels as though his heart will shatter if he doesn't open his eyes, is the mart-enitza which flutters its thin white and red threads, which still hangs from one ear of the kid's head. He remembers the bright laugh of the little one when she herself tied the threads to the little bundle of fur…If only it's just a dream, just a dream, he repeats it now and sees again the child's eyes, magnified monstrously, fixed on the kid's head, thrown down in the blood spattered grass. If only she hadn't seen everything, but she really could have, the child could still see quite clearly. If only I'm just sleeping.

He woke up on the edge of collapse. He jumped from the bed and tottered through the room on unsteady legs. He tried to remember that day and what happened later on. I cut the stalks of green onion and fresh spearmint, throw them into the pan and there the water boils and white bubbles bursts, I skim off the pink foam with a wooden spoon, I salt it, try the flavour., I stir with the spoon. I feel amidst the scraps something heavy, it's the head. I put in there to boil…I take it out and put it in a deep pail, the eyes are sticking out and whitened, that means it's been well cooked…I sit at the table: I pour out the boiling stew for everyone, keeping the head for me. I've added crushed onion in advance, taken out the bones and given them to the neighbour's dog. On the plate I've cut and set out the brain, the tongue, the eyes…God, Nebesna's sitting opposite me. I think to offer her brain. I laugh at her shock. I suck out one eye. Lord Lord Lord and the other. Aren't all men like this – didn't my father and my grandfather and his… In the whole village and the whole Stranzha, and the whole of Bulgaria and in all the Balkans and surely the whole world, didn't all men do this.

Why just my child, Lord God.

In the morning now, freed from the power of the dream, he re-told his nightmare to Fina. She vaguely reassured him, the business with Nebesna's eyes was hereditary, don't you remember that you also had weak sight.

This is what Fina tells Mavrud but she doesn't protest when Mavrud gathers a dozen men from the village's poorest families, opens the back gate and lets them take this year's kids down to very last. The regular St George's Day is approaching and the men, over-joyed with the unexpected present, begin joking and christening the animals with the names of their children and grandchildren.

A wolf in the eye. In the pupil of her left eye a wolf with a pro-truding scarlet tongue. Its eyes were like lit candles. It's gathered its tail, unmoving. It whines like a baby without its mother, like a stray dog. It could be a dog. It's dark with shining eyes, sad in its posture, sad in its whining. Defenceless in the dark night, in the whirling snow storm. Amidst the howling heaven, amidst the deep white snow, in front of the entrance gate. Amidst the universe, looking for a home, protection, love, looking for Nebesna's embrace. It snuggles trustingly. It licks her face with its thin tongue, and her hands. Don't cry baby. There's nothing scary, nothing scary at all. Good dog, sad dog. You're not alone. I'm not alone. We are two. Little golden dog!

Nebesna continued to talk sparingly to her family in separate words or short sentences. But out of her strange way of talking, one long sentence lodged in Fina's memory, to glow with light, white and directionless, but when Mavrud found out about it, the whole day from morning to night he repeated it under his breath as though in a fever: the dark is the light's cellar. This is how he interpreted it and together with Fina they interpreted their daughter's statement in different ways.

Several years passed by. Her body formed like a little tree, which filled its fruits with juice. She didn't live in complete dark yet and every day flowed into night and back into dusk. Her fingers didn't stop remembering, discovering. Contemplating.

She saw silhouettes, shadows, movements, sudden changes in light, but she was forced to imagine the details. That's why one day she saw the silhouette of a tall man and thought that her father's friend Father Peter was stepping towards her with his flapping cassock, unruly hair and deliberate gate. She turned to meet him, grab his hand and turn up her cheek for him to kiss her but she heard a young amazed voice: what are you doing girl, what are you doing. She shook with embarrassment, stayed rooted to the path. She breathed in the scent of a man whom she hadn't smelled. Like a woodsman, he smelled of wormwood and the honey of sun-scorched linden, but also gave off the sharp smell of leather boots, strong tobacco and barbers' eau de cologne and this scent so startled her that she stood motionless in front of him like a doe, with her thin nostrils, her eyes turned up towards his forehead and her half open tensed lips. And suddenly to the man's great surprise and to her own even greater surprise, Nebesna closed her eyes, sighed and said: you!

She was scared, she turned and went into the house, as she left the young man to ponder. He was the new driver of the narrow gauge railway, he'd come to find a room at Mavrud's.

And he was from the Thracian refugees from around Edirne, who had settled in Bulgarian Thrace fifteen years earlier. He'd found the Haskovo village restricting and set to learning a trade, and after learning to become a narrow gauge engine driver, he came to find work in the mountain by the sea. And it was as though fate's finger had pointed him the way and he'd found this narrow gauge railway which carried wood from Stranzha to the small port of Akhtopol. The Italian owner of the railway hired him immediately.

As soon as he'd crossed the mountain, Ilya would look on the level shore and his heart would quicken. The wagons behind him creaked, but he no longer heard them, in his yearning was directed entirely towards the big water. And then he'd stay on the shore and watch as they loaded the logs, how they weighed down the boat bound for Italy, and he imagined that one day he'd embark, without them noticing, he'd shift the logs and lie amongst them; and in Sorrento or some other Italian port, he'd disembark, he'd beat out the dust from his clothes, he'd wash in sea water and he'd set out smiling through the Italian streets. His smile would show off his white teeth, he'd doff his hat and greet everyone right and left. Buon Giorno, Signorita, Buon Giorno Sorento, Buon Giorno Italy, Buon Giorno Italians, because his dream was to go one day to Italy and nowhere else.

Back then when Ilya was fifteen, a dark Italian pushed a barrow selling malebi round the streets of Edirne, he'd shout his drawn out cry in ringing Italian and pour out little pots of malebi for the kids, jellied like jellyfish, floating in red strawberry syrup. He talked quickly in his language and smiled with his white teeth. Sometimes his daughter walked alongside him with a siren's gaze, a crochet dress, her tanned legs seen through the netted bell of the skirt, sandals with long laces, exquisitely tied high above her ankles. Other times she'd eye up the passers-by inquisitively and somewhat co-quettishly, sometimes she'd smile at them and her dark violet eyes glowed round as blackberries. Other times she'd stop, pondering and then her irises grew even darker to an impossible black. Some-times she smiled and her upper left crooked tooth made her pret-tier still. She was fourteen and smelled of her father's fruit sauces. One day their eyes met and so knitted together that for a long time one could not separate from the other, as though they'd been part-ed from their very selves and had become something independent, appealing and frightened at the same time, a ball of looks, gather-ing all the feelings that in one second had caught them unawares. When at last they came to and succeeded in unlocking their eyes from one another, taking them away and hiding them behind their lids, the two of them didn't even see that everything had happened in a matter of seconds.

They lived in a half dreamy expectation that they'd see each other again. He to feel from a distance the warmth of her pregnant look, to catch the aromatic wake of lemon syrup in the air, which floated above her dark cinnamon coloured hair, and she to greet his sunny eyes and to feel his embarrassment that she felt too… and thus they'd stand, two children sunk in their ignorance of what was happening to them, without being able to name it, and because it had no name, it could be everything that brought folk fatefully close, even from a distance. Most of all from a distance.

First of all she left. Well she didn't even leave like normal peo-ple leave, saying farewell, waving hands, looking into the other's eyes, coming up with words…She just disappeared along with her father and her supposed family. According to another malebi seller, they'd gone to Italy, because her father was scared by the approach-ing war, which was being talked of high and low. The boy went one day to the Greek neighbourhood, asked about the house in which until recently the Italian had lived and stood below the wide open windows. For a long time he breathed in the gusts of fruit juice

90

smells, they wafted still from the walls of the room. Only this was left of them – this and the name of the girl which only now the boy learnt from the landlady. Marutsa. She was called Marutsa. So unique from all the others that it hadn't been necessary to differentiate with a name.

When however he went home and shut himself in his room, he tore a page from his exercise book and with a biro wrote her name in big letters. He held the page before his eyes, stared at the letters, until his eyes netted over and suddenly he bent and kissed the single word and with his lips tasted the bitter biro ink.

Soon the war began and when it finished, after a certain lull another war broke out, very short. The Balkans did not cease to smoke and smell of gunpowder and blood, and when the second finished, immediately after this the Young Turk government expelled the Bulgarians from Edirne to Bulgaria. The boy left with everyone. This happened in 1913 and felt like yesterday.

The day when they found Nebesna in bed with the wolf cub was so dark, because of the blizzard outside, that everyone in the house woke up much later than usual. For a long time the clear sounds from the church bells had died out. It was Sunday, but because of the lateness and bad weather they weren't going to church. Cast down and somehow listless they trudged through the yard to breakfast in the old house with Mavrud's parents and brother, as they did on every holiday. Nebesna was not there, they'd thought she'd risen earlier and got there first, but they realized their mistake and Fina went back to wake her up. She went to her bedroom and saw the wolf cub.

Nebesna was still asleep. It had taken a strange position beside the girl, cuddled into her arm, but alert, ready any minute to jump up and pounce. Fina lost her voice, just covered her mouth with her hand and the wolf quivered and pricked up its ears. It watched the woman with its yellow eyes, without any other movement. They stayed like this, the blizzard, the woman and the wolf cub, its eyes fixed on her. And because time had passed and Mavrud got worried, he arrived and an extraordinary picture unfolded before his eyes.

Nebesna is sleeping, next to her a dark wolf with golden eyes, almost a baby, opposite them Fina on the threshold left with no voice, she stands and doesn't know what to make of it. Without strength to step closer, without the strength to get away.

In the first moment Mavrud froze as well, next he feverishly assessed what to do and how to do it, so as not put the girl in danger. While her father was thinking, Nebesna moved in her sleep, and turned towards the animal and hugged it and it obediently snuggled into her arms. Mavrud made a sign with a finger to his lips. But Fina couldn't call out anyway, her voice had not returned. The man left and in a little while came back, carrying a lasso with which he caught dogs to swing them on the day of the kukeri, he approached the bed, ready to slip the rope over the beast's head. He waited for Nebesna to turn in her sleep and leave hold of the wolf, and he threw the lasso over its head. He tied it to the strut of a nearby chair.

The beast thrashed, growled, the girl woke, sat up in the bed and when she recognized her father's silhouette, cried out: leave the baby. What baby, that's a wolf, at last Fina's lips came unstuck and Mavrud who had managed the wolf cub somehow, barked at his daughter. Are you crazy, do you see that baby or no baby, it's an animal. Nebesna grabbed her head in her two hands and shook it: didn't you realize, didn't you understand that you and I don't see the same things.

Mavrud loosened the rope and took the lasso off. Fina silently left and waited for her husband in the corridor. Both of them stopped by their daughter's door. They heard how she calmed the wolf cub down with a long statement: don't be sad, don't cry, there's nothing to be scared of…they just couldn't recognize you.

My eyes are full of birds. They fly to and fro. It's easiest to imagine a sky with birds. I'm scared that my eyes, wide open and darkening, won't stay empty forever, so I never stop imagining, blue sparkling tails, plumage with dark black feathers on both sides of a snow white path in the middle. Their pupils are dark and shining, black as prunes, like wild hard grapes. The stare is unmoving, harsh, far removed. This rounded vision is frozen, as though for centuries the bird has been looking at one and the same thing and left its gaze forgotten there in a different time.

Here it is present with its wings and that's sufficient for me. Sky full of birds, flying to and fro in my eyes, so it's not empty with them. I like skylarks the best because their song fills my skull with light. I hope that the wolf cub doesn't chase them away, let's hope he recognized them, no other way, he has to recognize them and not bother them.

Mavrud found out that healing water ran in the Stranzha interior. It cleaned diseased eyes, clarified sight. He loaded Nebesna into an oxcart one March day, they put the wolf cub with the yellow eyes in her lap and set off. They arrived at dusk. Down a steep path they got to a stream, there from the crevices of a huge cliff flowed white water. With beating heart Mavrud led the girl. Nebesna splashed herself, threw handfuls of stringent water into her wide open eyes...she threw until their whites grew red and her hands froze, but the miracle didn't happen. Only at one moment, while she was catching her breath between two handfuls of water, she suddenly saw a woman, tall and silver: her hair flowed into the sky, where she had set it free, it splashed the icy spring water and her image was crystal clear, frozen in the otherworldly emanation of light concentration. And everything around became crystal clear for one moment. The tree branches glowed against the sunset, the grass became transparent, you could see how a thick green liquid flowed out from them and the silence above their tips quivered like the wings of a huge butterfly, and the image of her father was magnified for a limited time and Nebesna saw his quiet grief. And she saw the golden eyes of the wolf cub, wild dedicated and inspiring.

She shut her eyes and the vision disappeared. She said nothing to her father, so as not to feed his hopes in vain, but long after that, as they returned and the wheels of the ox cart creaked monotonously Nebesna thought over what she'd been given to see. Either it was a sign that Nature mourned for her deprivation, her not being like all others, and had granted her the favour of understanding that, or that it pointed out the opposite, that fate had deliberately chosen Nebesna to be not like the others But maybe she had simply projected her yearning for a stronger vision, which she was never going to possess.

She lifted her head towards the sky and through her fog she caught the quiet glow of the stars and moon amidst that glow, no bigger than Fina's round silver brooch, which on holidays she pinned over the folds of her grey velvet blouse. No bigger than a brooch…

On the next day Fina looked into her daughter's eyes. It seemed to her that they shone ever clearer than before, clean as the March sky above them. She sighed and brushed away a tear that crawled down her cheek.

Mavrud kept the memory of his first vision in the inner room, he told no-one about it, not even Fina. It was special, this memory. Unforgettable. It was more alive than his life and the man sometimes asked himself whether in reality there did not exist other kinds of lives, which go onwards simultaneously, whether a person cannot cross easily between these lives, without even realizing it. His world whirled at this thought and he scratched his head. Unlike that nightmare with the St George's Day kid and little Nebesna, the vision was not so alarming as Mavrud often reminded himself. And so one evening, when he saw through the window the glow from the garden fill the inner room, his heart trembled. He opened the door noiselessly.

And again the woman is sitting with the child in her hands, in meditation, the stretched fingers are knitted together, round the head of the child like a cradle. Her tar curls are damp from the sweat of sleeping, her face is calm, her long eyelashes cast a gentle shadow, just as though two dove feathers have been stuck below the eyes. The bowl is full to the top with warm milk – that it's just cooled can be seen from the bubbles that make a delicate chain on the surface. And again the snake lifts its head and two shimmering drops of poison fall into the milk. The woman does not touch the bowl. Her head leans over the right shoulder and the glow that quivers above her moves a little. The man is also there, moving in the gloom. The skirts of his cloak fold on the floor and when he gets up, it billows. He moves slowly, leans over the woman and with one touch on the shoulder brings her out of her meditation. After that he squats down, he lifts the bowl in his two big hands and begins drinking. The woman makes a sharp movement, trying to stop him. The man elbows her away, the milk splashes and runs on his neck. Furious, he bangs the bowl on the floor. The snakes come to life and slither frightened through the room.

Mavrud gathers all his inner strength and manages in his head to mutter the shortest prayer he can come up with, it helped. Lord help her and straight away felt the weight of his body, His hands moved in front of his eyes… He's here and he's here in body and he must get involved, he must do something, it's no accident he's been granted this vision, it's not in vain that this is happening in the inner room of his house.

Before he is able to think up anything to get rid of this man: his cloak spells danger, his beautiful eyes spell danger, their mousy colour and the dimple on his left cheek like a tiny mouse spell insupportable harm and danger, he feels the force of the unknown. It nails him to the floor and in one second Mavrud stops moving. It's as if he's a child who's scared of taking a first step. Small, subjected to force. Pathetic. That one looks at him with his mousy eyes, instructs him. After that with a sudden movement, he pulls one of his hands out from under his cloak. In it he's holding Fina's shears, from the night of the birth. *Cut her tongue out, because when she speaks it rings and hinders the world, when she sings, when she cries…* He gives this order and puts the shears in Mavrud's weakened right hand. Then he leans over the woman, opens her mouth with iron fingers, the tongue appears, all silver. Cut, the man orders. Mavrud stretches out his hand, the shears shake. I can't, I know who she is. I don't want to. The man smiles beautifully. For as long as you live, you'll cut out her tongue three times, with your own hands. He takes the shears and throws them into the dark corner of the room. The woman lowers her head again, restlessly eavesdropping on the child's dream.

Fina found Mavrud lying in the one corner of the inner room, grasping the old shears. He was breathing heavily and shivering in his sleep. The woman stroked his forehead and got scared. It was as if she'd touched the wall of an oven. She shook his shoulder and then he cried out: cut off my hands, so I'll never be able to cut out her silver tongue.

Ilya lived in the lean-to which Mavrud had put up to be a summer kitchen, but didn't use because in good weather they moved straight out into the yard under the grape vine, there they opened up a long table and set benches. The building was turned into a hay barn and now he added a thin wall and separated out a small room. They soon got used to the man, as with a close acquaintance that they accepted as their own and unconsciously began to trust. That's why they were completely surprised when one day he didn't come home and because the next day too, he did not appear at all, they became seriously worried. They hadn't heard any rumour, that something had happened to the goods train, but the narrow gauge had been built through the mountains, up steep ridges and had many unexpected twists, and that's why they thought maybe that something had happened. The postman, however, who brought a postbag from Akhtopol delivered the amazing news. Ilya had found a deputy for one or two months and disappeared from the little town; they supposed he had hidden in the boat when it was being loaded with wood and setting sail for Italy. And supposedly the captain had spotted him setting up a hiding place but had pretended not to see anything because he'd seen the yearning in his eyes for a long time. A yearning for Italy could in no way be mistaken for anything else, he'd made this comment to the local Greeks, who sat in the harbour tavern and drank from misty glasses of mastika and watched with pleasure how the mastika crystals sparkled and the ice cubes brought from the cellar icebox clattered in the glasses like icebergs in the North Sea.

With the news Nebesna felt a tightened abstract fear under her bodice. She called Sharko and went for a long walk in the nearby forest, where it smelled strongly of scorched camomile, of bitter wormwood and various other herbs, but without understanding why she sensed the faraway wafting of heady aromas of male perfume and sharp tobacco. She even heard the squeaking of a man's leather boots. She got angry with herself and hurried to get home on her toes, bashing into the odd tree trunk. After her ran Sharko the wolf cub. At the edge of the wood she was met with a wondering girlish voice: You're as scarlet as a tulip, Nebesna, where are you running like this, when you can't see well. It was her friend, Antula, the Greek girl from the end of their street, with whom she'd recently become close. I'm running because I haven't run in ages, Nebesna answered and her face flushed even more.

Let me whisper something in your ear, said Nebesna and Antula brought her head close to hers. Never carry out your dreams to the end, Antula. It's very important, your most beautiful dreams should not be completed. Because they're more exciting that way, unfulfilled.

Not one Italian girl had eyes the colour of blackberries. Not one Italian girl had hair the colour of dark cinnamon. Not one had at the same time violet red eyes and hair like a cinnamon cloud. Under the clear Italian sky on the shore of the blinding sea, there was no Marutsa with a crooked upper right tooth nor a smile like a flower. And where there is no Marutsa, Italy is not Italy.

Like an onion skin, like a walnut shell, like a snake's skin, like
the shell of a tortoise, like every other wrapping, our body is peeled
from us, makes us naked, stops protecting us; we have no need of
its protection, at last, at last it's not necessary, we become unknown,
proud of ourselves, we see everything, without it being even necessary to lift our eyelids, they're no longer needed, we dig down into
our memories, our dreams, our illusions and at the same time, no
better call it outside time, we continue to live in our past life, we
dream our present and we remember our future. The trees there
have glowing crowns, the grass is transparent, and we are all fur-
nished with eyes like those of the icons in the inner room, the eyes
there are not eyes, but sources of light, our eyes are skies, birds fly
to and fro inside, and we are outside life, we're heavenly and don't
suffer. I can't wait to go there, at least for a little while, to peep for a
second. I'm telling you the truth.

Antula was concerned. Is that death?

No, it's not death. This is before death and before life. It's between times. I think that every time is a circle, times expand or
contract and lives are the same, sometimes faster times overtake
the slower times and when they catch, a person can live both at
the same time, one all the time, the other from time to time. And
what's more, this life, which a person lives out, sometimes is imagined by him alone and in due course it's forgotten, and whatever
he's imagined in advance, that's what his life will be in the end, but
when he forgets what he has foreseen, a person will ask himself why
is my life like this. But someone else has imagined the person and
that's the way we are, worlds within the worlds, imagination within
imagination. I imagine now and forever, my living is a circle, my
times catch each other up on the way. I creep into my memories
here, into the dreams there and…Most of all I want to be there
where the times are separated for a little and then, so as not to fall
out of them, heaven takes us. And then…Antula did I fall asleep?
How long have you been here? How did I not see you!

When she happened to fall into such a state, her lower lip suddenly began to tremble, and her fingers visibly twisted. Her body rocked and Nebesna began to pronounce words which they hadn't heard her say when she was calm. They were used to her question-answers which consisted of two-three words, no more. Fina began secretly to write her words down, to think them over later... Antula was the most frustrated, when Nebesna talked about wrappings, about human bodies, which are no more than onion skins or the shell of a tortoise or snail, or some such, she was startled. What's happening to you, she'd whisper. I like my body so much. Touch and see, how firm my breasts and legs like a deer's, he told me so. She whispered some man's name in her ear and she laughed throatily and happily, just like a woman... Nebesna paid no attention to her.

And so Antula whispered more hotly, you, because you don't know, you haven't tried it yet, that's why you talk like this, I'm not lying to you Nebesna, it's wonderful we have bodies and yours is wonderful, don't you feel it at least? You speak such rubbish that I get scared...that you'll depart for there all the sooner...Where is there, Nebesna, when everything is here, Do you want to make your body sing, girl. Nebesna nodded her head abstractedly in a sign of agreement. Antula breathed out.

Antula's laughter is both a ring of the bell and low and throaty, warm and engaging and the young leaves of the tree beneath which they are sitting quiver with it. Nebesna cannot see this but feels a light breeze from the branches and knows it's because of the Greek girl's laughter. From time to time, the two men laugh, frustrated at the beginning, getting freer later. Antula talks whatever comes into her head, caresses the man who's sitting closest to her, supposedly by chance, on his hands, shoulders, face and his laughter becomes more abrupt, still more stifled. Let's go for a walk, my boy, aren't we here supposedly on a walk and here we've been sat like old fogies. Nebesna you're lagging behind and you know me, with my winged feet. I'm not waiting for you, but I'm not worried because I've found you a companion. Come on. We're off.

Nebesna does not even manage to object and hears how Antula's laughter subsides in the distant bushes, how suddenly it turns into a deep vibrating moaning and this goes on a long time and the man who's gone with the Greek girl suddenly begins to emit stifled cries. Antula, my love, Antula, and as they were singing in two voices, they knitted their groans together, then suddenly fell silent. It's quiet. And after a while, again, again, the Greek girl's seductive laugh. Nebesna listens enflamed, she's buried her head in her lap. The other man, beside her, doesn't speak. At some point she feels his breath on her neck, as though a caterpillar is crawling on her skin. She feels his hand sneak under her skirt, higher and higher up her bare leg. Nebesna doesn't move, afraid to breathe. In a little while she'll learn how her body can sing. With the other hand the man unbuttons her bodice, his fingers tremble as they take hold of one of her firm tender breasts. He leans over her, sucks at her round nipple. Nebesna doesn't move, suppresses a cry of disgust. Nebesna trembles violently. The man's hand under her skirt has reached a place she does not know, one coarse finger makes some move. The man sucks and she draws back, frightened. She tries at last to pull away but he does not allow it. His fingers between her thighs move again. Nebesna again thrashes as if struck by lightning. Don't, she barely manages to say it. It sings, it really can sing. My body. Leave me be now. And she pulls back far away. The man doesn't want to stop, you have to help me, you can't leave me like this now, he says in her ear and sticks his tongue in there; a woman doesn't leave a man in such a state. Help me finish. What are you finishing, she asks. The man has no way of explaining to her because his whole body is in spasms, wound tightly to her. She feels the hardness of his body, the smell of salt which comes in the end and also her own bitter, sad unfulfilment. It's not that her body is frustrated that the song was interrupted, another bitterness spreads from inside: her soul does not call out at all; it's ashamed and a grey fog streams from its depths. Nebesna cries quietly.

What have you done to her, didn't we agree, that you wouldn't go the whole way! Antula runs up as if from nowhere and without listening to the man's explanations, takes hold of the girl by the shoulders and begins to button up her top. Don't cry now, nothing happened, absolutely nothing. You have to learn that it's not easy being a woman is it. To maintain you're not a woman isn't easy. I don't recommend you to wrap yourself in yourself and not be like yourself. When your time comes you'll know it. Did you see that even you are from this earth, Nebesna. So what about your name, being Heaven, you're from mud like everyone. Don't weep tears over rubbish, they're not your heavenly blah-blah-blah, but are here and now, human.

Late one evening Ilya came home.

Are you sure? That everyone sees one and the same thing? What else do you see, does Daddy see it too? And Antula? Everyone of you sees the blossoming pear tree in the yard? Not a cloud? Not a snowdrift? Not a ball of wool? Or something else? It can't be everyone seeing the same thing…

In the beginning the wolf cub growled and pulled away from neighbouring dogs, but little by little he began playing. It was very strange to see how often he would step back, without rising to a challenge from the puppies, even though they were the same age. Any reckless dog who jumped him, he easily rolled on its back and nipped its throat gently. Nebesna could only make out its eyes which even in the darkest night glowed like crocuses. The dogs appeared as playful shadows with no outline, Sharko was all eyes, full of light. Nebesna could see him even when he was at the far end of the yard. That in spite of her half blindness, she could see something recognizable, clear, not to be confused with anything else, it was her secret hope that at some time she would see. She shared this with nobody so that her family wouldn't have false hopes, but she was almost certain that while the beast was beside her, the miracle would happen. Its proximity encouraged her so much that Nebesna forgot her disability and walked boldly, as if everything was all right. And as though he'd smelled this out, Sharko did not leave her side, followed her always when she went any distance from the house.

Once when she was fingering the air for support and was walking, the wolf cub was behind her, Nebesna suddenly heard him growl, this turned into a frightened snarl. She turned to find out what was happening and with two bounds he caught up with her and grabbed the end of her wide skirt in his strong jaws. He pulled Nebesna back so strongly, that she tottered from inertia in the opposite direction until she fell at last in the dust of the street. Only then did the wolf cub release her skirt which hung in rags. Folk ran up, frightened, helped the girl to her feet, they began to cry out. If it hadn't been for the beast, you'd have fallen in the lime pit Nebesna

Little by little in the village, they stopped being frightened of the wolf. He didn't attack their animals or provoke folk, he just nestled at the girl's feet or played with the village dogs, always so good natured. That's why Nebesna was extremely surprised when one day Sharko jumped at Ilya. One winter early evening he was coming back from work and from a distance saw the beast standing by the gate, staring at the sunset. His eyes burned as though afire, his hair was bristling into waves, made pink by the strong light. Ilya bent down to stroke him, as every other time to run his fingers over the hairs of the wolf cub's neck, but the beast unexpectedly bit his wrist. Surprised the man tried to free his wrist from the jaws, but the teeth were so long that spots of blood spattered. The engine driver decided not to move and the two of them stayed that way, he immobile, the wolf with his teeth sunk in and eyes as hot as coals, fixed on Ilya's eyes. And there was such a wild stillness in the wolf cub's eyes, such a penetrating hatred, that the man felt his legs go weak and he fell to his knees, at just the moment Nebesna appeared at the gate. She heard the muffled growling her heart missed a beat, as she recognized in this growling something unknown, threatening and dangerous. And her astonishment poured out: what are you doing, you haven't forgotten what you aren't? Didn't I say that you shouldn't be a beast?

There was something else going on with Nebesna, the neighbours decided when Mavrud sheltered folk from another village in the inner room of their house. It was one of the heavy winters in the mountain, the snow came up to people's heads and the slats and ridges of the fences were invisible. They didn't leave their houses, just cleared paths with their spades, to reach their animals and feed them. After that the snow filled their footprints inn seconds. It piled up as if it had something to be revenged for in this God-forsaken village. Of the houses only the smoke from the chimney could be seen. On one such day Nebesna stuck her nose to the window pane and spoke shortly, as she used to her in her childhood: a big black smudge in the snow? Person? Beast? Mavrud jumped outside. It was a man, covered in a heavy black cloak. He was shovelling the snow in front of him with a spade and it looked as if he was doing it with his last strength. He fell at one time. He sank into the snowdrift. He disappeared from Mavrud's sight. And when he tried to walk through the snow towards him, he suddenly saw that behind the man's back were oxen fastened to a wagon, and under a blanket, a woman wrapped to her head swayed to and fro without saying a word. Just when he saw how the woman was rocking without uttering a sound, Mavrud's heart skipped in apprehension. The outsider got to his feet and carried on digging, didn't even look up when Mavrud called to him. He dug and dug and dug, and hurled the snow over his shoulder and it fluttered like flour caught in the wind. Mavrud found it necessary to grab the man's hand and at long last the man stopped, and looked at him with such terrified eyes. Just for a moment the man looked at him but Mavrud felt his desire to sink into the snow and become invisible, to disappear from this world. He turned to leave. Then at the threshold of his house, he stopped, stood with head bowed down, gathered his strength and came back again. This time the man muttered some words, although he looked at him with the same eyes. We've been in the snow since yesterday. We took the sick child to Akhtopol to Doctor Savichev, the white guardsman. But when we entered your village, what happened, happened…

The woman continued a swaying heap, with a whole foot of snow over her back, her head, her knees. Seconds passed before she fixed her empty gaze on Mavrud and could scarcely unglue her lips. No-one wants to take us in with a dead child… We've got an inner room, Mavrud said, thank God we've got an inner room.

And he took them in, into the inner room. Fina and Nebesna met them in silence. They sorted out the bed with a clean cover and the men placed the unusual guest there. Nebesna brought her favourite dress of sky blue woven cloth with white buttons to the bottom, and a knitted white jacket. She and Fina dressed the girl.

They dressed the man and the woman with what they could and led them after that into a warm room to defreeze. Mavrud warmed up the rakia, he mixed in black pepper and began pouring it into the mouths of the outsiders. Their locked jaws barely opened, the liquor leaked down their chins. In the end the heat conquered them and they sank into a heavy forgetful sleep. They came to only on the next day and then the man relaxed and began to speak, although with the same eyes, alienated from the world, gazing at the floor. She's our only one, but it would be the same if there were ten. I'm not poor, I'm not a refugee. I'm local. I moved from Yambol to a neighbouring village. She fell sick a week ago, and her lungs were weak. We set out before it snowed a second time, but on the way a second blizzard caught us. I walk and clear with the spade, walk and clear. And she begs me from the wagon, sing to me, to ease me, sing to ease me. When she fell ill when she was young, I'd sing songs to distract her and she quickly got better. But now, what the heck… sing while I'm shovelling, snow filling my throat, and what kind of song, just a howl comes out from my mouth. The whole way I swore

104

at the snow and got angry at the weather, but it's all the same in the end, as if I was murmuring against her. And I didn't sing for her. If I had sung, she might have got better, the song might have helped, what do I know. And maybe she had some spiritual need, I wonder, she needed not to be alone there, where she was going. She needed a song to accompany her…

It poured snow that night and the snow had no intention of stopping. It piled up and piled up. And it wasn't soft and gently, it was heavy and solid and it wasn't going to melt quickly, that kind of snow. The men and the women went into the inner room to hold a wake for the girl as was the custom. Fina had lit candles, the thurible glowed by the iconostasis. They left them with their deadly grief and retreated.

They slept on and off and woke up. They felt a wondrous presence in the house. After midnight they drifted off from the ordeal and exhaustion. At break of day, a quavering voice woke them up. He was singing with long pauses. The voice was like a wolf's howl. Nebesna's wolf cub nervously pricked up his ears in the dark and she began to stroke him between his ears to calm him down. The two of them were quiet, Nebesna and Sharko listened in alarm. It shouldn't be like this, he had to save his voice. He had to calm it down, so what the dead girl had wanted could come to pass. But the man turned it into a howl. You can't do it, you mustn't do it, Nebesna repeated. The deeper the grief folded into the voice, the more savage the pain was growing, the more the insupportable the anger. The girl could not hold back, she jumped up. She took the wolf cub with her and entered the inner room. She put her hand on the man's shoulder and he lifted his head and looked at her and she said: you see, it's started to melt, you see, it'll melt, however hold up now a little. Let me take over from you, because it's not good for her like this…For you, it's better, but it's not for her. Go and rest in the other room. I'll take over. The man obediently fell silent, wiped his tears with his sleeve. He put his trust in the girl and left.

Nebesna sat herself on the chair by the bed. She was silent, then she coughed and began to sing. Her voice gradually strengthened, her tension eased. In the raw night, the melody was quiet and unsteady. Soon however the girl let her voice go. She sang this way until the dawn broke outside. She sang all kinds of songs, filled with hidden pain, some kind of unattainable joy. Beyond the walls the man and woman silently listened. Ilya listened too from his room. Mavrud and Fina listened: Good Lord, what songs our Nebesna had inside her. I've always thought so and now, whispered Fina and Mavrud in the dark was on tenterhooks: well, I mean to say our daughter, Fina, where does she know these songs from? No-one in our village sings them, so where has she learnt them…The neighbours also listened on this tense night and crossed themselves and the blizzard stopped at that moment without anyone noticing…

Nebesna went back to her room, when it was light everywhere outside. She lay straight down on the bed and only then felt how much her lips hurt. They were swollen and cut and she tasted blood on her tongue, without realizing she'd bitten it, because the words were very difficult in the songs she'd sung this night by the girl's bed.

Fina writes secretly at night. She's printed out Nebesna's words in her mind and now licks a pen and put the crooked purple characters on paper: *today it was harsh summer the year 37 drought and roast from the sky and our daughter with Mavrud Nebesna was again rocking as she sat her skin was whiting out her face was turned sorrowful and as I looked at her my heart turned to mourning and she began talking one person against another person don't believe, don't want to believe that someone could understand how much the other suffers, nor even that someone can bear another's pain nor does it matter that the pain is one and the same as the pain of the other if they're hurting for one and the same thing and don't think that peace is better than worry that the wild is more scary than the tamed that what's seen is more real than the imagined and finally she stopped trembling and I saw her clear eyes and*

106

Nebesna, would you like it if I drive you to Akhtopol so you see the sea. There's no way you won't take it in, it's so big that even a person with no eyes would see it. Ilya got mixed up but Nebesna pretended that she hadn't heard this stuff about eyes. She turned towards the young man, didn't speak and then she said: they say that my eyes are stronger and deeper than your sea, brother Ilya. Because they regarded the driver as one of them Mavrud allowed Fina and Nebesna to climb into one of the wagons which had been loaded more lightly with logs and the train started creaking on the mountain bends. Ilya blew the whistle at the front – from the time he'd come back from Italy he'd been unapproachable and silent, but recently he'd become like a new man. Nebesna sat frozen, but this was on the outside. The smell of the grass, the drops of sap from the tree branches, the wind that buzzed like a warm bee and also a real bee, intoxicated by the honey scents, which flew before her eyes and Nebesna took its measure like a flaming spot, the smell of wood logs, rough, damp, numbing...There was another way to feel the world and to be happy. On this day she felt how inside her something was singing, and around her the same, and she wondered suddenly that perhaps the soul is everything which surrounds us in very special moments in our life, quivering, and so the soul is not just in us but we are in it for some inexplicable reason.

In Akhtopol it smelled of figs and damp box bushes, of fried fish and swept yards sprinkled with water, but above all these, there hung the bitter overwhelming smell of the sea. Nebesna breathed it in with lungs at full stretch and when at her entreaty they left her alone on the shore, her heart beat faster. This was the smell of some special solitude, sufficient in itself alone, huge and for this reason, terrifyingly relentless like some Godly being from a child's book of Ancient Greece, which Fina had once read her in her drawn out stuttering. Together with the sea they became a pair and shared with each other. This could have consequences, more probably for her than for the sea. She didn't know what yet, but she felt it.

Ilya who had waited for the logs to be unloaded at the port, was in no hurry to get back. Fina had to go round the shops in the town, so he took Nebesna to the café in the centre. Here they sold malebi. She might like it, was his embarrassed explanation, when, according to her wish, he installed the girl with her face towards the broad blue water beyond the shore. They brought them bowls, the jellied malebi floated in cherry syrup, do you smell the syrup, Nebesna, do you smell it, no I don't smell it, brother Ilya, here now everything smells of the sea.

After that her mother came and all three set off towards the train. Every one of them was pleased with this day. Fina because she found the greatest variety of balls of wool in all possible colours. Ilya because he'd treated the girl with malebi and Nebesna, because she'd had it confirmed: that the world is a lot more than you can take in with your eyes.

She dreams, that she dreams, that she dreams. She's alone in bed, with her golden hair, with her eyeballs moving restlessly under her sleeping eyelids. In the first dream she sees herself: also in bed, slightly befogged, lifted above a tree. The bed rocks slightly and she's sleeping in it but manages to see in some way: she's bald, her bare skull shines moonlike, her two eyes are closed but one blindingly white hand with no body draws a new eye, stretched over the crown of her head, bright, open wide, blue and unmoving. A deep set eye, awake, all-penetrating. While her closed eyes sleep and they dream the next dream, and she sees a real bed in which the real she is lying, with golden hair spread over the pillow like straw and at the same time the third eye sees colours which rotate dazzlingly. The stars fly, winds blow up, people fly aslant the endless blue sea, talk in some strange language, gesture to understand each other, but this doesn't happen, no-one understands the others. Among them is her father, wrapped in a dazzling coat. He alone talks comprehensibly, quotes the bible desperately. *Fear, fear, in the face of death, through the whole of our lives, fear which makes us slaves,* The Holy Apostle Paul. I believe you, that it is so, it is so, and so teach her, teach my daughter to see. I cannot. Or at least teach her Apostle, not to be scared, of the dark! The dark is the sister of death, fear, fear of the dark in my child is overwhelming me! Nebesna knows she is dreaming the prayer, while at the same time in the next room, Mavrud looks up to heaven in his sleep, and she tries to tell him, you're making a mistake, but no sound comes out of her mouth and this is so painful. And because in the last of her dreams, there are two dream visions, one asleep and one awake, Nebesna, in her three dreams, decides to get out of them at once; with an effort she manages at first to move the fingers of her hand, after that to wake up, to free herself from their weight, but it's not an easy task to emerge from three dreams at the same time. She touches herself nervously, her forehead is smooth and hot, her hair is in its place, the crown of her head is calm, not a trace of that drawn out all-seeing eye. Thank God, Nebesna crosses herself. Thank God that I'm still here. She turns over on to her side and sleeps without dreaming.

Isn't it time to let the wolf cub go, Nebesna? You can get too attached to him. Shall we let him go?

Everything which is my fate lies before me.

Even more rarely did Mavrud enter the inner room, although he continued talking in proverbs. He was scared. That man with the mousy scar would turn up again, he'd leave the shears in his hands, he'd give the order: cut out her tongue…Fina started going in there, to set about her womanly work. Against one wall, she assembled a loom and Mavrud didn't object, he even helped her put a stove in the middle of the room, a portable metal stove for additional heat-ing, burning coal through the winter. Gradually the floor was covered by numberless balls of wool, there was every kind of colour. Like a wise goddess of colours, Fina prepared her festival, patiently and self-absorbed. She plunged her hands in, she stirred up the wool balls, let them roll loose to mix up more and only then set to creating the harmony which was necessary for spiritual peace. And for something else, which made her thoughtful then enlightened, but she did not know its name.

Nebesna often sat next to her. Fina began to name the colours out loud: scarlet, mother of pearl, electric, beige, wine, sky, sky, black, violet, Morello, morto-mauve. Both of them trembled when Fina pronounced the name of this last colour. Morto. Dead. Dark. Sorrowful. When at some time the morto-mauve ball finished, Fina asked Ilya to get another one from Akhtopol, he asked her, puzzled as to why she needed this colour exactly. Morto means dead, Auntie Fina.

Fina was worried but she did reply. As there is life and death everywhere, so they're present in colours, Ilya, you'll bring it for me if you've got time. Buy me morto-mauve. The names helped Nebesna to see the colours: electric had the colour of lightning, there were also orange, lemon, sunflower, rose, strawberry, raspberry, dove…Defined in this way, the colours came to life, it was as if they each had a smell. Apart from that Nebesna began to identify them almost faultlessly and in another quite peculiar way: this ball burns my fingers, so it's scarlet, this is grassy, because it cools me down, walnut is grainy, Morello is smooth, electric pricks me like a lightning spark…Fina didn't quite believe that it was possible to recognize colours in this way, but still she witnessed the fact that most times, Nebesna identified the wool with her eyes shut tight.

But as for the morto-mauve, the girl never touched it.

Fina began to weave and when she needed to use this colour she always put sunny yellow next to it or scarlet or orange, these colours would counter it with their light warmth, so that it would not be allowed it to gain control. She didn't discard it, she used it sparingly, but didn't reject it. How can you discard something which exists for good or ill! Every colour, according to Fina, was created for a Godly purpose, because all the colours together became the light. When the light failed, they'll turn back into messages.

Nebesna was left to go to Akhtopol on the train on her own, because Fina did not want to leave the loom, so as not to stop her inspiration in weaving the colours and Mavrud didn't even hesitate, go, walk around, my child, see the world. Ilya made up a convenient spot in one of the open wagons, helped the girl to settle and sat in front. The little train creaked around the bends. Ilya blew the whistle. Nebesna took into her nostrils the familiar smell of the freshly stripped log-corpses, and however much this was incense for her soul, the words still repelled her. It was autumn and the mountain was aflame with the Indian summer. The smells this time were dry, scorched, the earth breathed like a mother relieved of her load, snakes hissed in the unexpected warmth of the sun, a strange bird gave a lonely cry and Nebesna felt that her joy in touching the mountain's secrets was more measured, more stifled than before in the spring.

In Akhtopol Ilya helped Nebesna to get down. He caught her under her shoulders and for a second threw her in the air as light as a feather. She flew to the ground, he held her in a strong hand and felt her warm breath, and without the man wanting it, his other hand lay on her head, and it stroked the dishevelled straw curls and slipped down her back. Her shoulders were thin, straight and quivering and Ilya felt a sudden tenderness. Forgive me, Nebesna, he spoke apologetically and pulled back. She could not come up with any reply, her voice had disappeared. When she came to herself, she whispered her plea to be left a little while on the shore, on her own. He didn't ask her anything, helped her sit on a rock.

When after an hour he returned, her hair had greyed from the salt sprinkling from the waves, her face was damp and smiling. Before setting off back, Ilya again took her to the café and ordered malebi with Morello syrup.

I'm not sure that the sea is what you say it is she threw out at me today and my daughter Nebesna doesn't want to explain whatever it might be she doesn't want to tell me I won't like it she smiles abstract-edly Daddy won't like it either that I like what I think it is…our girl expresses this deliberately sometimes wants to avoid answering how-ever much I insist on her uttering a word in the end and I think what more can the sea be there a big lot of water but I can't grasp it look at the trees she says about the wooden material that Ilya transports in his wagons and it twists my heart…Nebesna is sensitive and it's not good for her when I think of her handicap Ilya transports corpses of trees she whispers deep in thought someone kills the trees the foresters will surely kill the forest in the end Ilya transports the corpses and as the skins are peeled off they smell sad and their smell drifts wide and because folk don't want to admit what they're doing they call the dead trees logs it's not supposed to be the same and it doesn't sound scary

Mavrud and Fina weren't at all surprized when Ilya, shifting from foot to foot, asked them for Nebesna's hand. It's the right time for her, the woman murmured and wiped a tear. Mavrud paused a while in silence, before pronouncing his latest biblical proverb, this time from the Gospel of St Luke: *Can the blind lead the blind. Will they not fall into the pit?* He was confused a second but then began to explain: You, Ilya, you're not blind, you see very well, but you're pretty obsessed with this Italy of yours. You become blind, you keep talking about it, it's really close to your heart, that's why I don't know what to say…When a man looks in one direction, he can't see any other, it's as though he's blind, that's why I said what I did. Forgive me. First of all ask Nebesna, does she want this or not…

Nebesna was indeed transformed, heaven like, her expression lit up. Ilya blinked opposite her. But she gave no answer, neither accepting nor rejecting. She just put off her answer, so as to think it over and Ilya waited restlessly. After a day or two he met Mavrud.

We talked with Nebesna and I don't know what to tell you. It's like she's scared of something which she can't express or doesn't want to share. In the end she agreed but I get the feeling that she doesn't want to be a burden to you. You can see it, my girl will manage by herself, that's not your problem. However I want to quote you one of Solomon's proverbs. I'll change it a little, if the great king allows: it's better to live in the corner of an attic than with a man who is a stranger in a big house.

And the wedding passed and Nebesna remembered her whole life, how in the church, Ilya squeezed her hand and didn't want to let go, as though he was afraid that she'd run away from him, and the singing of her father's friend Father Peter, she remembered her father's sigh which he let out behind her back and most of all she remembered how amongst the festively burning candles in the church she distinguished two especially bright flames that didn't quiver like the others and while she tried to think about what to do to send him away, the wolf cub made his way through the crowded church and stationed himself to Nebesna's right.

After the wedding the pair of them lived in the eastern half of the house.

I see colours, Sharko's eyes, dreams, I see Mum's voice, Ilya's fingers, I see Marutsa, he's told me everything, from the violet eyes to the crooked tooth. I see the seed within me, smaller than a lentil seed, I see in the future, hair like straw, eyes like the sky, sadness like the sunset…I see a black rose over a milk white shoulder, drawn deep into the skin with a pen…I see very far, all the way to another Fina and another Nebesna. I see, see, see.

Nebesna's belly grew. It was winter and her time was approaching. Two months left. Fina restlessly turned over the balls of wool on the floor in the inner room, she brought them close to each other, compared the colours, pondered and remained unhappy with herself. One day she began a new task, this time she set to knitting. The big needles rattled in her hands, glinting in the glow from the stove, beside which she sat late into the evening with the knitting draped over her lap, thick and fluffy, and the colours lined themselves up, white to red, green to sunflower, blue to pink, orange to brown, black to mother of pearl, colour to colour, they sought and found themselves and each helped the other to blossom, to be highlighted as unique. After ten days of zeal, Fina was close to finishing, but suddenly she began to dither. She let her hands fall on her lap and had second thoughts. She dug out the morto-mauve from the balls and knitted a thin line at the end of the piece. She became worried. She undid it. She went out into the yard to breathe fresh air and to think again. She returned and stopped on the threshold, opened her mouth in wonder and froze.

A woman sits on the floor. Next to her is a little boy with black curls. The woman has turned her head to the right, a curl falls over her forehead, a wine robe folded gently. In her hands she's holding Fina's knitting, the needles rattle and give off sparks. The stranger is knitting in the morto-mauve and she looks Fina straight in the eyes. With her lifted clear eyes she smiles. She looks encouragingly, steadily. She leaves the knitting on the floor, picks up the child and disappears into the void…

Fina knelt, lifted the blanket indecisively, held it in her lap with her floppy hands. At last she carried on knitting. She knitted in the death-colour and from time to time she dropped her hands with the knitting on to her lap in amazement. She finished and sighed. She'd worked a blanket for Nebesna's future child and there was nothing to add, she unfolded it on the floor, stroking it with a gentle hand, and falling in love with her imagination. She'd knitted every colour in every combination, because she'd readied herself for this a long time, collecting wool for years, thinking through the combination of dyes, the volume of the knitting, the delicacy of the nap and now the blanket glowed with all the colours. Fina had heard that light originated from them and they really overflowed like some heavenly meadow. That's how Fina imagined a heavenly meadow. Not one colour was missing. It was all light, light for Nebesna's child, light. God, you who are light, don't deny it in your mercy!

Antula's laughter, her nimble steps. Her little footprints in the snow. Nebesna-a-a. Ilya is dazed, he can't believe his eyes. Hair like a cloud of dark cinnamon, sprinkled with snowdrop sparks, violet red irises, rounded eyes, rounded as if in wonderment, whirlwind gait flying over the snow, happy giggle, Nebesna-a-a. She flies again. Ilya grabs her by the hand and feels her breath fresh from the frosty morning. I am Antula, don't you recognize me. She tosses her hair, a thin orange fragrance wafts. Ilya loses himself utterly. When he comes to, she's already gone.

Nebesna's belly looked like a small mountain, her knitted fingers rose and fell without stopping. Antula often stuck her ear close to the rising swell and noisily proclaimed her joy, it kicked me, it kicked me with its foot. Nebesna was pleased that her friend began to bring the news to her every day, because her flighty babbling and ringing laughter distracted her from bad thoughts.

Sometimes when he came back from work, Ilya came to see them, I'm not going to be in the way, you talk, this is woman's stuff, I'll just sit by. And he sat down where he could. And was quiet. Are you here Nebesna would sometimes ask. It was as if Antula didn't notice him. She concentrated on chatting, laughing, cuddling Nebesna, stroking her belly. That wolf cub of yours, Nebesna, he's a beast and nothing else, if you only knew how scared I get when he stares at me with his yellow eyes. Like he's eating me up with them. Why don't you go and tie him up. I'll stop coming, you'd better believe it. And that very day after the guest went, Ilya tried to fool him with kindness, gave him a piece of red meat and slipped a noose round his neck. He himself was amazed how easily he did it. It was as if the wolf cub had surrendered. As though he wanted to tell him, that he had his own will, but for unbeknown reasons, his choice was to submit to another's will.

On the next day at dusk after work, Ilya met Antula in the street. I'm just now coming back from Nebesna's, she's sleeping, don't you go and wake her, and the baby kicked me a whole seven times. It was snowing thick and bitter and the girl's curly hair quickly got white. It's really good that you've tied up the beast, Ilya, as if you knew I was afraid…As they stood together she suddenly grabbed his hand, squeezed it to her breasts. She rose on tiptoe, brought her lips to his ear and in a throaty voice spoke quietly and seriously, where did you pop up from, where did you pop up from…as though it should have been Ilya who asked this question, as though every time he saw her the same words didn't jump to the tip of his tongue, In the complete oblivion of the moment he lost his face in the damp of her hair, shut his eyes and breathed in her fragrance of soap and geranium which wafted this day.

They stood like this an eternity. In the end Antula peeled herself away, releasing Ilya's hand and as she slid from time to time and laughed, she continued on her way through the blizzard. The man brushed the snow off his shoulders and went to the inner room. It was his turn to visit her and craft a wooden cradle for his future heir.

Who tied up Sharko, why have you tied him up, immediately untie him, right now, don't you know he's not a dog, he's not a person, he's not from here, he is free!

A white cradle of linden wood, fresh white shavings, Nebesna sometimes entered the inner room, happy that Ilya had found precisely this wood, light and fragrant. The man lifted his head, caressing her belly with his eyes and continued after that to manually smooth down the slats, Nebesna stayed in the sawdust and quietly celebrated.

One early evening he again felt her presence and smiled without lifting his head. He continued to plane the wood smooth, covered all over with shavings. He felt a small tender hand, passing over his hair and brushing away the debris, and her fingers knitted themselves into his thick hair. He started to help her but almost stopped breathing: a trail of lemon fragrance over his head, breathing a burning whisper into his ear, low laughter, he squeezed

116

a delicate hand tight by the wrist, you can't do this, girl, don't play with fire, the cinnamon hair fell over her eyes, covered her face… Through the plats, violet irises shone, as though sparks were flying. It's me, don't you recognize me, you've been seeking me so hard and you don't know me…It's not true, says the man. You're fantasizing. I found Nebesna and I don't need anyone else. You're spouting lies Ilya. Nebesna's not the woman for you, nor the woman for any other man. That's typical of the women in this house. She hurriedly stroked his face with icy fingers, her index finger stopped over his lips, scratched them with a nail, and without realizing what he was doing, Ilya sucked the tip of the finger like an icicle. The rest of her fingers were white from cold and icy, he sucked them one by one, so as to separate them, at last he took her little hand in his and blew into it to warm it with his breath…And Antula coiled around him like Stranzha ivy and moaned in his ear, my body's singing for you, Ilya, my skin is singing, my eyes are for you, for no-one else. I now know why I was born.

The man tore her away from himself, he squeezed her tighter by the wrist and pulled her to the door. He shoved her forcefully, Antula went flying. Don't set foot in here anymore, girl, not one step. He closed the door, drew the bolt, sat among the piles of shavings and as he found his head with his two hands, he stayed like this a long time.

The day came and it was early evening and new clean snow was falling just like when Fina's time had come. It hardly covered the ground, in places black protruded. Nebesna felt the first distant twinge and smiled. She set off to give the news to Ilya first, she didn't want to raise worries in the house. She knew that with the first baby, the early stages should be kept secret and up to the last minute. But the end was not going to be soon, because this is what it was like for women in her family. It could go on for days. Ilya was not in the inner room. The floor was swept, the shavings were gathered into piles in one corner, the cradle stood by the wall, white and fragrant. Nebesna brushed it with the tips of her fingers, smiled and suppressed a new pang. She continued looking for Ilya through the house, she didn't find him and went out into the snowy yard. A thin volley of snow blasted in her face. She opened her mouth to take a breath, laughed quietly and set out towards the shed. The door was half open and was rocking quietly in the wind. Nebesna could not sense Ilya's presence here either. She turned back and at that moment stumbled in shock.

From inside she heard Antula's low throaty voice. Her moans lifted like a song. And a male voice arose, his song twined with Antula's. After that Antula cried out something as though out of this world. Then the man. At first Nebesna didn't recognize Ilya's voice, she'd never heard him cry like this, in their shared nights, she'd only known his hot short breath and his abrupt silence. In her embarrassment she had thought that her friend had brought one of the men from the village to this lair, to be hugger-mugger this winter day. They were just a few steps away, behind a thin wall. But as she could see neither the thin bare legs with golden skin and hair bristling from the cold, twined about her husband's waist, nor the stretched neck nor the hair pouring like amber, nor the throbbing vein, nor the man's thrusting, causing Antula to sing and because she didn't want to see all this, Nebesna decided to tip-toe away. While she clenched her teeth against the next spasm, she stepped back. And then she heard the man's swooning cry: you're sweet, you're sweet as malebi, Antula-a-a.

Nebesna fleeing in her semi-darkness stopped in mid stride. Marutsa-a-a, Antula-a, Marutsa-a, Antula-a-a. On tip-toe through the yard, through the snow, through the pain, quiet so they don't hear me, quiet so they don't see me, quiet, she soothes the pain as though she's caressing a sick child. It's nothing, stay quiet, just because it's come out of the blue…otherwise what's the big deal…a man and a woman…and another woman too and a few stupid words…far too stupid…and funny…Quiet, Happened what had to happen. Quiet,

118

I tell you, because shouting with no voice is deafening. I can hardly stand you. No-one should hear us, no-one, because we're giving birth for the first time, me and you. Quiet, Sharko, quiet my boy, just to get dressed and a scarf to wind round you. There, I'm putting on Daddy's fur coat, it's thick and warm and fur lined boots too, with the woven laces on my feet, so they don't hobble; quiet, quiet, just so they don't hear, afterwards it's easy, and we know the way…

On the thin snow, through the sleet, down the empty street, on to the rails, which gleam… Still uncovered, like thick threads. We know the way, you and I, and as long as you're with me there's nothing scary; just stay quiet, don't growl, as we're the two of us together, there's nothing scary.

Nebesna and the beast like two shadows in the whiteness of the snow, little by little, quietly on the rails, further and further through the silent mountain, sunk in thought: two hours, give me time, give me time, Lord, and I'll get there and I'll be saved. God gave her two hours and Nebesna walked the six kilometres through the Stranzha mountain on the rails, along with the wolf cub, with his gold eyes, gleaming in the dark, with the warmth of his body to which she sometimes clung to warm up. I knew it, that you'd be my fate; he was suddenly brushing her legs, an inherently dedicated companion through the church of the forest, where the candles were the bright stars. A mystery how Nebesna saw them through the muslin of the quiet snow and smiled; her smile parted from her face, it rose smoothly and turned into a star; with her still infrequent birth pangs which hammered her for seconds, and with the distant life-saving presence of the sea, of the huge solitary, great water; at last she felt it from the smell of salt, of iodine and of something else which had neither smell nor name. Nebesna knew it, because this was what she yearned for. When she reached the shore at last and heard the boundless measured noise of the waves and the terrifying hum that came from its depths, she knew she was saved.

She waited a moment, silent, and then put her frozen hands to her mouth. She shouted with whatever voice came, loud to the heavens, a cry as long as a spasm. After that she shouldered the great loneliness and set off back.

They were two and sharing everything.

Shout as much as you want, Nebesna, cry as much as you can. I'm talking to you girl, you shouldn't be doing this, you're chewing up your lips. Scream Nebesna, it's an inner room, no-one's going to hear you. Your mother Fina, when they called me, because of you, we found her, as if she'd been slaughtered, in this same room. I helped get you out alive. After she'd been cut by the shears, her blood nearly ran out. And yours will run out if you don't shove a little. Put some effort into it, girl, because we'll cut you too. Shout, girl; Nebesna shout out 'cos you're a first-time mother. Shout out to God that he came up with this palaver, a person to be born out of such a tight slit. Shout, call God for a reckoning, and while we're talking, that stunt you pulled today, I don't understand it. Not that it's my business, but it's downright mad. Sometimes the pain brings out some wild ideas in first timers, you thrash and bite wherever you can, but I've never come across anything like what you did. If it weren't for Grannie Anka seeing you, whose house is behind the station, if she hadn't gone round to your folks to tell them, what she'd seen and how you hadn't come back from your walk, with the hours going by and it was dark and deserted, and you with your belly up to your mouth, and so the woman gets dressed, as she's crippled and poor, and tells your folks, if she hadn't done this I don't know what would have happened. Where didn't they look for you all this time, your father, your Uncle Niko. You'd have turned into an icicle or you'd have lost your child, just as well they met you with horses, the fact that they shook you up a bit, that's good for the birth, that's one good thing coming out from this madness of yours…Remember from me, girl, whatever comes into our heads in this life is not worth our human suffering, because early or late, comes the great forgetting. And be-

120

cause I don't see any serious reason for your taking to your heels, I reckon it's some madness, nothing more. You're talking rubbish… Do you see now. As they're words, and stupid at that, it can't be the reason for such an ordeal as yours…Shout now, because I'll cut you and my eye won't blink. And tell me that it's because of some stupid words, so your folks don't have to guess, so they don't feel guilty about you. You don't want anyone else to feel guilty, because of your thoughtlessness. And now shout. I'll be stitching you in the end.

Antula flies over the icy waste and quietly laughs. Her face is fresh, her hair is cloudy, her fingers are frozen. A heavy sunset burns alarmingly. She doesn't notice it. Sunsets don't interest her. Only the unrelenting song of her body interests her. Beneath the thick shawl in which she's wrapped, her skin wafts the scent of soap, boiled in the dew of the garden carnations. And the dew that breaks out over her upper lip after her session with Ilya has a hint of toffee. He really likes that because it reminds him of the taste of malebi. It sometimes seems comically stupid to Antula, this stuff smells of bewilderment, for a strong handsome man like Ilya to repeat these inappropriate words, you smell like malebi, girl. They're somehow vulgar, they don't resemble words of love, but an incurable disease. They've told her that she's got eyes like stars, eyelids like basil leaves, legs like a faun's, body like a poplar, she's heard all this because the men in the village are singers and she accepts their clumsy comparisons, untypical of their peasant mouths, ready prepared from the songs, but no-one has thought of saying anything like Ilya. There's no doubt the words are more than strange. They're sick words, but spoken with such yearning, such a break in his voice, that Antula feels her insides turn over. When he whispers in her ear, a strong light spasm begin to circle low down in her tummy.

The pot rolled over and still found its lid, Antula thinks now as she flies over the snow towards Nebesna's house to see the new baby.

And then, barring her way, stands the wolf. Again the scary sunset burns in his eyes. He growls quietly with deep hostility. Antula steps back, the wolf takes a step forward, he stops again, taking up an intimidating pose. Oh God, the beast no longer has eyes but two penetrating points…Antula doesn't know whether to stay on the spot or run. And while she's pondering with no drop of strength left, the wolf comes up really close. She stays on the spot, sunk in the snow, rooted. The wolf lifts his front legs and put them against her breasts. Antula doesn't move. She only feels how her bladder begins to empty and hot urine is running down her thighs, making a yellow stain in the snow. The smell of urine, mixed with a hint of toffee. And now she sees what's in his eyes, it's not hostility. She doesn't know what it can be, but she stops being afraid.

They stayed this way until at some point, Mavrud and Ilya were passing by and as they exclaimed and apologised, Nebesna's father unfastened the wolf from the girl.

When the shot reverberated and was swallowed into the blizzard, Nebesna didn't realise that it came from their yard, from the gun which for as long as she remembered, hung on the wall of the barn. A few minutes passed. In that time she unwrapped the baby, changed her, wrapped it up again and fed her. Only when she got up, a sudden thought left her breathless. She jumped with the baby in her arms, she stood at the front door in the frosty day. A stain over the white snowdrift, dark grey, motionless, with two dying golden eyes, something smelled sticky and thick, wild and sharp, it numbs the snow. Dedicated and protective as if for the last time, the real and imagined, together. The dark pool ran it crept through the yard. Oh God, it's happened. I was afraid and it happened. How. It can't be. He's not a beast, nor is he human, he's not from here or anywhere. But he didn't do anything to Antula, he could have ripped her to pieces, but he's not a beast, he already knew he wasn't. He was my fate, my hope, that I can look anywhere in the world as I see with his irreplaceable eyes.

She said all this slowly and distinctly in her head. At the end she turned her face to Ilya for just a second. And he understood.

122

∼ *PART 4* ∼

IN WHICH IT BECOMES CLEAR THAT TIME LIVES IN PEOPLE, AND NOT THE OTHER WAY AROUND, AT LEAST IN THE IMMEDIATE MOMENT THAT BETHLEHEM AND HER GUEST FEEL THINGS IN THIS WAY, AND MORE SO, IN THAT THE OLD WOMAN UNEXPECTEDLY GROWS YOUNGER AS SHE BEGINS TO TALK LIKE ANTULA AND HER EXCITEMENT COMPLETELY RESEMBLES THAT INNER STRENGTHENING WORK OF THE MIND FROM WHICH ARE BORN IMAGINATION, SUDDEN LONG VISIONS AND STRANGE EXPERIENCES, CREATED BY ONE STRONG THOUGHT, PASSING UNSTOPPABLY THROUGH TIMES, FROM PERSON TO PERSON.

"You are the second Nebesna, out of the womb of the second Fina."

"Call me Anastasia. I prefer my own name."

"And you call me Bethlehem. I'm not any older than you. I am older only on the outside. And only by years. It's impossible for one person to be older than another. Time is an inside job."

"OK…Bethlehem…I repeat that I prefer the name, I'm used to."

"If in this mountain and on this street, you're not called Nebesna, where else, my girl…"

"My mother also preferred to be called Maria, she kept her other name hidden. Everyone called her Maria. Only my father Mattei the dolphin called her the other name. Being called Fina didn't appeal to her much."

"I know that. After Mattei's death she left her birth name behind. Kept it for festivals. More than not they didn't happen. Celebrations, I mean. However the name Fina really suited her, I know her from a child and I assure you, it was right for her and for no-one else. But because, darling girl, we scarcely live time, it mostly uses us, lives us, as it thinks proper, forces us sometimes to find refuge in another name, in a different place, in another life…"

"I don't think that in this case a name is so important."

"It's important and even more so. It can't be that your Grannie Nebesna didn't tell you that. I remember your great grandmother Fina, Mavrud's wife, Both Finas, your mother and her Grannie were similar. In the kindness of their eyes, in their voices, in their silence. And both had the habit, when they were quiet and thinking things over, to close their dove grey eyes tight. Your Grannie Nebesna opened her half blind eyes wide, their whites appeared beneath like an arc…"

"You knew them well, all of them."

What are you saying, what do you mean by *knew*. You don't know what we were all of us together, you don't have a clue girl. My whole life I waited for someone to come after them. Not that I expected you exactly, but you came. And I recognized you, in spite of not seeing you since you were a girl. And I knew the rose on your shoulder, and your hair like straw, so what if you've blazed it orange. Who else could be coming but you? I am Bethlehem, from Antula's womb and my mother named me after a star, to be go along with the name of that first Nebesna, your Grannie, my mother's best friend. And you've remembered quite a lot. So, just as you've kept stuff in your memory, you may have missed something, now if you'd like to listen to me? I can't believe it! How can I believe that just because of this you were dragged through yesterday's storm! I cannot believe you at all, that you've found me for this. You've given so much meaning to me, when Vassilaki said to me yesterday, that my life has been meaningless and empty forever…I've waited for you for years, I've thought up at least a dozen ways of telling you. I repeated them to myself alone, while my tummy swelled like a hump, misshapen and full of my big loneliness, my childlessness and whatever else… Best to start, the same as though Antula is telling it, it lingers on my tongue the easiest. My mother was sweet tongued and when I'm on my own with myself, I talk for hours like her, just as though she's doing it. Just as though I am Antula. Though she passed away so long ago, my mother. We were about ten years old Maria-Fina and I, and I still remember. I remember the stories of Marguda, my Grannie and Vito, my second father. I'll tell her story and its human truth also, because I have to talk instead of her.

…I am Antula. When the Greeks left for Greece in 1914, because they expelled them from Stranzha, for the Balkan states to exchange their mixed populations after the dust blown up by our wars, my father put on a show, but he stayed in Bulgaria. This was the place for us, our house, our land, our life is here, where should we move into other lands and lives. Nations didn't interest him, his nation was his wife, his child, his field and vineyard, and he himself, the nation was in them and not the other way round. When the migration began, he loaded us into the ox cart, as everyone was doing and set out with the rest; we said goodbye to our Bulgarian neighbours, who were crying over our departure and when she saw how they were crying my mother began crying too, that's why I think my father hadn't mentioned his intention to her, so she didn't slip up in front of his fellow migrants. And because we set out at night, our cart creaked along behind the others for some time, but then turned sharply away towards the vineyard. No-one caught on to us. We reached our vineyard, we unhitched the wagon, my father pulled my mother to one side, they whispered and she returned to make me a bed from a folded blanket in the shed. The two of them lay in the cart and in my dozing I heard them quietly talking. We waited a day or two. No-one saw us in the vineyard because it was late autumn and not a person appeared. But because it suddenly got cold, my father decided one morning, Come on home, whatever happens, happens. And we returned, no-one said anything, our Bulgarian neighbours fell over themselves to celebrate our staying. And the powers-that-be shut their eyes, what's been written is written. I was a little over two years old then, but I remember everything like yesterday.

The second thing that I, Antula, dimly remember from later on, is how at the upper end of our street, Mr Mavrud demolished his house. Something he didn't like and he pulled it to its foundations. A brand new house was being built by then nearly to the middle, and he took to knocking it down as well. And dust rose to the sky, his mother cried and crossed herself, he stood and watched, and rubbed his hands. His brother Niko cried, you're crazy, brother, you've got a screw loose, it's not just your work you're destroying, but ours as well who helped you. Mavrud paced back and forth, joyful and satisfied. For the first and last time I saw a villager to be pleased that he's destroyed something ready for use. His wife Fina said nothing, I heard later from Mummy. This was typical of her, not to be interested too much in such stuff as building and demolishing a house. When I was growing and I became friends with their daughter, Nebesna, I felt from up close how much Fina wasn't like the other women. At the time I remember now, Nebesna hadn't been born yet, her mother Fina hadn't yet been cut with the big scissors with which they sheared sheep, and her blood hadn't been infected. My mother Marguda said that a miracle happened. Nastasia, the Greek, who just like us had hidden with her children and stayed in her house, was the village midwife, she maintained, that she'd poured Algeria wine down her throat. Forced it down a whole two hours, she's opened her mouth with her strong fingers and shouted, drink Christ's blood, woman, drink Christ's blood and the wine will turn your blood into new, and Fina revived, just that two days and two nights after that she didn't wake up, she lay numbed, more to the point drunk from the wine. That wine has real power, just so you know. They put the baby to her nipple, and she didn't feel it, she was so exhausted sunk by drink into unconsciousness.

When Mavrud demolished the house, and he almost went mad from happiness and excitement that he'd thought to do this in time, his daughter was not born. Nebesna was born in the inner room, you know it. Four and a half years after me. I think that I've remembered how the whole night after this, Mr Mavrud sang different songs. His voice was heard at our end of the street, I remember how my father teased me: joyful songs, but he's singing sadly, because a girl child is not for joy, but for worries.

I remember Nebesna from that time when she stepped into the street, carefully feeling out the air with her hands, as if reaching for an unstable support. That's when everyone understood that something in her eyes wasn't right. And they were clearer than clear, so that I had to blink facing her. When I was invited round there the first time, she took me into the inner room, made me sit, straight against the wall facing the iconostasis, and she says: Eyes not? Not eyes? That's how she talked in the beginning, in short questions, in which she was not asking at all. And she pointed at the iconostasis, and I saw that the saints' eyes were special, frozen in unearthly trance. And something else shocked me. It was as if these eyes looked through the barred window outside towards the sky, which appeared far away. Is cell? That's what she said about the room. Cell for their lights? She didn't say their eyes, she said their lights. I remember it well. When I went to their house years later, in this same cell, which wasn't at all narrow, but on the contrary, was the roomiest room in their house, my friend set me down and began to walk round the walls. At that time they hadn't been plastered and painted. Nebesna touched brick by brick with the tips of her fingers, stopping by every irregularity and announcing, here it's printed by a grass stalk, this brick is pitted all over by summer drizzle, here I'm touching the print of a pigeon feather, here's the footprint of a deer: he'd gone to drink water and stepped on the brick while it was still damp…she came out with this kind of stuff; because someone who has no eyes, starts to make things up, certainly so folk don't think them half human. More to the point, so they don't think themselves as inferior to others. Then she showed me scarcely visible scratches, supposedly from butterflies, from mosquitos, and whatever else you can think of. She stopped abruptly, smiled and said, is the cell roomy? Is it no different from the outside?

"Nebesna, what do you think, why is God so high up? Why so far away?"

"So we have a road, why else is he so high up. He…

The wolf cub was severe with honey coloured eyes. Haven't you seen honey from acacia, yellow and transparent. That's what they were like. His little ears savagely pricked up, his tail continuously quivering. Nebesna loved him very much. In the beginning she carried him in her arms like a baby and kissed him on the forehead between the eyes. Later, later when he grew, they set out walking side by side. The beast never parted from her, that's how she was more confident moving without another person. When I saw him for the first time, I liked him and we even played, but in years to come he turned into my enemy. We'd grown up, my bust was developed, when Nebesna confided in me something, and I can't forget it. That wolf cub, she said quietly, he's neither a dog, nor a person, nor real. I've imagined this wolf and all of you believe he's real. I thought him up for courage and protection. And because of the light in his eyes. But you took to believe. And now you see a severe wolf cub with yellow eyes, only that. Because all of you see one and the same. You see the world in one and the same way. Why is that? Why can't you see: eyes are sometimes nasturtiums, another time candles, sometimes live coals, another time two suns. Look, now I'm seeing them as something out of the ordinary. But I'm not going to tell you exactly what, I'm not going to. Because, Antula, it's time for you to begin to see things differently from the others. Look, I see differently and that's got nothing to do with my weak sight.

I got angry with her. She who had practically no sight was teaching me to see in ten different ways. Well what person can, I ask. And if you begin to see the world differently, doesn't that mean that you're not all there. For some time I didn't go to theirs, and so she looked for me at home. She came with the wolf cub, which rubbed itself around her bare legs. Don't be cross, Antula, that day I was joking. I don't see anything, I imagine this stuff. Only the wolf cub's real. He's not imagined, he's real. A common or garden wolf cub, from the forest. In the winter he came to the front door, there was a horrible blizzard and I took him in so he didn't perish.

I quickly cooled down. In spite of not believing the stuff about the wolf cub this time. Now I was more than certain, that she'd really imagined him and that all of us saw a product of her imagination. There, what sorts of strange stuff, this Nebesna provoked me into thinking sometimes. And one day I actually saw.

Certainly from fear, eyes of fear are certainly large, I saw something unseen. It's black night, with no stars. There are such summer nights in Stranzha, which are impenetrable. I'm rushing to get home, I'm late. I stumble, I fall from time to time, because the streets are steep and stony. Suddenly, a light above my head, clear but not blinding. I lift my eyes, I take in the view: a sky blue wolf is flying, all over as if in flames, just though the light, which shines doesn't give out heat. Cold bluish flames flicker in every direction and sometimes outline the twists of his body. Get away, devil, sss! I shout at him, God, cut him down, the Satan, amen, I scream with a dry throat. I'm scared fit to piss, but I know that the devil, if he hears God's name, disappears in a second. Nothing of the sort happened. I took to calming myself down: couldn't this be a force for good, which lights my way so I don't hurt myself in the dark. And as I calmed myself, I saw that it was no wolf at all, but the moon, appearing from behind the clouds, huge and yellow and lighting me. So without realizing it I got back, without falling again, not once. Just as if I was walking on the surface of a sleeping river, in spite of having my head lifted towards the sky the whole time. Out towards our street it's the most potholed and stony, but I didn't stumble any more. It was so bright in fact that, even walking with eyes closed, I wouldn't have fallen. Never again would that kind of moon shine.

In the morning I ran to Nebesna. I stuttered and screwed my face, and I tried to tell her what happened. You've had a dream, she interrupted me. She shook herself and went into the house. But I stayed to think this through and reached the conclusion that Nebesna's influence over us is so strong that we begin to see her visions. They just suddenly start to turn into our own experiences.

Soon after this we parted for a long time, because I'd grown up quickly and she, four or five years younger than me, was still a child.

Antula, how beautiful you are, Antula, I heard this all the time from all sides. I didn't really like myself. I was always wanting my breasts to be more tender, my legs to be more rounded, my hair to be blonder, not black like the night, and my skin to be whiter. They liked me, however, as I was. Surely there was a reason why, unless it was a common delusion, which passed from person to person. From man to man. There was a Stefan. He made up a song for me. Antula, fair skinned Greek girl, Antula, Stranzha flower, who will pluck you my Greek beauty, fragrant lily… we called wild irises lilies. I was fragrant, really. My mother Marguda knew how to make soap, in which she put different scents. We had violet soap, soap from geraniums, roses, lemon balm, lemon and orange peel. The woman had thick fingers, but she didn't give away the secrets of her soap to anybody, she only made it for us. Only to me her daughter did she reveal it, and later I passed it on to my daughter Bethlehem, I left her the secret written on white paper with ink from gall. So, I'd scrape my skin thoroughly, pour water over my body in the yard in summer or in a big pan in the kitchen in winter: I filled it with snow, which melted in the warmth, poured hot water from the pan on the stove and got in, and I would sit for hours; I liked being clean, and I rubbed my skin with soap foam, so I'd smell of soap a long time. One day as I was bathing in the yard, I felt a look from behind the thorn fence. I felt it on my back. I knew it was a man, like it was on fire, my shoulder blades were burning. But instead of shouting, or running to the house, I made out that I hadn't realized. I stayed and continued putting soap in my hair, to dig my fingers in and scratch, and I just happened to turn around, so he got a good eyeful: how the foam ran down my neck, how it poured from the tops of my breasts and how firm they were, how their nipples poked out from fields of soap bubbles, black as ripe mulberries. And then men found out that I bathed in the yard, every time I'd sense their dazed presence. First one, then another, they didn't stop pleasuring themselves.

Sometimes I'd stay with my back to them, so they could get a good view of how fit I was from behind, and how strong my thighs were. Another time I'd lean to the front, supposedly to wring out my hair, so they could see my breasts from the side. One time, just one time, I swept my head back and my hair fell down my back, and I opened my thighs, because it was Stefan behind the fence. Through my senses I knew it was him and I wanted him to see me all over.

I gave myself to Stefan first. He was first to pluck my lily. I was sweetened up by his song. It was dusk and I was coming back from the meadow. I was late and he met me. He practically grabbed me round my waist, my legs grew weak and I lay myself down in the hay. He threw himself on me. So what if his song was beautiful, he was rough, he didn't even consider that he might be my first. It's possible he couldn't accept that he was my first. When he realized, he moved away from me and stared at me amazed, why didn't you say, my girl, look what we've just done. He really hadn't guessed.

That's the sort I was, why hide it. I liked a man's hand to crawl over my body and for it to sing. I didn't think there was anything shameful. In nature isn't it just the same. Ladybirds scramble over each other, stags jump on deer, stallions do the same with mares, cocks over hens. Why not folk doing it out in nature like all earthly creatures and enjoying their bodies. Why did God forbid it for folk, allowed it for all other living creatures. My cries were a joyful song and men liked it. They found out that my enjoyment was real, when they jumped me and that at the same time I have some kind of gift in bestowing pleasure. And I didn't get a name. The men turned out real gentlemen. Neither did they mention me in the pub, nor did they boast one to another that I'd tumbled them. Not that I went with all the men, not many met with my approval. But it wasn't just one. I was young and beautiful and I gave myself to men as a present, and who did this in those strict times in this God forsaken place. They didn't even think of calling me a floozy. They knew that fun with men was the last thing floozies wanted. I didn't reach out to married men, however much they circled me. The most I'd do when I smelled them behind the fence was to do a twirl so they saw my beauty, so that when they got home, they could make their wives happy. And I didn't give Stefan a second go.

You don't ask me how my parents didn't realize. I forgot to tell you that my father worked as a woodsman in that time, for Vito the Italian, he was killed by a huge tree that hadn't been properly cut. This happened before I'd started bathing in the back yard. My mother Marguda became a widow, and so distracted by having to take care of everything she didn't sniff out my quick development. My brothers were young, squatted with fishing rods on the river bank.

And without realizing it, Nebesna's bust filled out, but her womanly beauty was tender, transparent and somehow distant. Whether it was because of her unearthly eyes, clear and turned upwards, so that white arcs appeared over her lower eyelids, whether it was because of her semi-blindness, or because of her light filled hair, which nobody else had, smooth as straw and shiny…but maybe because of her words she looked like this, those words which rarely fell from her, but they were strange and somehow other worldly. She began rocking, nonstop, clenched her eyes and went white, she'd recite them hurriedly, and her mother Fina, tense all over, would strain to remember them and then write them down ungrammatically on paper as she licked her biro. I found these mauve pages later and as today is a day of truth, let it be the whole truth: I discovered them one time in the inner room when I could still go in there. Fina wasn't there and I took them out of curiosity, so as to see what Nebesna was saying and why I could not reach her ability to talk. After that I had no way of returning them, and I took to destroying most of them, but that's another story. Bethlehem will tell you later, if you want to hear it; and she can give you the pages that survived.

Bethlehem stops at this point, stops making out like Antula, and speaks in her own voice with her own words, these pages, my girl are for you: their mauve has paled out a lot but the marks of the pen are still there, I'm sure you can restore them through touching and feeling. When I finish telling the story, I'll give them to you. And now I give you this soap, it's at least thirty years old. It's mixed with geranium and linden, and thyme, these fragrances go together.

And again Bethlehem stops being who she really is, but embodies herself into a young fragrant woman, passed over in time, but return- ing for a little while to share, to ask forgiveness and only then to leave forever. Once I, Antula, did something that I was ashamed of till the end of my days. I knew that Nebesna was still inexperienced, no man had touched her. I realised that her body was still asleep. I thought that someone had to wake it up. But an underhand thought came into my head and didn't let up. I didn't want Nebesna to be above me. I wanted her to be like me. This could only happen if I succeeded in driving her into the hands of a man. And so one day I tricked her into going for a walk. I convinced her that every woman becomes a woman this way, to prepare herself for her future husband. As if everyone does it. Fina would hardly have talked to her on this subject, in her house the women were abstracted, they only thought about other-worldly things. Her father Mavrud would never have had such a talk, fathers didn't talk to their daughters about this. And he wasn't all there, Mr Mavrud, he just gabbled biblical proverbs, people learnt to keep away from him, because it wasn't nice for someone to point at your life, even with biblical words. Life is for allowing things to happen as you want, isn't that so. If we start to interfere, look how it punishes us. Like I messed with Nebesna's life, and my conscience has punished me from then on. But more about that later…

It was a lovely day, the wild pears were blossoming. The forest smelled of young leaves, sunny drops fell through the branches. And Nebesna's hair shimmered like corn cob silk. I prattled and giggled the whole time, while my eyes just darted to find a suitable spot. I made them stop in the thickest part. We sat. I continued to talk all sorts of rubbish. The man who'd come because of me was joining in. The other, whom we'd lined up for Nebesna, there was something worrying him, you could see. At some point the moment had come, the guy beside me was pushing every which way, if you get me. I had no more strength to put him off, so I got up. I reassured Nebesna that we'd be close by and we snuck into the bushes. We finished quickly, because we'd been warmed up in advance, our insides were turned upside down by cryptic banter and petting. And as I got up and fixed my skirt, we crept up on the pair. Through the leaves and branches I saw how Nebesna had buried her face between her knees. I saw how the man moved right up close to her, their shoulders were touching. Nebesna didn't even change her position, nor did she lift her head. The man's hand went under her skirt, you could see how it was moving under the material. At some point he thought of unbuttoning her bodice and he put his other hand inside. This time Nebesna lifted her head. I saw how embarrassed she was. But apart from the embarrassment, I caught some shy curiosity. And some quivering anticipation. I let out a sigh. Nebesna was like everyone else. And with this, nothing could stop her being like me. I could control her without her even understanding. And I wouldn't be the white crow in the village. Not that anyone had called me this, the men continued to treat me as their sweetest secret. But it was me who felt this way. I really was a white crow, amid all the women.

The man's hand moved under the skirt and I saw how my friend's body jumped, as if struck by lightning. I realized what he'd done. My lover huffed and puffed and I elbowed him in the ribs. Her body shook a second time and I thought of grabbing my pest, who was staring like a tomcat, and pull him away so as not to be a hindrance. But at this moment Nebesna pushed the man away, opened her eyes at last and I saw.

I saw a remorseless grey fog well up in her pupils. I saw how her hair had flattened, I saw the desperation, her face darkening like a frost-withered flower. And I realized that I'd done something irreparable. Up till now Nebesna had accepted her body and soul as one whole, that's how she'd felt them, I am sure. I thought now that I did not know her and it would never be granted for me to know her. I saw a solitary tear run down her cheek. I turned back through the bushes, over the mole hills. I bumped into tree stumps, and I screamed as if from far away, I'm coming Nebesna, don't worry. I'm here. I'm coming to you. I dashed and stumbled into her legs and I held on to her ankle as we lay on the ground. I was blind. Blinder than a mole. And so much blinder than Nebesna, let's not talk about it now.

Only at this minute when my Bethlehem told me everything, how I am outside time and the times, how I'm outside life and lives, death and deaths, how I'm not what I was, at last I begin to see.

Out of Antula and Nebesna, you cannot make one woman. What do you say, darling girl?

When Ilya turned up in the village I didn't take any notice of him at first. I was overfed with men. I soon got tired of them and

I easily left each one behind, as my curiosity pointed to the next. As we say in Stranzha, they'd begun to stick in my craw, like when something sweet becomes too sweet, but there's nothing else and it starts to taste bitter from the sweetness, that's when your mouth wrinkles up. If you throw yourself into a whole tray of baklava, your tummy will swell up, your mouth will dry up from all that syrup, the tip of your tongue will burn. I'd had more than enough of men's caresses. I went about the village like a bee heavily laden with honey, swollen up all over with nectar. The women had begun to suspect something. From the glow of my sated blackberry eyes, from the aromas I gave off, my indolent walk. And my mother, Marguda, the firewalker, saw it.

She frowned one day, clutched my wrist tight and pulled me into one of the rooms. She yanked my blouse, baring me from the neck down, and she saw what she saw, she said, we'll wait for these shameful marks to pale out and if I find a single bruise on your body, I'll strangle you with these bare hands, so that my ten fingers will leave their marks forever. I knew my mother wasn't joking. Just as she would step out on hot coals to dance, with the very same aplomb she would rub my presence from her life. I calmed down, I promised that I wouldn't touch another man in my life, unless he was the man for me forever.

This went on a long time, until one day I met Ilya. I mean to say, not for the first time, but when I *really* met him. His and Nebesna's wedding had passed. And I was there, that's how I remembered the pair of them. Their faces were lit up by the candles. Nebesna's eyes shone like suns. I remember how Ilya held her hand and how the wolf cub came into the church and snuck up unnoticed to stand beside the bride. They left him there, so as not to interrupt Father Peter, and he stuck to Nebesna's leg and stayed there to the end without moving.

I bumped into Ilya one winter day. I'd speeded up on the ice and slid, falling straight into his arms. Nebesna was heavily pregnant

136

and I was going to see her, to celebrate her growing belly, to feel the little one kicking me, and to distract her from bad thoughts. As he held me, I saw his face change, his skin paled, his eyes widened in amazement and he quietly moaned. He looked at me as if he'd seen a ghost. It even made me uncomfortable. I peeled myself away, shook my hair and brushed the snow out of it. I said to him, I am Antula, the Greek. He came to and looked at me like no-one had looked at me. I lost myself in that same moment. My body trembled anew, again my body sang from its innards and little spasms crawled low down there, only when I saw this man from a distance. But something new. Some kind of spiritual sweetness, untasted bliss. I didn't know what could be stronger than the blessing of a woman's body. I just gave myself to him completely. At night I tossed in bed and I burnt on coals, then icy shivers convulsed me. In front of my eyes his taut body appeared, his work hardened hands, his face windswept by the mountain and the sea and his eyes. His eyes most of all. Amazed I realized that even if this man didn't touch me my whole life, just looking into his eyes would make my soul sing.

It turned out that what I'd imagined was not enough for me. I began following him. I was a real she-devil, but he didn't realize it. There was no-one to tell him to guard against me. I thought up a dozen ways to snuggle up to him, just as the wolf cub would do with Nebesna's legs. I'd get in his way. I'd brush him with the tips of my cinnamon coloured hair; everyday I'd get in the tin tub filled with hot water and change the soaps, and my hair would become even more fluffed out and its perfumes wafted ever thicker. There was no way my mother Marguda wouldn't catch on. She grabbed me one day, as wreathed in steam, I was getting out of the bath, and she pinned me to the wall. I let her inspect me from head to toe. Not finding anything suspicious, she waved her finger: don't forget what I'll do if I find a bruise on your body. Whether it's from a man or something else I'll still do it.

One day at last it happened. It was frosty, the earth rang from cold. My fingers were like shards of ice, the skin on my face was taut and my hair was frosted by the sharp snow. I climbed up the stairs and went in without them realizing. I stopped in front of the door to the inner room and I heard a soft rubbing. I stole inside. It was him. He was smoothing out the boards of linden wood by hand. He was sunk in shavings. I approached and without even meaning to I dug my fingers into his hair. He caught my hand, turned and when he saw me, he lost his breath. He got up, without dropping his gaze. And what was meant to happen happened. One by one he sucked my fingers, like trying to separate bits of ice. He rubbed my hands, you're frozen Marutsa, he'd mixed up my name. He folded my fingers in his hand and began to blow, to warm them with his breath. And as he was doing this, he suddenly remembered himself. He grabbed me by the shoulders and shook me roughly. He pulled me by the hand, pushed me hard and I flew into the corridor and he bolted the door.

I was happy, I was delighted. I was senseless. I snuck out of the house and got back home through the snow. Every day I began to go to Nebesna. At dusk when he came back from work. No-one suspected anything. Sometimes I went to see Fina in the inner room. There we unfolded the many coloured blanket. Once I felt the stares from the saints on the iconostasis. All of them were looking at me with their silent eyes. They were Nebesna's eyes, they all had her clear eyes. I got scared and hurried to leave the room.

You know the rest, don't you, so I won't make Bethlehem tell it. You don't know everything? But you'll let me rest and gather my strength. And in a while we'll carry on.

*A Short Interval in which They'll Gather
the Strength to Continue Further*

Why did they stop? Because the worst is coming? Or the most sorrowful? Or the most wonderful? Whatever it is they need the strength to continue. Bethlehem often lies back on the bench under the awning and sees how the heavenly clouds move in flocks and change their shapes. Vassilaki is scraping the yard with a hoe. Nebesna sometimes goes to the house at the other end of the street. In the inner room of Mavrud's empty house, she's installed the old computer. This is the only thing she's brought from the town, and her scarlet cotton dress; the dress is older than the computer. Nebesna-Anastasia looks at the monitor's blank screen. You're living an uninspiring life, my girl, that's what a writer-acquaintance had written in a flash of friendly openness. But the more uninspired your life the more talent you show in your writing. Illogical, but it's a fact…As far as life was concerned, he was right. Mistake after mistake after mistake. Her life was a spiral of mistakes. But she wasn't sure if it was true about her talent for writing. By herself, being hesitatingly honest, she wasn't so confident.

Sometimes she translated for a common-or-garden local magazine, other times she wrote words that she expected to come to her…She didn't take it seriously now. In spite of writing and publishing a dozen books in this way, she experienced an uncomfortable feeling on telling anyone she was a writer. Her computer had not been put to work in two years and this was not professional whichever way you looked at it. She sat in front of it, sometimes between two books, but did not touch the mouse. The mouse which would have eaten up her book. The book of her life. The slim scraggy, skinny little book of her life. Even mice don't allow themselves such a life. Her computer had no defence against viruses. The old programme had run out and she hadn't installed a new one. Whatever came, this was it. Just like life. She'd never vaccinated herself against the flu virus. And she either caught the flu, or didn't catch it, question of immunity. However, recently, when she felt the urge to write, she was very careful with the keyboard. No more delete. It was life and death, no delete.

Today is the first evening she'll sleep here. After a thousand years away. It's getting dark, from the bricks under the plaster, you can hear the first slight sounds. The willow leaf stirs, the bird feather stirs, the deer stamps its hoof, almost immediately the river flows. Maybe old fashioned, maybe stupid, maybe it's an illusion, but so what; illusion and imagination in this house is a way of life. Apart from this, it's important not to be alone.

The old house breathes. The inner room is also alive. The times have flowed through the house leaving the timelessness in the eyes of the saints on the iconostasis on the eastern wall. She's still not looked at them and they haven't looked at her. To peep into another's eyes is an infringement of their freedom, although it's not obvious. Hidden violence. Penetration through the eyes requires a mutual vibration at an equal frequency. Just like her vibration with Anastas.

She hasn't even thought of this and on the computer screen his name appears. She dons earphones and connects. His voice unwinds from the distance, but not alone, he's trumpeting in excitement, at last, at last, I've learnt the language of dolphins, after so many years. Just listen. And Anastas speaks for several seemingly endless minutes in unusually rounded dolphin words, just like from his childhood, but this time he translates and she listens with an open mouth. Hello, how are you, life is wonderful, dangerous, endless, life is a festival, a weekday, a pain, a joy. Her brother says whatever comes into his head. She smiles at his game. But at some point it's as though the sea is really splashing in her ear, she catches

140

how the dolphins plunge, diving and re-emerging on the surface, she feels the salty spray dampening her forehead. She thinks she's breathing next to Anastas, she thinks she's sitting on this shore. Here they've never murdered dolphins. Don't you remember because of that I ran away from Burgas, to find the kind of place where no-one wages war with creatures like me. I really found it…She sighs. Don't you miss your birth-place. She poses the same question every time they talk. And now she gets an answer, which if it wasn't Anastas would sound pathetic and insincere, but she knows that he's convinced about his words: Oh come on, our homeland is the whole earth, don't you understand, how small it really is really, compared to infinity…If we hadn't parted, who knows how many words would have passed between us in our lives, but we'd maybe miss the most important thing, Anastasia. When someone is far, far away, he finds a few words that will mean a lot…She's thought the same thing in the same second. I love you Anastas, she says to him and hears his abrupt laugh. Do you see we used to live regularly, would you have dared to say these words freely. We are afraid to talk face-to-face, we're scared of looking funny and that's a fact. Anastas trumpeted in the end and translated: Here is everywhere and everywhere is here, don't you understand. Surprised, she says nothing and they stop. She's sure that this thought of his was sent telepathically.

She continues sitting, staring at the advertisements which change on the computer screen. At some point she opens the note-book and closes it again. Today words are not working for her. Words cannot express that which is greater than them. Today she's scared of the words. She gathers courage and turns to the east. To turn east in this house needs courage. To look into the eyes is a little daunting. Not to mention how you can look into something which is just eyes and to understand that all of them are the eyes of that distant Nebesna.

After midnight the noises behind the plaster stop. A last slight sigh. It's so quiet that at once she wishes she's not come.

Not stayed in the empty room, not listened into the various deer hooves clip-clopping and pigeon feather rustling. Imagined stuff that has survived the interior of the house. Alone in such a house, means alone against the world which at one time they said was everyday. And so what if you're on your own in such a world. Is this what she's managed to achieve in this life, in the inner room of her life.

She logs into her ICQ again. She chats sparingly.

Hi I'm Tango.

Hi why are you Tango?

Because I like Tango.

Why do you like it?

Because it's got rhythm, which draws me into oblivion.

There's more to it than that.

What is it?

Ask me for a dance and you'll understand.

What's your name?

Sparmannia.

I'm sending you this crimson rose instead of an invitation.

Thank you, I've put it in my hair

Let's dance.

First let me put on my black backless dress. And my shiny red high heeled shoes.

Come on then let's dance.

There's no music.

Put on the gramophone

I'm putting it on.

Relax, you're a little tense.

Let me tell you something. In the tango the man is ninety percent. He leads.

Relax then. Completely

I'm feeling faint.

This isn't a waltz. This is a tango.

I know, my head is spinning.

You didn't tell me what the most important thing was.

The tango will tell you, Good night.

Out of all dances, only the Tango requires sharing.

She sometimes chats. That's how she becomes ageless. A woman of no years. Like this evening. She doesn't know who Tango is. How old he is, what colour his eyes are. Today women don't need them to pick roses from the garden. They send them imaginary ones. Or they bloom on the monitor. Or they have it drawn with a black crayon over the shoulder. In the old days when the first gifted rose should never fade. Forever on the shoulder, a black Dutch rose with a velvet interior like a secret. She doesn't remember who picked it. Nor who tattooed it. She tries to remember but she cannot, and that's good for her spiritual health. Partial amnesia, darkening of the intimate, of the lyrical in her life, whatever you call it, it's not important, because the man has not stayed in her memory. What's important, the rose has stayed. She writes these thoughts in the notebook and pushes it away again, with revulsion. She lies straight on the bed. She falls asleep, before taking off the imaginary black dress, before kicking off the imaginary red shoes. And the whole night the imaginary gramophone plays tango, until at last the needle begins to scrape rhythmically and loudly and Anastasia wakes with the dawn.

From the notebook:

Why write. Why do I sit in front of Mr Hewlett and record my visions, the advent of the thought, the flickering of the feelings, my own assumptions, and others' stories. Why did Fina write Nebesna's words in a purple blue. Why do people write their thoughts at all, what is writing in itself? Imagination. Don't imagine anything as it's in heaven or on earth. I wonder if there isn't a heavenly taboo hanging over writing. I wonder if it's a sin, underlined twice. But it could be a prize…But what for? What is writing, someone tell me! Awareness of something that has meaning. And it's something otherworldly, deliberately hidden, so we seek it out, to enquire with our pathetic five percent brains what it is. A yearning towards the meaning. Wow how stupid! Yearning for something, you don't know what it looks like. Nor why you need it, nor whether it exists at all. Well now, what if things have no point?! Someone is dreaming you or you're dreaming everything, practically this doesn't change the idea. And even so where does this yearning come from? There now, I clicked!!! The desire you remember, it is your blood. Something more, the words teach you to remember the desire. The urge towards the unreachable (underlined three times). If it's unreachable, how will you reach it! In this line of thought, is not the meaning meaningless? The pointlessness of writing your thoughts of gathering them into a strict order. Twice I write: fuck it, because words have set out to speak out themselves. What can I do to stop it. No-thing. I write because the words flow out like floods into a river, it then rushes to pour into something bigger. There, where have flowed the written thoughts of so many people from before, now and ever after. Where in spite of vast numbers, it's quiet and entranced, or as the mood falls, loud and festive or even stupid and disorderly. Altogether there, where the sentence is irreparable. Where the spoken word is a stone thrown. Sometimes it occurs to me that to begin to write I need life experience. Some other time. Experience is needed, but the kind which doesn't have so much in common with my life in the herd. No-one less gifted than me has lived on this earth. No kind of story, no kind of personal subject. But I write. Because the writing does not come from me. I'm not its source. Someone, some time, has lived in the inner room, full of eyes. Another someone has written without full stops and commas with a biro, as it sputtered laboriously. Someone has started before me. And so further back and further back. To the beginning which was the Word.

Note: Sparmannia, calm down a little. Who are you to preach. Who are you to preach to yourself.

144

What follows is underlined several times. In fact, it's very simple, everything. Writing is an escape from reality. But as you create another reality in which your heroes also try to escape reality, what is the point of all these realities? Mother of God!

Her Granny, Nebesna didn't live long. Soon after Maria and her children left for the big city with the pickup driver, the old woman returned from the seaside to the house of her birth in Stranzha and sickened. Probably because she seized up, shut in that inner room. Before her time. Or it was ordained in advance.

Most likely the latter. She used to come to her every summer and to this day she remembered her careful movements in the corridor when she had to get up to go to the toilet or to wash at the kitchen tap. She'd hurry to get back to the inner room and wrap herself from the world again in her little nook. Why had my Granny become like this. She doesn't see, now she doesn't talk, she doesn't go out, she scarcely breathes, when she sleeps, curled like a cat at one end of the bed cover. Is it possible that this old woman is the same Nebesna who Maria-Fina would talk about so much. Sometimes it doesn't look as though there's anything under her covering. As though there's nothing left of her. As if it really is some kind of covering, like a bean pod, like the shell of some century old tortoise, like the dried skin of a snake, the same as any other covering, fallen on the bed by chance. On this bed, once, Fina gave birth to her, then Nebesna had given birth to Maria Fina, then she had given birth to Anastasia-Nebesna, in Mattei the Dolphin's boat. Enough. There's no more Fina-Nebesna-Fina-Nebesna. Continents disappear, civilizations, stars, galaxies, why shouldn't all the Finas and Nebesnas disappear. Who would notice?

She remembered how one day as they passed down the corridor, her Granny suddenly stretched out a hand and grabbed on to the sleeve of her dress. You, who are you, she spoke with difficulty, wheezing, with her chicken lungs. You…She lifted her eyelids, looked with unseeing eyes into her face and suddenly everything around glowed. I recognized you. I really recognized you. You are me, my little one, you are. She leant confidingly towards her grandchild. Soon I'll have to look for the wolf cub, my golden eyed wolf cub was lost years ago, the time has come for me to go out and look for him. This will take a lot of time, a life, two lives, five…But I'm thinking of finding him. And you remember, don't forget your heavenly name…She stopped, stood motionless, just as her chin trembled and her hands, hanging loose by her side also trembled. They had brown gnarled skin with white-yellow spots, like some enormous ladybirds which were trying to fly away in vain. Her eyes glittered as if bigger than the ancient face, covered in a cobweb of wrinkles. Oh come on, she said in the end, she slipped into the inner room and they never met again in this life.

Her mother Maria Fina, daughter of blind Nebesna and granddaughter of that Fina with the dove grey eyes, lived a long time comparatively. In the driver's house in Burgas, little by little, she began to relax her hardened body. On one moonlit night two years after her second marriage, the husband, who every time he tried in vain to pour the stars of his fluid into the source of her body, heard a quiet ringing, turned back for a second and once again he thought he saw something move like a huge shining tail and silver scales scattered in the bed. The man swore the next day to Maria that he'd gathered them and filled a glass jar with them, and at dawn he had thrown them into the back garden, but the wind had blown them away. The twins, who had heard their conversation, went into the back garden and it really seemed to the girl that in the clods of dug earth, scales twinkled like fish, but Anastas tapped his forehead, those are the clumsy trails of snail slime. One way or another, there was no way of finding out what exactly had happened but from that day onwards in the late hours of the night, they began to hear their mother's smothered laughter and her newly hastened chatter.

One morning, as they were having breakfast, Maria looked at her husband somewhat strangely with her half closed eyes, and sud-

denly said: You can call me Fina, I feel sorry for my birth-name…
From this morning onwards the sharp knives, shot from her mother's eyes, thinned out and disappeared, her irises glowed with an intense blue and her words took on light transparent wings. She kept that way even after the death of her second husband, she lived through the loss wisely and with the dignity of someone who can measure this event from the viewpoint of life, rather than death. God gave me a comrade in life, who was in no way different to what your father would have been, had he lived, she told them, ten days after the burial.

When she took to her bed, for longer than a year, Maria Fina began to have a premonition. She demanded to return to the village. How far is it from the town, you'll pop by and look in on me when you can. Her daughter held her tongue, unmoved. Her mother made no more demands but curled like a guilty child under the blanket. Anastasia pulled it, dragged it off and got down to changing the urine soaked nappy. Every time when she did it, the blue eyes of the old lady looked at her guiltily. She hurried to clean her with perfumed wet-wipes and sprinkled talcum powder over her. She lifted her and pulled on a new nappy. She avoided looking at her pathetically skinny loins with their seldom plucked hair. She hurried to finish and get away. To throw away the old nappy, to sit in front of the computer and to continue the cursed translation, which kept limping at such moments, for reasons that were unclear. But she hurried even more, because she knew what would follow. But this did follow as every other time. As soon as she did up the nappy and pulled the nightie down, her mother began in whatever voice had been left her, please mum, sorry, sorry, mum, sorry mummy's girl, sorry for everything. Nebesna, sorry Anastasia…She wasn't apologising just for the nappy, nor because of the efforts exhausting her daughter. She was apologising for everything she felt guilty about, and this was really everything. It was her unstinting inadequacy, such an insatiable symptom of her illness, so unbecoming her heart, enough to gather all the worry in the world, it was her dried up paralysed legs, it was her bedsores which Nebesna-Anastasia treated with all kinds of spirit and ointments, but they didn't go away, one would close, another two opened…It was the Middle East war, it was the rowing of the neighbours, who could be heard from below, it was Mattei the Dolphin's house, abandoned by her on the beach, it was her lost youth which shone eternally beyond reach like a golden heavenly Jerusalem, forward with the future of her memories…It was her feeble walking, which she dreams of often, I walked again Mummy. I had light shoes, I didn't get tired at all, walking the whole night, it was her daughter's shoulder, damaged by weight, it was the enemas, which she did once a week…it was the inner room in their abandoned house, full of eyes, which peeped through the window, it was her mother, Nebesna, and before that, her Grannie Fina, who now kept her informed in the guise of two sparrows on her window sill, and she begged for bread crumbs to be put out for them, but Nebesna-Anastasia often forgot, it was the day of her birth, it was the blanket of light knitted by her Grannie, in which she was once wrapped, find it, find it please, and keep it for your child, it's in a cupboard in the village. What children are you babbling about, mum, mine? Her daughter snapped, at my age with no husband, and on top of that children. It was the whole truth, conceived from a sometime indescribable life and she apologised for herself, for her daughter who didn't use her real name, for her son Anastas, lost forever in the wide world…for everything with all this world's mercy, she apologised.

She couldn't bear it, she quarrelled furiously with her mother. Then she went out into the corridor, buried her face in her hands and cried soundlessly a long time. The Dutch rose on her shoulder folded its leaves, turned into a mossy black beetle which tried to crawl on her skin and escape. It did not succeed, appearing once more as a rose and quieting down.

She lost herself every time when the feeling of impending death overcame her. When childish helplessness hampered her resistance. Just like that faraway day.

Yellow rubber gloves up to her elbows. The nappy with turds. The wet wipe. Sorry mum, sorry. The bed sores open like wounds on display. Oh my girl, oh my girl, I'm sorry. The spirit burns into the wounds. Strong spirit. Sorry-y-y Mummy-y-y. Visnevski ointment…Sorrr…And suddenly a breath like a chicken's peep. End. No breathing. Suddenly frozen face. Death with her mother's face. A tear in the corner of the eye, it rolls slowly. Silly thought? If I could just gather it in a little bottle, glass cup, mum will continue to live, like a tear.

Death was in her mother's face but with the look of a child, caught unexpectedly in front of something unseen that stopped her breath. Forever gazing in wonder in front of her in shock. A look not seen till now, in the first second of her mother's death she herself looked in the direction those crazy unmoving eyes were staring.

She left her to lie and stare. She threw away the nappy and finished applying the ointment to the sores. After the burning spirit, the soothing ointment. The big nightie, to cut away the nightie mouldy from urine and washing. To wash the wrinkled skin with a damp sponge. To clean the thighs, sorry as sparrow's legs, And these hands with arthritic fingers. Death with her mother's hands. Small dry with brown old age spots, two enormous ladybirds landed on the covers. Hold on to my hand Mummy, I'm afraid of the dark. Now to throw away those nightie rags. Throw away the gloves. We'll get out new clothes from the cupboard, for your funeral, Mummy, I've put them right down low, so you don't buy new ones, I've crocheted the lace myself, it's really delicate, they call it peacock's eye. There we are. Now let's put on the shoes. Look you've got shoes on your feet again. Death with her mother's feet. With brand new shoes. You're ready…Suddenly the bladder releases the delayed urine for one last time. It smells. Doesn't matter, we'll change the nappy again. From inertia, she'd changed the nappy. There this time you really are ready. Everything is OK. Everything is OK.

She lay below her shrunken body, she buried her face into her spilled tummy, in the bosom of her own life, with the smell of mother, of acidic urine, perfumed wet wipes.   Everything is OK. Everything is OK.

After so many years when in spite of all, she returned and entered the old house, and dared to enter the inner room, and she'd sworn not to do it while she was alive, as though the room didn't belong to her, nor did she belong to the room, suddenly she felt a premonition of the imminent past loss. Her mother had wanted to die in this room and not in any other, but she'd not taken her last wish into account.

IN WHICH EVERYONE RECOUNTS THEIR LIFE THROUGH ONE ANOTHER, AND THEIR MEMORIES CATCH UP WITH EACH OTHER, ADD TO EACH OTHER OR RIGHT OUT CONTRADICT EACH OTHER. BUT THIS DOES NOT HINDER THE COMMON STORY LINE, BECAUSE TO RETURN TIME IS THE SAME AS TO READ THE BIBLE BACK TO FRONT, OR MIXED UP, AND STILL GET THE MEANING, IF THE MEANING OF LIFE IS ANYTHING WHICH CAN BE GOT AT ALL.

Well what I've told you up till now, that's going to be that. I'm tired of Antula's wonderful life. It's not easy to be Antula. It's not easy to be from Antula. Darling girl, now I'll give you these worn pages with Mother Fina's purple writing, your Grannie. Read them, only when you talk to him. If he can still talk. I haven't heard tell that he's dead, that means he's still alive. He's twenty three years older than me, work it out, how biblical to become a fisher-lighthouse keeper.

My bones are creaking. From the damp. The damp in my life is rather too much for me. Life too is too much. That one who lets lives go, I wonder if he's forgotten me. And how can I tell you, what with my mumbling, so you won't understand anything. And I don't remember. I remember how I fought in the last war, I reached right on to the river Drava in Hungary. There one day the machine guns sang out in joy: chata-chata-chata-chata because we won in the end. I can't remember exactly who we beat. I remember the victory. And before that the little train which I drove for years through the mountain. I remember it. And when I became lighthouse keeper, here on the shore, I remember. And the fish I caught in the nets, I remember them. I remember them because of their eyes. When they thrash about alive, their eyes go wild. And I threw them back. Because of their eyes I returned them to the sea. I fished every fish in the bay and I returned every one. That's how it was. But folk, I don't remember them, I forgot them. And now you don't believe me? Because they were unforgettable? I don't remember people. I remember fish eyes. Gaping. Unmoving. So you get scared. Whole life, fear of fish. Nothing more than that. Fear of fish. Of their gaping eyes.

He sees with eyes himself, unmoving like fish eyes. She tries to wake a memory in him. Marutsa, Nebesna, Antula. He looks at her with vague eyes. Fear strikes at her, as though a centuries old fish is looking at her, emerging for a second from the depths of the abyss and has fixed on her. She gets ready to leave. The further the better from this old guy who is turning himself back into a fish and scales glitter on his forehead and his hands. In a moment she holds out her hand for goodbye, and then, confused, she withdraws it, hides it behind her back. After that she leaves.

At this very moment, she hears his voice, she stops and turns around. He's looking at her with a gaze that's suddenly changed towards the human, and there's such yearning in his eyes that feeling even more confused, she returns. She walks towards him, drawn to those eyes as if by a magnet. I'm waiting for a boat, he confides in her, I'm waiting for a boat to Italy. It'll come soon. I feel it. The boat to Italy.

Do you see, Bethlehem got tired talking to you. My old woman surprised me, I admit. So many words, where had she kept them. Surely in that pillow, in her pretend tummy, I mean to say. So many years, she's been stingy with words – for good, for bad, and now you can't stop her. Now that she's tired herself out, I can tell you what I know. And the century old Ilya didn't tell you anything as far as I've heard. Listen now to what I know, old man Vassilaki.

Mavrud built his new house with an inner room to be hidden, so the madness of the folk inside the house wouldn't get out. Everyone there had something to chip in, if you get me. When Fina started to give birth, Mavrud went and left her in the midst of her pains and raced off to throw himself on his knees to God in the church. He forgot himself in his prayers you know. At this point a stranger entered the house, dark skinned with a ragged cloak and mousy eyes. Well you might say, twirling a tail behind. When he saw Fina racked with pain, he took his hand out from under his cloak and held out a pair of rusty shears, so big they could cut a calf's head off, he opened them and shouted, I am the heavenly midwife. And he tore her legs open and cut her with the rusty shears. My mother, Nastasia only just saved her from death. With that wine from the black Algerian grape.

I remember too how Nebesna sang one winter night. There was a dead one in the house, all of us neighbours around, saw how Mavrud took in the outsiders and in spite of it being a really hard winter, the rumour spread from house to house. No-one had wanted to take them in, that's death. No laughing matter. I was an impressionable child and I remember how my mother Nastasia crossed herself and prayed: help Nebesna Lord, help Nebesna Lord. I realised something irregular was happening in their house at daybreak. Joyful songs were heard. We recognized that it was Nebesna. I'm telling you, but it wasn't the time for such a thing. I even remembered some of the words of one of the songs. There she sang about a river, which dragged its waters and the willows were bending to touch the ground and the rain drizzled on the earth and the sun was made of gold and more like this and she said in the end: so you won't feel alone, my girl. As if she wouldn't realise there is no place lonelier than this. The wind had died down and the blizzard calmed and that's how you could hear clearly. It was horrible. The girl was laid out in the house, deader than dead, but Nebesna came up with a special set to make your hair stand on end.

And the words were very meaningful, that was obvious. Something happened to her sometimes. She wasn't entirely all there. The girl was defective. My mother, Nastasia, said no-one in the village sang these songs. Where Nebesna had learnt them, no-one knew. It's a shameful thing to sing when there is a death, a madness overcame her. When she stopped, because she'd run out of strength, she just lifted a tremulous voice: aha, aha, it'll break. But happy, I tell you. We're all from them, she cried, we're all together. No-one can be alone, because it's not granted to us. And even if they closed you up in a room, you're not alone. And if they dump you alone in the earth, you're not alone. As we share our lives just once, everyone is together here, and elsewhere. Who was she saying these words to, you tell me if you can. It's a lie and a confidence trick that: if there's anyone lonelier than a corpse, you tell me.

I remember her wedding with the engine driver, Ilya. As they left the church they threw wheat and rice as if it was raining. I squatted to pick up the sweets and coins and through the people's legs I saw how Ilya kicked Nebesna's wolf cub and it moved away and there was such despair in its body, that it was practically crawling on its belly, it was the wild dog in it. It was a wolf and nothing more. They say such nonsense. You know my Bethlehem isn't really all there, she imagines a sheep in wolf's clothing. There's no such animal in this world and it's not about to appear in Stranzha. But when I looked it in the eye, there was no doubt. It was a wolf that could love and suffer. On the other hand, if it gets the chance, isn't it going to sink its teeth into your throat. What do you think. Nebesna's wolf could have torn up anybody, because it felt on edge, because it felt what was going on between people and according to its notion of right and wrong, it could get really seriously involved. On the other hand what do we know about these wolves, found in the darkest forests, like white crows, if you get my meaning. But whatever we say, that beast was a dangerous wolf, looked at from any side. I heard Ilya demand that it be set free in the forest, but Nebesna said something like: better set it free in the mountain, and her husband refused. That's why in the end, what happened, happened.

The wolf jumping up at Antula, I remember because I was there. I also saw when after a few months the angry engine driver pointed a gun at it. I was just passing. I think that he did not believe himself that the beast was looking for a bullet. Ilya was certain that outwardly it looked a wolf, but it was something more than animal and more than human in its behaviour. When we believe in nonsense, such things happen I'm sure he meant to save it, but anger had flared up and had the driver in its grip. When the gun went off, the beast flew in the air, then fell to the ground in spasms. And what I won't forget for as long as I live, is that it looked towards Nebesna's window with a sorrow and a pity you've never seen. And then it looked as if it would talk, the wolf cub. It lifted its head to the sky and I heard words. There now, cross my heart: mercy, it said, without opening its mouth, it said it agonizingly slowly. It was obvious that it wasn't asking mercy for itself. Just in case you haven't understood, I don't believe in such stuff, it seems devilish to me. But I heard what I heard. If it was devilish, why would it pray for mercy from heaven. Mercy, it repeated, mercy for all of you. Maybe I was in a trance, hearing and seeing all this. I was a sensitive snotty nosed kid at that time. At last Nebesna came out with the child in her arms. She stood, eyes fixed on the beast lying there. She rocked, turned and went back into the house. She didn't make a noise, but now I think I heard her utter heavy terrifying words.

I remember too Ilya coming to his senses. His anger had passed, he sat on the ground by the wolf and took its head in his two hands. He was a moderate man, but this time he'd made a mistake. That's how it was, I'm not lying. I think now that we don't tell the truth when we do something unforgivable; we say that supposedly we didn't mean to do it. But if we did it, we meant to do it. Maybe this is hidden deep in us and only pops out for a second, and it's done. We can't mend it. That's why I like calm folk, who ponder seven times before cutting. My Bethlehem is like that, she's not at all like her mother Antula, you'd better believe it.

Bethlehem was born a few months after your mother Fina, daughter to that Nebesna. Later Nebesna's second husband, the crippled outsider, christened Fina a second time, gave her the name of the Virgin, so she'd look after her. Bad things had happened to little Fina and he added the sacred name so she'd be protected in later life. I was fourteen then and I remember Antula being pregnant, because her pregnancy made her very ugly. Everyone in the village talked about it. As if God was punishing her for having too much beauty before and most of all because Antula had known how to use it. My mother was her midwife one autumn evening and when she returned one autumn evening she said that Marguda had gone grey with pain. She was an upright woman and Antula giving birth without a husband stuck in her craw. God was her witness however that Marguda had strained every sinew to put her careless daughter on the right path, but she didn't know…she didn't realise that this was Antula's path, this and no other. She'd walked down it and her beauty had shone untouched, though she'd given it out in handfuls. Anyone else who'd done what Antula had done would have been called a bitch on heat. But she had something inside her that wouldn't allow you to open your mouth and abuse her. As far as the rest is concerned a person has to live out their own life.

Everyone in the village could set to calculating when and where and by whom the seed had been sown in the Greek girl. Everyone wondered what would happen when the conscience of the man who'd planted the seed pricked him, but they soon stopped wondering, more shocked than astonished. Antula told them something else. Just like this, she stood up in the village square. She'd heard the women talking behind her back, put her hands on her waist, lifted her head and loudly proclaimed: It's not known, only I know it and I don't want to share which man made me pregnant at this time, it could be every man in the village. Every one of your men was also my man, if you didn't know up to now, you know it now. So that every man in this village is father to my daughter. Everyone's the father. She said this out of spite but it was effective. The women didn't provoke her any more. Just the men admitted being with her, one by one. Each overtook the other in looking after the single mother and her child. One brought them firewood, another cut it up, a third fixed the roof so it didn't leak, a fourth dug up the garden, all wanted to show their concern for the two supposedly lonely women, Marguda and Antula. And everyone took a furtive peak into Bethlehem's face to descry their own features. But they'd been sculpted from her mother's skin, no-one could recognize anything. But they didn't stop caring for them, as though they owed this to her.

Ilya was confused by the situation. Surely he'd worked it out and wanted to accept it and look after Antula's little girl, but my mother Nastasia found out that Antula had said the same thing to him. And so Ilya remained really mixed up. With a guilty conscience, he feared to look after his daughter by Nebesna, he didn't have the courage to look her in the eye. And so soon after this, he left the barn which he'd moved into and set off towards the sea. And he gave up his narrow gauge railway job. Everybody thought he was planning to leave in Vito's boat for Italy but he didn't do it, he started work as a lighthouse keeper and he's been there to this day. And you had the joy of seeing and talking to him recently. In the beginning he sent fish by the new train driver, lots of fish by the basket load, but Fina distributed to the neighbours and he stopped doing it.

A few years after that Vito the Italian, an old bloke, set in his ways, moved in with Antula and the women sharpened their long tongues till they bled. How could he come to like her in her situation. No-one understood. He was a widower, he had no mind to repeat the experience. What we think and what we do are not one and the same thing. Antula bewitched him and he circled her like a crazy man; she was an enchantress, everyone knew this. Vito stopped going back to Italy, he set up something with the authorities; he just dispatched the boat and met it, watched it being loaded. And he looked after Bethlehem, he was a second father to her. Soon after our wedding, he passed on.

That was what Antula was like, I can bear witness. Restless, remarkable from a distance, unforgettable. Her beauty might have faded on the outside, after the pregnancy, but the beauty gradually turned inwards, you could see it in her eyes.

Don't, Vassilaki, don't pretty up my mother needlessly. If you knew, if only you knew…

I didn't think that I'd know this feeling, but I felt it with all its nastiness. It's untypical of my nature and why did I let it crawl over me like mange from head to toe, I don't know. An inner mange under my pearly skin. On the outside smooth and gentle and underneath scabby mange. What's your beauty here, turned upside down inside. I, Antula, got uglier, spreading everywhere.

Ilya left and i hated nebesna and everything about nebesna. I hated big fina and little fina, mavrud and his proverbs, i hated the house and the windows, the pear tree and the bees in it, the horses in the stables, the hens in the hen house, once i even cut the head off their stupid nanny goat. And i hated the eyes on their iconostasis. I now thought that they'd left those eyes to watch me, to follow me. As they looked out through the windows, do i know what they see. Their eyes reach all the way to our house, they penetrate my bedroom. Everything in that house seems to be to blame for ilya's departure. I felt he left, not because of me, but because of her. Who is she to make ilya feel guilty. Who is she that he feels so conscience-struck in front of her. Who is she, not to want her husband, and to render my conscience defenceless, so that i don't dare desire him anymore. Where is human justice here. At some point i began to express my hatred of nebesna in a strange way. I'd go out in the morning, when the village was asleep, and stand in front of nebesna's window, put my hands on my waist, and look up there with my head cocked. As if i was shouting, come on nebesna, come on, take me on to see what for. Once i even made a rude sign. I wished a plague on her, as they say, i felt better, i turned and left. That's it.

Vassilaki, when I listen to someone else talking about my lives, and especially when they get muddled up sometimes, it's something I can't put up with. But even so, who knows me, your Bethlehem, better.

I am Antula and Bethlehem simultaneously. I told you why, darling girl. Listen and work it out on your own, which one is talking. I interrupted Vassilaki to confess all this about the mange, because it was very important for me to do this now, when Bethlehem talks to me. What I didn't manage once, I'll say it now with my mouth.

It's true that my beauty decayed. I look at myself in the cracked mirror and see how my hair has plastered down, how my eyes have gone dark, how many spots from the pregnancy have not cleared up. Nebesna's skin became clearer after the birth, mine roughened. It's not important. Not at all. Bethlehem is important. With cinnamon powder in her hair and purple sparks in her eyes. From all the craziness of my body, a pure and gentle result. So, what's there to talk about, think, judge. Even more so now my body is still. It's stopped singing. No man excites me. And from the time Ilya left me, it's as if he never was. After that business with Sharko, which wasn't a simple shooting of some forest beast, it was as if I'd dreamt Ilya.

I put up with the wolf cub, with all his yellow hatred, which turned unexpectedly into forgiveness, with his paws over my breasts, with the urine that I'd released and which ran down my thighs, and my shame in front of Mavrud and Ilya and the spectacle I'd made of myself. I put up with him because I continued to believe that he came from Nebesna's imagination and it was no coincidence that he had come into our life. And he had a reason to put his paws on my breasts. I don't deny it. And it being so, Ilya had no right to touch him. He did it out of pity for me, that's why I feel downright guilty. I don't like to be made to feel guilty. When I do something myself, it's another matter. Well for the first time in my life, I feel insupportable guilt. This makes me another person. I'm imagining it because I'm not used to looking at myself, as if I'm unremarkable. Disgrace is disgrace, and to survive it you need inner strengths and at that time I didn't have them, and the mange crawled over me, it made me horribly ugly.

I thought, Nebesna, why should I like her. She overtakes me, she carelessly cuts across my path, she met Ilya before me and he saw her before me and they mixed up paths and lives and the stars in the sky surely got mixed up because we are one whole in nature, surely there's such a link between us and the world, between people and the stars. What do I know. But as I'm mulling it over this way, look what strikes me. If three people mistake their paths and lives and for this reason they mix up the paths of the stars, that means they mix up the fates of many other people. Because the stars are for everyone, aren't they. Imagine how much we influence each other with our mixed up paths, without even suspecting. I am sure, that Nebesna and Ilya meeting earlier is a fatefully mistaken mix up. That's the reason for the restlessness, anger and uncleanliness within me. Do you know what anger means? Poison. That's what it means. I'm angry, that's why I can't like even little Fina. I'm expressing myself really carefully because I'm scared to name the other feeling I have towards her. I do everything I can for it not to be like this, but I can't manage it. I pray to God to help me, but he seldom gets involved with people's stuff. Whatever God says to himself, Antula's a grown intelligent person, so let her rethink matters and clean off the shit that stinks up her soul, so that she herself can't stand it.

Sometimes I just remember the wolf cub with golden eyes, how he put his paws on my breasts and his look expressed something to me. He shared something big and beautiful with me the second I shamefully let go and released warm urine smelling of lime tea over my thighs. Sometimes I wish to know what exactly he was trying to tell me with his forest eyes and why this is so important. I don't have the skill to find it out and I suffer. Along with the hatred, this torments me, so it becomes unbearable. I think it's telling me that something glorious, something wonderful awaits you, Antula; but it's not to be believed, I continue to hate and that's that.

I wonder if you haven't loved before this, whether you'll hate. Love and hate, it seems, walk down one and the same road. Night captures day, death captures life, hatred captures love. Good, that another time it happens the other way round.

Mummy Antula, Mummy Antula, a falling star. A star's falling from the sky!

A man is approaching. Thickset and windswept, he smells of salt. I'm sat in the orchard under the apple tree. I'm in my baby cradle and I'm playing with the green apple, which broke off the branch and fell next to me. I try to sink my teeth, tiny as rice, but I don't manage. I get angry, I whine. After that I smile against the sun and sneeze. The man offers me a hand, I find out his index finger, I begin to babble. He smiles too, looks around stealthily and quickly leaves through our orchard gate. Antula arrives and begins to sniff the air though widened nostrils.

…I identified the feeling and I'm clear with myself. As if you diagnosed a deadly disease. I got used to its implications. And I calmly accepted the implication for me, what I've become. And I carried on with the mange under my pearly skin.

I saw little Fina again through the window. She was walking in the street, stepping carefully, with arms spread out, taking care not to slip. And I say to myself, just let me see those bright eyes, let's see when those sky blue eyes cloud over and you'll stop seeing the world, because that's what you deserve. I realised the horror of the curse and I made the sign of the cross, I bent in a deep bow before the iconostasis at home, for heaven to forgive the unworthy thought. A few days later – again Fina totters down the street, she's fixing her bright eyes on something of her very own. And again my thought, as though separate from me: there's no escaping it, my girl Nebesna, you too will be blind as a slow worm. Because that's what you deserve, who plunder folk's fate without permission. And on top of that you light up with your eyes…What rubbish I managed to come up with. As though if it's fate anyone could avert it! But month after month my relentless thought established itself, that the folk in that Mavrud's house deserved retribution, all of them, who'd been granted otherworldly eyes and plundered others' lives with them. And it went and happened. I saw it with my own eyes.

The kids were playing in the street, the boys were boisterous. One of them stripped a thick mustard stalk, that hadn't dried yet, strong and fibrous, he blew through the hollow in its stem, then lifted it, like the first cavemen lifted a spear, he flexed, and from my yard I heard how the wind whistled through the hollow, powerful and terrifying, as though a storm had broken out within the stalk. The stick flew a long way whistling straight into Fina's eye, it struck straight into the heavenly eye. The girl fell as if mown down beside their house's fence and didn't utter a cry. She just went limp. I heard how the children shouted out, how her Grannie Fina screamed, I saw how Nebesna ran and grabbed the child. My legs folded under me and I sat down so as not to fall.

They treated the little one as they knew how in the village. The eye was black as a rag and flowing with blood, as though it was a pool of blood and not an eye. They put fresh cheese on it and leaves of sempervivum and fleawort, and wet compresses of linden, and ice from the pub cellar. This carried on for months. I picked fleawort from our orchard sent my mother Marguda to take it to them. While from behind the curtain I watched her enter their yard, I cursed myself ten times for what I was doing. Ten times my conscience called out like a man fallen down a well. You've never been a hypocrite, Antula, what are you doing with them now. If you want to hate, hate out in the open.

The little one's eye cleared up, just a purple shadow stayed a long time under her lower lid. Within the blue looked like a scilla flower, but very dark in colour, somehow extinguished. While this was going on, every evening I stayed in front of the iconostasis and prayed for God's forgiveness and I carried insupportable guilt. How many ages have passed, what an eternity remains, and I still carry it. Little Fina never again saw clearly.

As I mentioned, this event made my conscience call out ten times. Ten times I cursed myself because of my hatred's hiding place. The kind that lurked in my very depths, unexpressed and unemployed, it could poison my very own blood incurably. And one day when I was unconsciously thinking about this, I jumped up and ran to their house, up the stairs, down the corridors. No-one met me, no-one stopped me. I open the door. Nebesna is there with knitting on her lap; she's not knitting, she's staying, head resting against the wall, not moving as if numb. I've come to tell you that I hate you. I hate you three times over and even more. And it's you and Fina I hate, may you not see a good day in this house. It's fair this way. So you know, Nebesna, it's fair this way. I said it in the most normal way, just as though I was sharing some village rumour. I turned and left and felt revenged.

I didn't walk home, but flew, sure of my right, that it wasn't me, but Nebesna, who'd killed off my love.

Quite a long time before this, shortly after our separation, I became aware that Ilya was coming round here. He had a free day once a month and then he got on the train and came. He stayed in the station room and didn't go out. He just stayed silent, they said. He slept the night there, and the next day, as they were loading the logs, he sat behind the driver who'd taken over from him and gone back to the lighthouse on the narrow gauge railway.

One evening, Bethlehem was still in nappies, I felt his presence in the yard. I remember as if it's happening now: it's a moonlit night, and the house is dark everywhere, but the yard is lit white and I see him under the apple tree. Sorrow grips my heart, hot grief overcomes me. I go out on tiptoe, so my mother Marguda doesn't hear me, I barely call out to him, and he comes close. I'm still angry with him. Without wanting to, against my will, I rest my head against his chest. We say nothing. His heart beats to bursting. I pull myself away. She's yours, I tell him. But don't come close to her. Because of what is humanly right, don't. Go where you have to. Where you have to, go there. He scarcely touches my hair, his eyes shine under the moon. And I'm shaking all over. I didn't want to say these words, I'd imagined quite the opposite, what I'd say to him if I saw him. You're mine, you're ours, I'd imagined saying it so many times. But there, other words lined up on my tongue, because human truth is stronger than anything; and I understand, for the first time with my inner beauty I understand why people have to meet up together on this earth, it's stronger than hatreds, than loves, than sorrows and joys, than words and silences, because it's all this together. I pick him an apple from the dark tree, I offer him a green apple. He slips it into his breast pocket and steps backwards. He doesn't speak and looks at me, and fingers the apple. In spite of not being sure now when I said these words, then or quite a lot later, a long time after I broke in on Nebesna in the inner room and haughtily declared my hatred. Years later Ilya came again. It might have happened then. Because such words are not uttered when the poison of your hatred is on the tip of your tongue.

The woman hanging over my head is like the sun when she laughs and like rain, when she cries. I smelled the first scents of this world from her skin. The Man who stealthily visited me smelt of salt. And wafted various other mixed smells, I'll remember these, when I myself become a woman and realise this is the smell of a man, who lives in nature. This man and this woman never stood over me at the same time, I don't remember it happening.

…Only when I pushed him away for good did I understand that I was preserving my love in this way, that I'm wiping her face from the mud.

…I feel my eyes are fishy. I don't need to look in the mirror or in the clear river, or in another's eye, to understand what is happening to me. My eyes can't move in their sockets. There are scales on my hands. They're embedded in my skin from the time I pulled out the nets, full of bonito, mackerel, sturgeon, bluefish, glofus, spearfish, garfish, goby… Silver glittering scales. At night my skin shines like the chainmail of an old time soldier. Like a gleaming fish skin. I'm a human fish. I can still speak, mostly in my head. To think up some short thoughts. When I learn how not to do it, I'll be a fish. If I forget the words. If I have dead eyes staring into the marine depths. If under the grey locks of my hair, my ears turn into gills. I think I've already got them on the left, but let's be entirely sure. And the lighthouse is gradually turning into a gigantic fisheye. A one eyed sea monster. Once its yellow eye is lit, it will surely wink at equal intervals as always, but now there's no need for it in this place. Its shaft is overgrown with slippery moss, venom-green and greasy. I talked to it for years and it listened. It'll listen wherever it goes. Otherwise my human conversation was with Stavros and Nikolai the White Guardsman, Whitey for short. They were younger than me, there's a score of years since the death bell tolled for Stavros from up on high. Beyond belief. He was wiry and plugged into life, but he kicked the bucket before me. I want to say he hugged a bouquet of seaweed, because that's what he wanted at the end of his life. We filled his coffin with green seaweed, seashells and dried snake skins, with fish scales and golden sand. A year later and we sent Whitey on his way: supposedly he'd left one to two hundred women in this life, who awaited their turn for him to make them happy but they had no luck, poor women…From Kolyo Whitey I learnt why the abyss is called *the bottomless*. In Russian the abyss is called *without-bottom*. In other words, you tumble into her, you fall, you fall, you fall and there's no end to your fall… They left the two of them, who so enjoyed living, like children love honey. But me, who can't wait to turn into a deep sea fish, am still in human shape and if I live, I live. I put all my hope in silence, the fish have taught me this.

Recently I tried to talk to that woman, who came, at I don't know what time. Orange, cigarette stuck in her mouth like a man, scattering ash carelessly over her clothes. I see her for the first time, and her eyes are so familiar somehow, that they even hurt me, those eyes. And I got scared. They shouldn't hurt me. I'll become a fish. Fish don't feel pain. But what do we know. In this world no-one knows what's most important for others in the rest of nature. Well but if fish feel pain? What will happen then for my hope to turn into a sea monster? What's the point of turning into a fish, when it hurts. Although I worry a little, because I suspect, that not to feel pain is also an illness.

That woman with the orange hair, and orange sandals on bare feet…the sun shone orange at her back and cut into my fish eyes. And the woman didn't move, she tried to learn. She said: Asturam. Anseben, Alutna. For quite a time I utter the names backwards. Even the only prayer every day I recite it backwards. In this way the words hurt less. It's not just fun. Asturam, Anseben, Alutna. And uttered thus these names say a lot. Alutna, as you look at it, is a name, worthy for a woman to bear. Asturam is suitable for some girl. An Armenian, Jewess, Sicilian. Anseben doesn't go for any round here. How would you define it. Eh? How can you call whoever it might be Anseben. People would be astonished, and wonder where this Anseben has come from…

Tell me, she says. About them. Maybe backwards.

I don't know I say. I'm a fish. And she looks at me and those eyes hurt so. And I turned away. I looked into the abyss. Dark. Cold. No sun, no memories, no life, no death. You don't see a second there or an eternity. There where there's nothing. If it's not like that, go on tell me; otherwise why are fish cold-blooded. Why are their eyes from a million years ago. Why are their skins like snakes. Only nothing has cold blood and empty eyes. When I become an empty scaly nothing, I'll stop speaking words at last. Never again will I remember a human name. Not forwards, not backwards. And words will stop hurting me.

Good, that you came back, orange woman. What and how it happened, I know best of all. So you preserve my last words. If you need them, use them. I'm not going to need them anymore, once at last I've said them. Keep these words. I'm silent after this. I become a fish forever.

…The light of the winter evening seeps through the cracks and holes in the slatted shed and inside is special with these holes of light. It's as if shining eyes watch them, as they've sunk the pair of them into the hay. Antula also shines with the white of her eyes. Her stretched throat pulses, her hair flows behind her like a cinnamon stream, her skin is soft and gentle like silt over a river stone. Her colourful woollen socks are pulled down to her ankles and her bare legs dart about, just like fluttering white doves in the half light. The hay underneath them smelled sweet and mature from summer. Antula-a-a, Antula-a-a…

At last Antula buried herself entirely in the hay, her teeth chattering and she laughed throatily, let me warm up, I'm turning into an icicle, only her head with the cloudy hair appeared, smiling broadly. She suddenly became serious, but why are you flying to me. Nebesna is one hundred times better and you've landed like a fly on my loins…She complains supposedly, but she's pleased. The man lifts her up in the hay and dresses her like a child. Pulls up her colourful socks. They stop talking at last, each in their own silence. Antula leaves first. She stops at the door, the snow sprinkles her head with icy flour, she brushes it off with one finger in her green woolly glove. She waves farewell with the glove, putting her finger to her lips, she slips out. Her steps are heard scrunching through the icy puddles. The man stays lying on top of the hay with out-stretched arms.

The tens of eyes at the cracks gradually turn off. The day is over. There's nothing else to do. The cradle is finished. He's cleaned the inner room. Nebesna will be pleased. Nebesna… He gets up. He brushes off the hay. He goes through the yard, looking at the windows of the house. At this moment Fina is lighting the gas lamp, her shadow over the curtain is magnified ten times. Just as Ilya comes in, the old woman calls through the fence. Low, urgent. Nebesna. Fina silent at the window. Her shadow, magnified mon-strously by the light of the lamp. Driving sleet. Niko and Mavrud with lighted lanterns, sheltered under their cloaks. And Mavrud's prayer to heaven, voiced unexpectedly as a threat: Lo-o-rd Go-od! The horses disappear into the dark, you can see from afar the glow under their cloaks. The lanterns are there, but the riders are like flying ghosts. Ilya looks after them, although he can no longer make them out in the dark, after that he sets out on the streets. They're slippery, whitened with new snow, here and there the black from the hardened earth emerges, in patches. A white winter night with black patches.

…When at long last I saw the flying ghosts return, I stopped at the gate. I waited. All covered in snow, I didn't think to brush it off. At the window Fina's shadow moved. They got closer and stopped beside me. Nebesna sat on her uncle's horse, wrapped up in Niko's cloak. He got down first, took her in his arms. She was holding the wolf cub, she let it go on the ground. Mavrud led away the horses. The others passed close by. Nebesna bent in half. She straightened up beside me. Her face a foot away from mine. She looked at me, unseeing, more accurately all-seeing. Unexpectedly she laughed. I mistook you for a blossoming pear tree, she cried. And laughed again. And left. And I felt relieved inside. A stupid unforgivable relief.

The same night Nebesna gave birth. In the inner room. Little Fina had their eyes.

A few months passed. And that day came which changed our lives. Antula didn't look herself. None of her bold beauty was left. Her face paled like a sail, at her feet a yellow puddle had formed and it was steaming. From then on she wasn't frightened any more, she was more passive, humiliated and bewildered. From afar I established this in a matter of seconds. The wolf was standing up, with his front paws on her breasts. The two of them didn't move. And at some point it was as if she and the wolf were looking deep into each other. Just as if they were silently exchanging unusual thoughts. Nebesna, or maybe it was Mavrud, distracted the beast with flattering words and Antula breathed out. And I came out of a trance.

However a black hatred stirred up in me. A black and sticky hatred began to drink my blood like a tick. It gave me no rest. Everything, which is not what we want it to be, drives us most often to hate it. Isn't that the truth?

We doubt, that we have the strength or intelligence to understand it and we make up our minds to destroy it. Easier supposedly. Our human nature. Total self-deception, ask me and I'll tell you. Total. Violence blackens the bright mind, which God gave us. Violence over difference. Who's told us, that we're strong there, I don't know. Guns are strong, not us. To think you're strong if you have a gun, is a dangerous illness. I thought to overcome the wolf cub. To overcome his secretive strength which at moments chilled me. To destroy him in secret and unobserved.

One morning I got up at dawn. I opened the window and gazed at how my breath came out in thin white streams in the frosty sunrise. Then I dressed, took whatever I'd prepared the previous evening and snuck outside. Nebesna didn't notice me. I stood under the shelter. I leant my back against the shed wall. I waited. I knew that at this time the wolf came outside, did his business exactly at this spot. I was numb already and was about to go back inside when he came out. He passed by me, as if he didn't notice me. He lifted his leg against the trunk of the frozen pear tree and while the stream spattered and steamed in the snow, I swept a noose over his head. I expected him to thrash about, to growl and I'd prepared a bag and a lump of oakum to stuff into his mouth, but there was no need to rush so much. He set out obediently after me, he just lightly dragged his belly from time to time. We walked and made tracks in the snow. No-one saw us. Quiet in the forest, spacious, only our breathing, his and mine could be heard. I tied him to a tree and left him there. He didn't resist. Neither did he pull nor growl. He just looked me in the eyes. So I avoided his eyes, but at some moment I hastily threw him a glance. And I saw ridicule in his eyes. I swear, he was sniggering at me. Somehow matily, as if he had set out to challenge his best friend. I don't know why, this drove me wild. The blood rushed to my head. Who is he to take the micky, who is he, to send a challenge. As he was tied up, I kicked. And again, and again. And again for a finale. He squealed something, surely from pain and once again began to snigger with his look. That's when my anger warped me. It made me savage as a wolf. I want to say like some other wolf. I broke off a thick branch from a tree and as everything went black before my eyes, I started to thrash him. I hit wherever I could find. He squealed and jumped and his blood ran. For Antula, I shouted. For your interference in our lives. Because you're making out as a human. Because you sleep with Nebesna. Because you protect little Fina like a big brother. For that day when you bit my wrist. For everything, that I can think of and mostly for everything I haven't thought of. I tore into him. You're a beast, a beast you are, a hateful beast. I left him to lick its wounds, just as he was tied to the tree.

I got back and slipped into the warmth of bed with Nebesna. I felt like a soldier who's carried out his warrior's duty. No shame, no remorse, no pity. Just the warming thought, that tomorrow Antula

170

when she realises the beast's absence, will silently look at me with gratitude and relief…And unsuspectingly I fell asleep. And in my drowsy state I thought of something really terrible. Had he provoked me on purpose. Didn't he encourage me to do all that.

Someone's gaze woke me, carefully fixed on my face. Worried, I opened my eyes, rubbed my eyelids. Nebesna wasn't in the bed. I heard them in the next room goo-gooing with little Fina. Just outside the frosted glass someone was standing. In the beginning I couldn't see him, but in a second his eyes flashed bright. It was the wolf. I got up without a thought in my head, I approached the window and looked. He could hardly stand, propped against the wall, wounds all over, he licked them and smiled provocatively with its eyes.

Someone's beaten Sharko, someone dark, terrifying, vengeful has injured him. The woodsman found him tied to a tree…It's cruel. It's inhuman. It's hateful. Please. Please find a doctor. Please take him to Akhtopol to Dr Savichev. Please, hold him carefully, carry him carefully. I feel pain the same way. I'm hurting, Ilya, more quickly, It's hurting me, more gently…save him, Ilya, please…

Through the wood again. Snow to the knees. The wind starts up. The wolf cub, under my cloak, hugged into me. He's crinkled up its eyes, breathing heavily. There where I'm holding he is encrusted with dried blood. He lies exhausted with his head on my chest. He's wheezing. Nebesna's eyes remain far behind us. Nebesna's pain and her crazy plea. They reach my back. The weight in my arms increases. An ill defined fear takes over me. I try to move more quickly. I stumble on snowdrifts, I often fall. The wolf cub half opens his eyes, looks confused. Turns up the whites of his eyes. My fear increases. To my surprise I start talking to myself: come on, now, you what are you up to…You're supposed to be a wolf, a tough beast, and strong. Don't give up…Sharko. Hold out a little longer…Hold out, I'm telling you, get a grip., aren't you a man…And because some kind of crazy moon was shining, in its pale light I see how he half opens his eyes and I catch sad laughter in his look. But this doesn't irritate me anymore. The important thing is to get there in time. The important thing is to convince Dr Savichev that Sharko is not a beast, that he's not dangerous…What's important is that he laid its head on my chest.

I somehow convinced Dr Savichev that the wolf cub was not dangerous, and he took us in. He worked on the wounds, and in the end shook his head. Amazing thing, this is a wolf, and how easily he let himself be beaten. That really amazes me, believe me.

We returned the same way. Only that now, when I was convinced, that the beast was better and would live, the old hatred started to work on me again. The wolf cub surely felt this and this time didn't lay its head on my chest. The wounds healed quickly. As they say for dogs. And again that hatred filled the tick with blood. And left me no rest till the end of winter. And one March day, when new snow had piled up and the wind shivered from cold, we met in the back yard. Eye to eye. His eyes were yellow, piercing. Testing. Harsh. There was not a trace of a snigger. Nor of a friendly challenge. Cold. Two blades. Trying to stab me. To touch deep into my conscience. To give me some understanding. Wasn't going to happen. Never. He's a beast, an enemy. Uninvited foreigner in my life. To get the hell back to where he came from uninvited. To get the hell out. To leave into nothingness.

Days after this business with Sharko, the dolphins turned up. It had got warmer a little while, trickster weather, fraudulent, it misled everything in nature. The almonds and the peaches blossomed, the flies buzzed, the water in the river babbled in a new summer language, the newly grown frogs croaked… And one day we heard how the children were shouting in the village streets, lots of children, their cries were full of joy and wonder, dolphins, there are dolphins in the river, they scolded them not to disturb the quiet of the village with fantasies, but they protested against the grownups, we're not lying, we're not lying and the whole population set off after them. However much I had concerns around Sharko, I trudged there too. And what I saw, I'm not going to forget it even at the sea bottom, when I turn into a deep sea fish.

Two dolphins were ploughing through the water. It had flooded from the melted snow and now it foamed and boiled with the powerful swimming of the animals. Their skins shone, transparent water flowed over them, gilded by the sun. They were male and female, the female had a purple spot under one eye. The male stopped moving a while, nudged the female with the tip of his beak and said something to her in their language. I'm not lying to you, the dolphins were talking out loud, and the rest of the time they rubbed tummies, brought their heads close, caressed each other's backs with their beaks and as we witnessed such love, all of us fell silent, clustered on the bank. We'd heard, that once in fifty years two dolphins enter the mouth of the Veleka up to here, every time different, but always two, male and female and the female every time has a purple spot under her eye, and every time she's pregnant. And this time her tummy was swollen and as rounded as a globe, with which the children learn about the Earth in school these days. What kind of globe, the male dolphin circled her so carefully it was as if the female was carrying the whole planet earth in her womb. What a man, twice the man.

While we were silently watching, our faces transformed, suddenly we heard a strange howl, which more resembled a song. Nebesna's wolf cub, was standing at her feet, watching the dolphins, and singing for joy. Just as he was with his unhealed wounds, shaky and pitiable to see. Now I think with my shallow vapid brain, that Sharko was trying then to share the joy of the watery creatures, as if they had some common experience, as if they could understand and share with each other. And well it looked that way because the dolphins stopped going crazy in the foam, sharpened their hearing and it was clear to everyone, that they were listening fixed on Nebesna's wolf cub's song. And as they were listening, at one point they too began emitting sounds. That squeaking, which you've surely heard. It doesn't resemble anything else in nature, the sounds the dolphins were making were most unusual. Just so you know what came of it. They were listening to each other. I'm not lying to you, girl, they were talking. The wolf saying something in his language, the dolphins listen. He shuts up, they start. And this way they conversed a long time, animal to animal. We watched, we listened, no-one said a word. And then, when the dolphins swam back towards the river mouth, no-one uttered a word. Only Granny Anka called out sotto voce, that she'd heard about something similar from her mother, supposedly fifty years ago, two dolphins swam up the river to present themselves to the people and when that happened, folk needed to know that life will be go well with mutual understanding. Maybe that was it, because these weren't any dolphins. This purple spot under the female eye was a sign of recognition, don't you think. As such a female dolphin turns up at a specific time, maybe it really is a sign, that while she exists, we, the people, have hope for good.

However, what do you think happens, when the days passed and we forgot. The winter came back one last time, so biting and terrifying as a last winter can be. It burnt the tree blossom, it drove the little creatures away. And we forgot the dolphins, as if they'd never been. We quickly forgot nature's lessons, we have a short memory, even for what comes to us as an omen and like a warning. Don't you think, girl?

The winter re-entered my heart, if you understand what I want to say.

Look now, orange woman, what a miracle. My words are beginning to come back. I'm talking length and breadth to you, without even realizing it. I thought to this minute that I'd forgotten them. The words. Well if they're something that can't be forgotten. This blocks my intention of turning into a deep sea fish. It makes me unsure and agitated. And I haven't felt spiritual excitement for so long, I think, from my very engendering. That's not good because of my doomed purpose. I begin to think, that purpose doesn't come from us. It's good that you turned up, so I realise this…

When the gun went off, the barrel, shattered from age. But it finished the job. The wolf cub jumped in the air and smacked into the snow, the snowdrift immediately blazed red. He lay with closed eyes, suddenly he looked at me. I froze. His eyes once again smiled, eh God. Thoughtful and calm. If he had been a human, the beast, I'd have said, that he smiled at me in spiritual closeness. After that he turned towards Nebesna's window, he did it with his last gasp and his eyes projected sorrow like a quiet sunset. Why should I lie. It was like this. My heart tensed and I came to, as if waking from a heavy dream. Then Nebesna stood at the door. She was holding little Fina in her arms, wrapped in a blanket. She didn't utter a word. She just looked. And looked. With all seeing eyes. And there was no ending. She asked nothing. I understood from this that she knew everything. About me and Antula. That she'd known everything a long time back.

A pair who hate, love each other. Such a love resembles the moon. Supposedly, bright all over but with a dark stain on its face.

The same night he got on to the train. He wanted a path. A distant traitor's path. If possible to the other end of the earth. To the moon. To Italy at least. He lit both windproof lamps and drove the train. Up to a point the rails could be seen like black snakes with an icy skin, but when it got high up, it hit the snowdrift barrier and the wagons behind him banged into each other. He stayed sitting without a thought in his head, empty like a beaten out flour bag. At some point the snow stopped and the moon gaped. Quiet, just the cold tinkled. Occasionally frozen twigs snapped and that was all. He dozed and jerked awake. He was as numb as a frozen corncob. At last the thought occurred to him to get out to stretch his limbs, he jumped on his stiff legs into the snowdrift and filled his mouth with snow. He dragged himself out, and threw himself to the other side. There the snow barely reached his ankles. He set out with no direction. The moon gaped above, the night was paled out and cutting. The whole forest was weighed down, lumps of snow fell noiselessly from the trees. He warmed up from walking, and a sudden joy gripped him. It was an inexplicable feeling, it crept through his blood and it could have stopped him maybe, because it smouldered like a coal beneath the cinders of his dark despair. So what. What's the big deal. Everybody's alive and kicking. The two of them are alive and kicking. Nebesna gave birth successfully. Everything bad will be forgotten. Everything will all right. That's what happens in life. Sometimes things get messed up, but bit by bit they get sorted out. Just the wolf cub…

And it was then I saw them. The eyes. From every direction towards me – eyes. Like the candle flames in the forest temple. Like burning coals. Like stars, fallen from heaven into the trunks of the trees. Eyes. Ancient, wild, relentless. A circle of eyes around me. I closed mine tight and sank into total darkness.

Now I'll put in some effort. I'll come out of this dream. I'll lift my head and I'll see the dull January morning in the window. Beside me on the pillow the golden threshing floor of Nebesna's hair, her deer-like breath, her arm stretched over the blanket. Nebesna sunk in sleep like in summer hay. Calm, faraway, otherworldly, not mine, even so, Nebesna for me. However it can't be a dream. I look, the eyes shine. I remember the windproof lamps. Just to get to them and I'm safe. Wolves run from fire, I know that. But there's no way to reach the train, however. They ring me. I don't move. And then for the first time I speak the prayer back to front. Drol Dog Ycrem Drol Dog ycrem. I forget normal human speech, I try speaking another, some kind of wolfish or God knows what universal. It's as if I find out my own safe words from the beginning, never spoken until now. Completely new, untouched by any other meaning. It's as if I'm all over Word. For the trees to hear. And the secret evergreens. And the crystal river below in its banks. And the frozen moon in the sky which rings hollow with its broken hoarfrost horn. Ycrem Dog. Soothe my sick soul with your faraway hand. Lord God!

He spoke the prayer and something happened. A heavenly breeze came and like a strong funnel blew the snow from his feet. It revealed the frozen earth beneath, even so support as if from the land of his birth. And he stood over it, and looked from above. He saw: thick white forest, a dark circle in the middle of it, walled by the shining cordon of wolves' eyes. And him at the centre, cursed eternally. Stripped of feeling, fear and courage lost, overcome by indifference of one lost for life. And at this moment, he felt their lights. That's what Nebesna said about the eyes on the iconostasis in the inner room, and their lights. In that moment the wolf eyes looked at him with their lights. Ancient, relentless, penetrative. Penetrating. In them there shone an unerring warning, but most of all saving mercy poured out of their pupils. It was that same impossible, unreachable absolution, which Nebesna's wolf cub had sent him in its last gaze. He suddenly understood. The truth. He learnt the whole naked truth. His legs gave way from the shock and dark despair, his cry of horror echoed, God have mercy! God have mercy on me a sinner! Have mercy on me, a savage! Today I killed a child, An innocent golden eyed child…

I spoke out my guilt aloud. At the same time a whirlwind whipped up my soul, it swept up all my insides and my body turned into an empty dark tunnel.

Light began to flow from somewhere and without meeting any obstacles it poured through the tunnel, filled him from end to end, lifted him again high over the world; He felt ever lighter, ever more blessed, ever more wide open, with wonder he began to understand that really these were his true dimensions; he couldn't grasp himself in a look or in his imagination; but he felt stretched out in blinding light from one end of the world to the other. And although he felt huge in these gigantic dimensions, the man could barely stand the strength of that equally unbearable universal absolution, cruel in its mercy, which a minute earlier he'd seen in the wolf eyes, but now felt it fill him in one with the light…In one more minute all this stopped. The man shrank stripped of strength, he shrank to his human size and stepped stumbling over the ground, and around him the night darkened again.

And then the lights faded, the wolf eyes disappeared. The wolves had gone into the void, just as they had come. Ilya felt, that the times, which had stopped, now began again to flow. And in some of his own undefined time this man remained. Because that was the time, in which he had at last to understand, that evil is not always a wolf.

What do you think, Stavros, were these wolves real or imagined. Eh? Stavros looks at me strangely. What does it matter whether they're real or imagined. There's no difference at all.

Sometimes on rest days, he left Stavros to take over, he climbed on the train and arrived in the village. He stayed to sleep in the station hut. He didn't go out much, but from his spot, he could see Mavrud's big house through the window, and lower down the street he could spot the flaking corner of Marguda's low cottage. Sometimes in the dusky air he could catch Nebesna's washed face, standing at the window in the corridor opposite the inner room. He caught the glow of her hair, which had changed a lot, its shine was dulled, moonlike; he thought he caught her dove grey eyes. Sometimes Nebesna squeezed little Fina to her breasts, wrapped in a blanket. Her face was not seen from here. Ilya had to imagine it. He didn't try to fool himself at all: The window to Nebesna's darkened inner room was brighter than the other windows. In spite of her telling him he could see the little one when he wanted, Ilya couldn't summon the courage to cross the house's threshold; maybe for this reason Nebesna became more distant, and there was no way of changing that.

Sometimes through the window he saw Antula crossing the street in quick steps, in her wake a spray as if of cinnamon powder, her skirts flounced and lifted up a whirlwind of fallen leaves, but her face had gone dark, with thin shadows under her eyes.

In one brightening summer evening the man could not hold out. The moon shone and he sought the shadows of the trees, to get there unseen, he jumped the low hedge and stood in the shadow of the old apple tree. One of the windows was lit and Ilya stared up. Antula sat on a low stool, on the wall above her head a gas lamp burned on a low flame. She was breast feeding the little one and was sunk in reverie. Marguda could not be seen, she'd surely gone to bed. Ilya waited a long time in the shadow. He stared, without moving. Antula was the first to move. She buttoned up her breast, carried the child to the cradle, and carefully laid her down. She paused, turned quickly. She tiptoed to the door, and before the man realised, she was in the yard. Her eyes shone in the moonlight. Like the eyes of a she-wolf, Ilya thought and stepped away awkwardly. Without saying a word, Antula impulsively turned him about and laid her head on his chest. She pulled away immediately, unconsciously picked a green apple from the dark tree, and put it in his hand. She whispered something which anyway he didn't understand, and after that went back inside. He saw her rise on tiptoe, to purse her lips to blow out the flame in the lamp through the opening of an elongated glass.

Antula was extinguished in the night. Ilya set off and squeezed the apple, and it smelled green and bitter. I have this apple still. Believe me if you will. It doesn't rot, its insides don't go bad, it just toughens on the outside and goes brown. Everything in spots like mange, it looks like me. But if you smell it you'll realise how green this apple from Antula is. Sometimes when the moon is high and rounded, it looks like a big green apple; as if Antula has picked it from the old apple tree and thrown it up there. Smell it, I'll allow you to. Why do you think we sense smells? So we know their souls.

The same summer some women arrived in a dilapidated boat, foreigners. From that kind with red hair. You know what I mean.

They poured out on the quay, clucking like short feathered hens, there were giggles and good heavens, the town swallowed its tongue so to say. A woman was in charge of them with turned up lips. She'd drawn her eyebrows with charcoal, her fleshy breasts brought out like a sow on display, all over ribbons and bows. A sow I tell you. Walks with an umbrella. She twirls it and just pokes one of the women, she drives them down the road. She's driving them down the road, it's completely obvious. The women were six or seven, we won't count the madam. Give or take, the number of unmarried men in the town. As I heard they were Italian, I felt weak. I was sick, I'll tell you. Later I learnt that only one was Italian, a Sicilian, swarthy and white toothed like our gypsy, the others – a Balkan mixture. Rumanians, a Serb, one or two Croats, and there was even a Hungarian, white with dark eyebrows and she was silent, however she wound around Whitey like a snake, she sucked him dry. Afterwards he walked about grinning his face off and showing off his love bites. There were all sorts, but to tell you the truth I didn't see the women, I had no interest in the female world. Antula and Nebesna were enough for me and more than enough the two of them. That's it. I saw Whitey's and Stavros's joy and I wasn't too impressed. Women, men, bible stuff… The same as if they gave me the arrival of tinkers or paper collectors, or basket weavers or umbrella menders, or chirping Mesdemoiselles.

However one day, one of the females led me on. I saw her coming from a distance. Bright and in a hurry, hopping, and I think to myself she's one of those. She gambols like a goat on the rocks, she slips in the mud and tumbles. She shrieks, but gets up happy and again is hopping. She arrives out of breath, she brushes her skirts, sprinkles water over me. Flirty. I look at her, she doesn't look like a woman, but she's gone out into the world to sell love. On her face – bright, freckles crawl like little flies. She's applied two kilos of powder, but she can't hide them. And her lips are reddened in the shape of a heart, big lips, greedy as a child's. The men surely eat them in one go. Her eyes, green and narrow like willow leaves. Her hair is pink, cut unladylike over her ears and neck, and it's thin, pathetic like a child. Her body, half womanly, tall and straight like a poplar, dressed in a dark green dress with a yellow strip below and a yellow belt with a dark green silk rose pinned to it. And her décolleté – a sight to see, bare little shoulders, collar bone like a sparrow's, pitiable. Her breasts half bare, rounded and immature. She says something in her language, it's incomprehensible, laughs and glows all over. Didn't I tell you, a genuine child. She latches on to me and looks through half closed eyes, using her various wiles; I think, that I'm single, deserted in the lighthouse. That I haven't tasted female beauty. She takes my hand, licks it with her tongue, and that's as rough as a goat's and she laughs again at the salt. She's beautiful when she laughs. A child. And so I remind her of particulars, because she looks like an early budding wild plum. She comes close, sits on my knees and she wants to do something naughty with her tongue. I sense, she's poured perfume over herself by the handful. The smell of artificial violets is unbearable. Enough to make you vomit. I can't, I say. I'm not a man. At the moment I'm castrated. Don't touch me. And she laughs and teases me with her tongue. She started pulling at my gristle, you'll forgive me, but I'm not a pervert, to be tumbling an adolescent. Powdered, rouged, but still a child.

I pushed her away. She didn't get very angry, just sulked. She sat to one side with her bright apple coloured dress, with two apples in her bodice, and pretended to be cross.

That's when I stood up. I brought out this apple of Antula's, it was still green and sour. Look I say, I've got a green apple and how it smells too. I've got an unripe apple, I don't need you. Then I put some money in her bodice, so that old sow with the lips didn't scold her, and I slapped her bottom. I couldn't hold back, you know. As she jumped over the rocks on the beach and I watched her, I held the apple in my hand and sniffed it from time to time.

Sometimes I dream my life, as if I'm falling in love with it from a distance. As if someone has kindly allowed me to remember that I've been alive. Maybe my inadequate life revives in this way. What do I know of dreams and where they come from. Just as a guy lies down and gets to close his eyes. And sees. His own self, how he walks, how he caresses a woman, how he carries a child on his shoulders. It can be viewed from a distance, as through nine lands into a tenth away from himself. Stavros would say that death was the big sleep. Well maybe it could be a big sleep. Very big, give or take an eternity. In that case a whole eternity, I'll be caressing Antula, and I'll carry my girls on my shoulders. The good thing is that there's nowhere anymore. I lie down at the bottom of eternity and dream my fishy watery sandy dreams, that supposedly I was once a man. But I somehow don't quite believe in such a sweet death. It'll be different I think. But then again why not…maybe it'll be that one from the dilapidated boat. Look now, look! Why didn't I realise earlier! Well it's her, there's no doubt or deceit. Why do you think I remembered all of her and she made such an intriguing impression on me. That one with the apple dress, with freckles which crawled over her face like marsh flies, with a big greedy mouth and naughty tongue. Ey that sort of woman, flighty attitude, who smothered herself with perfume and smelled of artificial violets, fit to make you puke, I want her to appear in front of me sometimes, I want death to be a floozie and nothing more.

Very rarely do I get nightmares. Once or twice a year, but that's enough for me, I'll leave it for another time. One of them is so horrible, I don't even want to tall it. I'm scared of the words with which I have to tell it. If I find the words…if the words aren't scared of the nightmare and voluntarily find me and try humanize it, OK. I'll tell it.

I'm inside war. In its belly. I was in it in 1945, and I know it from the inside. And earlier I was in another, blood and gore. And both World wars. It's war whatever you call it, don't dress it up for me.

I've seen its eviscerated guts. Its gouged eyes. Its maggoty wounds. Its amputated limbs, which move and twitch far from their body. I know war. In it folks are enemies for millions of years all the way from the caves. Through humanity's different periods the man is always a soldier. He shoots arrows, thumps with a mace, stabs his knife, bangs his gun, shouts hurrah and accepts it. Accepts it. He stops feeling, like a real butcher. Without realizing he turns into a butcher of human meat. That's it: neither the blood nor the white bones bother you, nor the gaping skulls. You walk through the killing and kill. Your only human thought is to survive. The others to save themselves as they can. You to stay alive. He's no human who's facing you, but an enemy. It's war. That's your excuse. Disgusting, lowdown, belittling, pathetic and contemptible. Human excuses.

In my nightmare everything happens the other way round. The war is in me. Almost as if I am the war. My body is full of war. There's gun smoke. There are no people. I am all the people. I don't know whether you understand, I am all the human soldiers, both ours and the enemy at the same time. And everyone's striving to survive. As they cut off others' heads, as they rip out others' guts, as they shout Hurrah, in the name of their homelands and their families, in the name of the ants and beetles in these homelands, in the name of the mountains and goats on their ridges, in the name of the cows and cow dung, in the name of the clouds and puddles, in the name of the tadpoles in them… But that's not the nightmare at full throttle. You just wait. Because I'm all the soldiers at the same time, my own and the enemies, I don't have an enemy. I want an enemy. And he appears suddenly in the bright wonderful nightmare. The sun shines, gold and jolly through the nightmare. The multitude has dispersed, to goodness knows where in my belly. The roasting heat, it will melt me. From the sun two women appear at the same time. My mouth dries up. My tongue thickens. The bayonet on my gun glints like a sun beam. I take position. I'm flexed all over in expectation. The women move smoothly, beautiful and threatening. They don't step on the ground, they drift a foot above the ashes. The sun glows behind their backs, I haven't the strength to look into its eye. The women are now close. God. One of them is Antula, all over in red, with a dress of heavy silk and a red scarf, waving around her shoulders and with a white necklace over her breasts. In the sun her hair has become amber, they blow in the sky and the crooked tooth shines in her mouth, she's illuminated all over. The other is Nebesna. She's wrapped in a cloud of fog, only her hair twinkles like straw, higgledy-piggledy over her shoulders, and her eyes – lifted up, so her whites arc. In her arms, as you've guessed, is the wolf cub, ruddy all over in the light. It's so bright and frightening, horror turns my legs to lead. Antula and Nebesna, shoulder to shoulder and both pregnant, with bellies like rounded hills. And both of them smiling lovingly. It's getting more and more dangerous, more and more threatening. They are, what I am not and what I cannot be. I am the war. They are with gilded tummies. They are the enemy.

I point the bayonet. Savagely. First I stab Antula's stomach, I slice it lengthwise. I pull it out bloody and thrust it into Nebesna's stomach. I rip it too, I feel its softness and I get even more savage. They both slide sideways, shoulder to shoulder, head to head. Their hair knits together. From Nebesna's stomach creeps fog, white clouds come out, raindrops run, it's as if I've stabbed the sky.

Antula's stomach, I'm sure you've guessed is full of green apples. Just now picked, they're still with their branches and young leaves. They smell of apple soap and of hay in winter, in which the apples are buried. In just a little while something not so good will happen to me. I begin to feel tender. A man who softens up is no good as a soldier. I knit my brows. I wipe the bayonet in the grass, I squat by the bodies. That's when the wolf stands in front of me. It looks at me. His one eye grows huge, turns into a fiery abyss. It will soon swallow me up. At this moment I wake up.

That's it. Bright, bloody with lots of sun I dream the war inside me. A killer lives in me. Do you understand me…If twice a year I

184

stab the stomachs of Antula and Nebesna, if on top of everything
in reality you've killed a un-grown wolf, which isn't exactly a wolf,
the imaginary creation of a helpless woman, if you've reached out,
mixed up human colours, created a little world war. You get it don't
you? In the end someone whose own sin seems bigger than the sins
of others.

From the notes written with a purple pencil

*My womb…I feel it full of stars moons tangled hay with pale rays
with foggy clouds and the azure there inside there one golden seed in
the eternity of my womb…*(at this point the paper has completely
bleached out) *if you sow in heaven where will it root…*

PART 7

*IN WHICH SOME FOLK SHARE THEIR SOLITUDE,
SO AS TO GIVE THEIR COMMON LONELINESS
ANOTHER NAME, APART FROM THAT, ANTULA'S
SUNRISE WILL GROW AND LIGHT UP LIVES,
NEBESNA WILL DRINK MILK FROM THE CERAMIC CUP
WITH THE GOLDEN SNAKES, MAVRUD WILL TEAR OUT
THE SILVER TONGUE THREE TIMES, AND BENEATH
THE GREEN APPLE SOMEONE WILL COME*

When the cripple arrived, years had passed. From Antula's last impossible glowing dawn, before that, from Little Fina's and Bethlehem's first milk teeth, from the desert wind, which blew red sand from the Sahara, from Nebesna's seizure, before that, from that tar black one horned bull, which flew like a heavenly angel, from all touches, ties, approaches, rejections of human times, from which, electricity flowed invisible, similar to that of the heavens but without thunder. Only electric sparks spilled then and whoever could see them knew that they had seen the clash of those bulls' heads, which stand sentry so times are not lost. At least that's what Nebesna maintained in the throes of her seizures. This stuff with bulls may however have been the consequence of the appearance of the real one horned bull, which came down from heaven in the morning of Antula's glowing dawn and changed the times forever.

The cripple was unusual, not only because of his disability. They hadn't seen such a disability, and what exactly it was, they couldn't say. But they were sure that they hadn't met anyone else, who smiled so unselfconsciously, like a man, who has never met people like him up till now; and if by chance he had met them and noticed them on his way, in the next moment he'd have forgotten them. He doesn't remember because he doesn't need to remember. He doesn't remember because it's not essential to remember. It's essential to forget trivial things. To leave his memory for the other, the more important, is there a Nebesna somewhere round here?

And because he doesn't remember and forgets, after every meeting, he asks the next person, is there a Nebesna somewhere round here? They give him directions, point out the street, the yard, the house and he asks, stammers a-a N-Nebesna?

Look he doesn't forget the name, he repeats and repeats, because it's the essential. It's one. She's one. Nebesna. She's the essence. From when he heard the name, because just by chance someone from her village had mentioned it among other things, which didn't register with him and he heard it in the town, in the market, by the bowls of cabbage and turnips, he heard some villager say Nebesna from our street had a wolf cub and it was as clever as a dog. Nebesna, nebesna, sounds of Heaven, sounds strange to him, he asks about the village, breaks into the conversation and from this moment does not stop repeating to himself to the exhaustion of his thought, this one name is a proclamation, a question, an answer, an assertion, a denial, this name is a secret to be unfolded, and the cripple found the essence of life in unfolding secrets, which hindered him, because they were exactly for that. Otherwise everything would be readymade and then life would be just for living.

…Without even stopping in front of the house, he climbs up several steps, enters through the open front door, and asks Fina, the mother, who stands in his way: Nebesna? She was so surprised that she immediately pointed to the inner room. Silent, she stopped, looking after him. Before he got there, Nebesna opened her door.

A stranger. Cripple. Unseen till now. He stands at the door and looks at the eyes. At all the eyes at the same time. They've turned towards him, they're waiting. He too is a secret. The kind, who's stood at this moment and at all other moments on the threshold of the inner room. Neither stepping in, nor staying outside. Even without taking a step, he's entered Nebesna's inner room with one look and this means forever to him.

The stranger says to himself: whether imagined by someone or I'm dreaming, if they're unreal in this life, in some other they surely exist, both the room and the woman, and the deer footstep behind the plaster of the wall. Nebesna's thoughts cut through the air in this room like blue lightning, so blue and thin, a normal eye couldn't detect them. He even thinks he hears them: the world of the inner room is no smaller than anywhere else. No-one claims the whole world. It's as big as what you can gather from it into yourself. Nebesna thinks too, the world is what you see, what you hear, about what you hear, what you imagine, what you dream, what you gabble, what you think… The world is my freedom to live in the inner room. Freedom is so many things, why shouldn't it be a cell in the insides of the house of my birth. You can people it with whatever, Nebesna would think and he caught on to this. Solitude, which is once shared with the great solitude of the sea, now has a new name, she thought.

The cripple sat on the chair which Nebesna silently offered. He straightened his back against the wall. He sat like this and suddenly excited said, b-b-bricks are breathing, I hear them

Nebesna stays quiet, she doesn't want to say anything. The man doesn't speak any more. They sat, their heads leaning on the wall. Before full darkness fell, the man thought that now he's uncovered the secret.

You're blessed with a different solitude.

He left as he came. He got up in the falling gloom, opened the door. He didn't turn. He went down the steps and disappeared on his way. He'd unfolded the secret, he had to continue to the next. Still somewhere in the world he'd find it. He went an hour, he went two, he sat on a tree beside the road, He lay his head back on the trunk, lifted his eyes and his eyes fixed on the sky. Starry, with bright stars washed in the waters of the moon, alive, hanging over the earth, each quivering with its secret. Infinite sky, unending, alone in itself like every great creation. He looked a long time, as though this was happening the first time, him looking up. And suddenly he saw. And his heart beat ringing in his chest. Heavenly secrets are not for the unfolding. They are, in order for the sky to exist.

He stood up, and set off back. The sky lit him. He entered the village again, stopped under Nebesna's window, looked up. He laid his head on the wall of Mavrud's house. He waited daybreak, wonder of wonders like any dawn. He waited for people of the house to move around the yard, he climbed the steps and reached the threshold of the inner room: the young woman silently met him, I just imagined, you're not possible, for the first time I don't want to uncover a secret, you remain Nebesna forever.

Stay Nebesna forever.

I'm from here. Folk are misled by my name and call me an outsider. Supposedly I'm heavenly. I'm from here. From Fina and Mavrud, from the inner room, from the world with the deer and the blue butterfly, stamped in the clay of one brick, with some grass stalks, printed somewhere there and with little Fina who is growing up so quickly, so she reminds me that time exists even so and it's in the inside: in the inner rooms of our houses, in the hideaway everywhere and most of all in us. Then there's time. Time for everything. Whoever's outside, they must wonder what I do so much in the inner room. Well whatever. I live my life.

In the morning I do my everyday walk along the walls of the room, also from one wall to the opposite wall. One corner to the opposite corner. At least two hours I move through the room, that's my street at the moment. My road. I meet different things on this road.

Some bundle of sunrays pierces me, a cobweb crawls over my face, is the spider spinning, it spins quickly in the corner of my room. The cobweb is pretty much the most accurate way to measure time. If I manage to count its silver circles, I'll count the minutes of my time since I've been there. And children's cries from the street reach me, I meet the echo of the little voices and it's nice. And some song just comes in, then I sit and cry. My face doesn't move, my skin gets goose bumps, and the tears roll out automatically. I always cry more when I listen to a song. I sit down, it comes in through the window, as if it's alive, as the water's alive, which runs from heaven, as the air's alive, as the tree in the yard is alive and it sings me a song, listen. Nebesna, how unique and unrepeatable everything is in me: every word of mine, every cry, every quiver, hear what a holiday I am, Nebesna. I think and I'm sure that God also listens to our human songs, up there and is proud of us. One reason why God loves us more I think. Through the barred outside window I see and hear everything it lets me. The blossoming tree in spring and the fiery sparks of the bees in it, its green crown and fruit in the foliage like little suns, and the dry swish through autumn, the wind's snapping of the twigs in winter. I don't see distinctly, just like before, but my sight is as sufficient as to not forget the world. I'm not alone here. Everybody in the house comes to me. My mother Fina also likes to be silent, I hear the clicking of the knitting needles in her hands, and sometimes see flashes from them. My father Mavrud comes in to sigh a little, he utters one of his proverbs in the end and leaves, and he breathes a last sigh again at the door. Little Fina loves to babble, I don't know who she resembles, in our family there are basically no babbling women. Her words are bright, open, quick, but also a little guilty, whose guilt she's carrying in herself I can't work out. I detect this feeling, but I also detect forgiveness, in whatever Fina says. Guilt and forgiveness. They're there, both of them, in the depth of the words. They're there already and when she grows up and she uses them outside. I know, to the last, her words will be kind and guilty, to the end of her days.

190

That's it. I have a roof, a road, a window, a room. I have close family. As I said, I live life like everybody. But I don't go outside, because I'm missing him, irreparably and forever I miss the wolf cub with the golden eyes. Without him I haven't the courage to move independently through big spaces.

That seizure took place at daybreak. A pale moon was shining and the light woke her. A worry fluttered under her ribs. She straightened up and began drawing back the curtains, but the room revolved, the ceiling and floor smoothly changed places and Nebesna felt someone had hung her head down. All the blood rushed in her throat and she began to suffocate.

And when from the bottom of her eyes fog poured out and entirely darkened her eyes, her final thought was: am I going completely blind or perhaps I'm going there. At this moment two hands took up her relaxed floppy body, and her head lay over someone's crooked arm. She felt them bring a bowl full of milk to her lips. She swallowed a few drops and was surprised how strange its taste was. Sweet and cool, with a bitter aftertaste in its tail. It's nice like this, she tried to articulate slowly, but a gentle womanly hand lay over her lips. She stayed lying on the woman's lap and at the same time felt she was shrinking, until in the end she felt a child. She managed to look sideways; tar black curls framed her white forehead, pearl drops seeped from the roots of her hair, as big as rain drops. The woman whose face remained hidden, wiped her forehead with the end of a wine red dress and spoke in a brittle voice, now you are all my children.

After that Nebesna came to and was surprised that she was lying in her bed. She didn't remember returning to it. She looked around, seeking the presence of the woman at least as a winey shadow. In the room there was nobody. Just some sorrow lit the ceiling with a barely visible glow.

A woman. A woman helped me to come to. Dressed in a wine red dress. She gave me to drink bitter-sweet milk, she poured it into my mouth from a clay cup.

Fina sighed. She said nothing.

Mavrud sighed twice.

Years after that Nebesna tried to remember what exactly the woman had said to her: you are all my children, or all the children are my son. Sometimes it seemed to her that what her strange guest said was neither here nor there; in the next second doubt seized her, she caught a subtle difference and tried to define it as it should be, but didn't succeed…

…On the ICQ, a quick exchange of thought with Anastas: More, yet more, yet more I feel Nebesna. My second name is a refuge and a means of self-knowledge. I have no intention of using it to abscond, quite the reverse. I want to reveal myself to the world, to come out of the convenient anonymity of a woman-sparmannia. I am Nebesna too. Anastas, you to have to get used to this…

Today's Nebesna, with a new-old identity sits and writes in her notebook about Antula with words that contemplate her. That bring her to life. Notes that I'll transcribe into computer text if necessary: Antula is beautiful. Apart from that she's one in the world. Apart from that her world is one. Her small world. Safe, in the corner of eternity. One village. One street. The quietest in the world. Nothing of goodness knows what happens there. From time to time a new life dawns. From time to time some death. Everyone is born in their place. It's a blessing. Because Antula was born here, now she alone is to understand. The birthplace fingered by fate.

Note, underlined twice: a wolf cub under the green apple. So I don't forget the green apple and the wolf cub, which Bethlehem told me about.

A little before that dawn rising, Antula met Mavrud. Mr Mavrud I have to tell you something important. She looked around, put her hand to her mouth, dropped her voice to a whisper: Mr Mavrud, I don't know how to tell you…pass it on to Nebesna… tell her, that the wolf cub…I want to say, Sharko, her wolf cub, last night came into our yard. Released from the void like alive. He stood under the green apple tree in the dark, and his eyes glowed like suns. I felt that he wanted to warn me about something, but he just stood and looked at me…and so much…and so much…in his eyes there was so much…I can't put a name to it with words… Supposedly my most terrifying enemy, but he looked at me this way. My legs gave way…from good. And I remembered how once Sharko told me without words, be ready, Antula, for your glory and honour, be prepared for your own wonderful and unrepeatable. It was the wolf cub, I'm not lying to you. I caught this time too what he wanted to say: I'm not from the devil, nor from God, but I'm from you all. I'm imagined by you all, but especially by Nebesna… It's very strange for me, Mr Mavrud, that without wanting this to happen at all, Nebesna's imaginings began unconsciously to become mine. Tell your daughter all of this and say, if you can, that I…no, better for me alone to say it to her someday. I'm not ready yet.

Mavrud looked silently into her troubled shining eyes. Do you want me to tell you something, Antula? A person sometimes sees or hears, what he wants to hear. But when he hears what he doesn't want to hear, the business might really be serious. It's apparent, that this thing makes you sad and joyful at the same time and I don't understand fully why. I don't even ask you. Because, the wise Solomon said, the heart knows the sorrow of its soul and a stranger does not share its joy.

Antula has felt it, darling girl, she's anticipated. But she hasn't guessed what will befall her.

The cripple is without hands. Up to the wrists. An explosion ripped them off on the battlefield in the last war in 1945. From then up till now, in 1954, he walks in a broad cloak, down to his heels, which he clumsily wraps about his body and keeps his damaged arms underneath. Before the war he painted icons. Before that he'd been an atheist. He told Nebesna the improbable story, and she was, out of everybody, the only one who believed his every word.

Born in a Plovdiv village, the man enjoyed hunting in the valleys, he shot little partridges, wild pheasants and quail. More to show off, as he walked through the village, hung with garlands of birds, swinging head down from his belt. I was like everybody at that time, I was no different from the most brainless peasant. One day I went out early and by lunch even I managed to turn back, richly garlanded with strings of woodcock, but I felt sleepy. I lay down under a tree, the sun warmed me nicely and I fell asleep. I woke up wanting to take a leak. I finished the job under the tree, picked up my gun and got ready to go, and that was when someone put a hand on my shoulder. A man I'd not seen, otherworldly, with shining clothes and a huge shining cross in front, the same as a garden cross spider. I couldn't look him in the face like this, however many times I tried, it blinded me, and I closed my eyes and gave up. He gives me a thick clumsily rolled cigarette, full of some short sharp grass. No longer than the nail of my longest finger. I puff, I give up, the world spins. I throw down the cigarette and stamp on it. It can't be put out. Leave it, he says, it's not going to start a fire. He blinds me with his face and asks: you're a hunter? You shoot birds? Yes, I begin to boast, I'm the best in the village. Up till now I've certainly killed hundreds of birds. As you're so good, can you hit that target? I look in the direction he's pointing. I screw up my eyes: on the very tree, hanging from a low branch is the icon of the Virgin and child and she shines with a rare beauty. Can you hit her from five yards? He's joking on top of everything. I can and more. Let's see, he challenges me and I try to pull the gun off my shoulder. I pull the strap with my hand. Once, ten times, a hundred times. The gun doesn't move off my shoulder. It must have been the one hundred and first time that I got it off. I load it in front of me, lift it to my shoulder, I take aim. Big deal, easy-peasy. I pull the trigger, doesn't move. And I start again: once, ten times, a hundred times…at last I angrily throw the gun down. What's happening now, he asks, easy jobs are not for champions like you. Well whatever, I want to tell you that on this spot you've committed a great sin, insulted Petka…When you realize what your sin is, go to the church and pray to be forgiven. And remember something else, whether you're shooting at an icon or a bird, there's no big difference. Birds are created from heaven, don't you know this, little man. Has it never happened at least once that you envied them, one time at least that you've wanted to be like them…No? Then I leave you in peace. And as he stood in front of me, he put his hand under his cloak, which quivered like melted gold, pressed something and was lifted into the sky. Just as I blinked, he was gone. And there was no icon. I rubbed my eyes and began to wonder whether it had been a dream or whether all this had really happened. I decided it was a dream, but on leaving I saw the cigarette lying in the grass and it was smoking, without setting light to the twigs around it. I remembered the icon and my gun, pointing at it. And I felt something strange. My fingers began to go crooked, they began to move like living roots and fear overcame me, I thought, I'm getting paralysed. This carried on a week. My hands got stiff, the fingers never stopped going crooked, I couldn't hold anything with them. Day after day I thought who is this Petko, whom I've insulted without knowing it. My brain dimmed with the effort to work it out, but I didn't succeed. Petko, Peter, Petyo, Penka, Petra, Petrana…I counted everyone in the village with a similar name, but I couldn't remember insulting any of them ever. One morning I awoke with a clear troubling thought: friend, I said to myself, Saint Petka…back then you relaxed under a tree in the area of Saint Petka, a step from the spring. That's where everything else happened I thought this and in the same second the bell tolled from the Catholic church in the village. It called on me first, before the Orthodox church and I set off for it, and entered like a thief, I felt so uncomfortable. And I saw the same icon, like that on the tree. I stood in front of it. Words didn't come to me, I just held my hands outstretched in front of me and they trembled and twitched. I stood with eyes closed, at some point I felt it: my fingers straightened, warmed up, relaxed at last. Thank you, I said amazed, thank you and forgive me, if you can… There that's how faith found me on its own. From then on my gift emerged, my hands became the strong and joyful hands of an icon painter. I painted icons throughout all of Bulgaria, in all churches, both Orthodox and Catholic. Now I can say with certainty, that the church is not faith, but the faith is a church. Under a roof, within a person, under the open sky, in a tent, in a shed, faith is a temple… After that in the war, a mortar happened to cut off these two hands, She'd forgiven. It happened, but my faith stayed unchallenged. A new force to now and forever.…

Nebesna-Anastasia turns restlessly in bed. Through two streets a cassette player blares out, never mind the late hour: Madonna sings and reverberates through the Stranzha village. Nebesna wakes up. She doesn't remember what has happened, just a sense remains of something green, scented, faraway and wonderful. She turns one more time, moves her head, slips her hand under the pillow. And then touches soap. Wrapped up in lemon paper, Bethlehem's soap smells of the dream she just had, in which a single green apple shines on the top of an old tree. She sleeps again, the cripple appears and that other Nebesna with the half blind glowing eyes, she tries to talk to them, we are 2006 now, how did you appear like this young and pretty and alive, aren't you in your time, where is it, what is the time… They don't answer her at all, they're just silent and their silence fills with light, which makes Nebesna-Anastasia weep from joy, as she sleeps with eyes painfully clenched shut.

From the moment he was mutilated, he's got to know the world, without touching it. He's adapted himself. He hears thoughts. He uncovers secrets. He's developed compensating senses for the handicap. He sees Nebesna's thoughts first of all in the gloom of the room, as they dart like glittering fish in a deep pool. He can't always catch them, they're quick and slippery. Sometimes he grasps them more distinctly, before Nebesna has a chance to voice them. He picks up the essentials, which would help him unravel the young woman's secret. But as soon as he senses them, he hurries to kick them away, to distance them, to forget them. Because by now he doesn't want to uncover Nebesna's secret. This is the first secret in his life, which he doesn't want to touch. Nebesna doesn't detect his confusion. She lets him into her world every time he turns up. This man and the golden eyed wolf cub are the only beings, stopped at her threshold, who need to be more to her, than they seem to be. When the cripple turns up, her door seems to open on its own. And he turns up every month or two. He climbs the steps of Mavrud's house, stops in front of the inner room door, and every time Nebesna feels his presence and opens to him. He stays an hour or two, sometimes he sits till dusk, usually in winter, because winter days are shorter. And then the reverie of shared silence is all the more engaging and it's difficult for him to break away. There are days when they meet and don't speak a word. Not a single one. More and more they complement each other with their silences, that's why the hours he spends far away from this place seem to him like centuries.

Nebesna doesn't understand exactly what is happening. She's met many people of every kind, but such a man has never crossed her path. She suspects that their solitudes have sought each other out, so as to become something else. Shared solitudes, should be still solitude, just greater. However if it is peopled with words like these, which find her, maybe a person's solitude has the potential to be something more, similar to the great solitude of the sea: full of underwater secrets, enlightening like the flexible twisting of the deep sea fish. Because she's confided in the big water, Nebesna has the vague expectation for something to happen now, as back then on the beach, on that crazy and savage winter night with the sleet, with ripping pains low in her stomach and with the only thought that she had to save herself, because no-one else could do it on her behalf: before giving birth, to be born again anew…

Nebesna does not suspect that people outside are beginning to judge them, it's not bad for a couple like them to get together, aren't the pair of them handicapped, poor things, maybe no-one's faces are more beautiful, but both of them disabled, and so they're not going to be fussy. What handicaps, pallid Fina worries, she's overheard what they are saying about them, what defects, but she pretends that she's not understood the gossip and leaves it for time to waft it away, like the wind blowing autumn leaves.

One day when he'd turned up again and it was winter and snow flew about haphazardly. Nebesna lit the stove, sat close to him and says, I'll tell you about Antula's clear dawn, if you want. He didn't. He didn't want Nebesna's past, nor the people on her path before that. He wanted the unsaid, the sharing in silence, he wanted what would be from now on, and only here in the inner room. He forgot that inside was everything. However Nebesna still spoke, I haven't dared mentioning Antula's dawn till now, fear and guilt overcomes me. Sometimes we're guilty only just because someone has moved us into someone else's life, without asking us and this someone else, carries out their life's purpose, as they make us dependent one on the other. The man again refuses to hear about Antula's dawn and Nebesna feels alienated. She stands at the window and stares dimly at the day. She understands that her past is only hers and the man obviously has nothing in common with Antula, but in so far as he has something in common with her, with Nebesna, there's no way to not have something to do with that someone else. It amounts to two secrets in one. Nebesna thinks this, the man catches her thought and is amazed. And she begins to remember her friend's dawn on her own, because she needed to see this dawn, she's always needed to, from the time that morning happened, but she hadn't the courage to imagine it, because in imagination everything for her had to be authentic and unchangeable to the last breath. Nebesna strained her inner sight and beads of sweat broke out on her forehead and dampened the roots of her moonlike hair. She fastened her fingers

198

on the window sill and was on the point of refusing to do it, to stop bringing the memory to life, to stop that dawn from ruling in the sky above Stranzha. But it was time, after so many years, at last she had to look that day in the eye and Nebesna closed her eyelids and stared at the memory with every tremor of her soul.

She's sent Vito the Italian off to work, she's waved to him. She doesn't hurry to get back. Not a leaf quivers in Antula's orchard, nor a hair on Antula's head. The morning has a rasping chill, summery, fresh as a new-born. Right on the ridges of the hills a thin golden line begins to shake. There beyond, invisible to the eye, the dawn is born, which will fill the sky in no more than a quarter of an hour. Above the village which is still asleep, lies the shadow of the mountain. Dew drips from the apple tree, under which Antula, dressed in her scarlet cotton dress stands and greets the day. The tree is full of golden apples, it's time for someone to gather them. At long last the apples are ripe. First I'll meet the sunrise and then I'll stretch my arms into the belly of the tree's bushy crown.

She liked meeting the sunrise, the glowing summer sunrise. She's done it from childhood. At this hour the day is like an innocent child. This world had to made for this, to be exactly thus, and no one to interfere. The light begins to shower golden dust. Antula sees how some dust particles glitter on the nail of her index finger. She laughs quietly. She lifts up on her toes, she picks an apple and sinks her teeth in. The skin breaks juice runs down her chin. Everything is so small around her, but it's only hers. The apple tree, little Bethlehem's clogs with their purple leather straps left by the door, the white washing out in the open, so white, that they're almost blue, the broken bowl, in which a perennial sunflower yellows with a smiling round head, the opposite hill, thick with firs…As her eyes look, this world will still be this world. She looks at it with wide eyes now. The gold on the edge of the mountain visibly grows rosy. The quiet around is still intact, Little Bethlehem and Marguda are sleeping in the house and their breathing is audible from here. It occurs to her that if she sharpens her ears, she'll hear how even little Fina breathes in her sleep at the other end of the street.

Suddenly she sees her. Little Fina. She quietly opens the gate of their yard, and carefully steps out down the street towards Antula. The clip-clop of her wooden clogs scare the birds and they flutter from the tops of the trees. And little Fina is dressed in a red dress, with a white jacket, her hair combed damp, she's let down her plaits and they sparkle in the first rays of the dawn like straws. The ray has found them exactly, in order to emphasise their glory. The little one steps out in a trance, surprised at the world's loneliness. Good morning, she calls out from afar, with half a voice, so as not to awake those sleeping in a good morning. Antula understands, that, just like her, Fina too has felt the tremor of the moment, wanted to share it, and has found someone to share it with. She's coming to wish the morning to be good and to return to sleep. The woman, uncomfortable, blushes to the roots of her hair and begins to open her mouth and try to answer the little one, but in that second, what has to happen happens, according to the meaning of Antula's life.

The pair heard a banging. Somewhere in a side street the cracking and breaking of wooden slats. Something was breaking something with inhuman force. With a bang and smash a board fence was uprooted. The quiet was squeezed by panic. The girl and the woman stayed on their spots, as they watched from a distance. Antula with mouth open in greeting. Fina with a single ray in her hair.

First of all Antula saw it and at first she froze. Because the streets here are steep and Marguda's house is low down, it's as if the bull is descending from heaven. It swoops threateningly. It seems to her that heavy tar black wings are flapping behind its shoulders and it's flying with unearthly speed towards her. On its neck swings a frayed broken rope, white foam drops in gobbets from its nostrils, its only horn also shimmers in the first ray of the day and just this, just this and the world is not the same, threat, fear, numbness,

200

death, which is arriving by the shortest, safest street on this earth, death with a sharpened horn.

Little Fina in her confusion was standing in the middle of the street, and the only thing she could do was to hunch her shoulders and shut her eyes. And she did it. And the red dress flickered in the glorious pupils of the bull. The child opened her eyes, for a second looked at the woman, then closed them again.

There's no time. I have to break out of this paralysis. The bull is death, I, Antula am life. I'm still here and await my blaze of sunrise which cheers only me and that means the only one in the world. Because little Fina shared with me and now the two of us in this world are together forever, I have to move my cemented legs, because the moment approaches, the fateful wings are flapping, and there's nowhere to go, the little one is in its path, no escape, none, I am life for first and last. She tears her feet free at last from the earth, she rushes pell-mell, and now flies alone, flies diagonally, she flaps her red gloves, A little more, God, another second, she knocks over the little girl, and she falls amongst the overgrown nettles and the thunder of heavy hooves, shattered rocks, white gobbets of foam, threat in the bull's left eye, death in the right. But the dawn, Antula finds enough time to ask in amazement and repeat it aloud, and she stretches out her arms. It doesn't even cross her mind to jump to one side. Against the enraged animal with arms open. In protest, for shelter, for a hug, for forgiveness, for mercy. Her scarlet dress flares up, because the sunset at last crawls across the whole sky, Antula's festive radiant dawn, Lord God, have mercy on me, Antula, mercy for my radiant dawn. She hears her last thought and is amazed at how much her inner words resemble Nebesna's spontaneous words, she's always wanted it to be like that, for words to find her like they find Nebesna, in order for her too to be able to express her inner beauty… Pain stabs her, blinding as the dawn. Antula lies beneath the sky and it rocks her. With a final effort the thought passes through her head; maybe people live on this earth to learn about their lives and share their deaths, their unimaginable lives and deaths. There Fina entrusted her life to me and I succeeded, I succeeded.

God, to be thankful to her.

She closes her eyes exhausted.

And the shortest street in the world turns into a long road.

Yes she thanked my Fina for her trust and found the time to forgive herself. There was enough time for the most important thing.

The one time Fina, wife to Mavrud, mother of the first Nebesna. After that little Fina, the granddaughter of the first Fina…It just becomes more confusing. Not just the names, even their words are similar. The more Vassilaki and Bethlehem talk to her, the more unknown her mother seems to her. And in some unusual way yet more close. The little girl with plaits like straw, with one unseeing and one all seeing eye, and both as clear as the sky. The mustard stalk flew a long way and the wind had whistled maliciously through it. The stalk against the blue in her eyes, provoked by another's thought, and because of that it was immutable. The little girl Fina with rapid bright words. The woman Maria, abandoned her birth name, name of a festival. The old woman retrieved her birth name towards the end of her life. A name for love, called Mattei. A name for birth and name for death. The old woman Fina-Maria with nappies and bedsores, with guilty words of kindliness, a mother with a child's expression, rapt at the wonder of the invisible, at the second of quick death: the times have arrived, the human has met herself, become simultaneously a child and an old woman. Young and old Fina, at the same time.

As she remembered all of this, she clutched her throat. Her vocal cords swelled up fit to burst. She held them gently in her hand. The skylarks. Mummy Maria, my throat is full of skylarks. One day she pushed herself into her mother's skirts, it was such a long time ago, but now, in this second, after more than thirty years, she heard the worry in her voice, what's happened? I drank lots of skylark eggs and now they're hatching inside me. Maria looked at her questioningly. Her voice was expressionless, when she said: and now what, one talks to dolphins, the other fills her throat with skylarks, well did I have children as a marvel for all to see! The mother fell silent, continued standing, looking amazed into her little one's eyes. After that suddenly she burst out laughing. Her laughter was all at once expansive, sunny, it gurgled in her throat like white water, it tinkled like silver and couldn't stop for anything in the world. Tears poured from her eyes. Maria wiped them away with the back of her hand, but they rolled and rolled down her sunburnt face, with its high cheekbones. I began to laugh too. The skylarks in my throat fluttered but didn't scare me now. My laughter became more confident, ever more ringing, just like Mummy's. We laughed a long time, the wind blew our tears from our cheeks and they flew around, they fell on the grass and glittered there like dewdrops. Mummy stopped laughing first, she held me round my shoulder in a tight hug, she squeezed me close to her and whispered in my ear, well what would our kids be, what would our kids, mine and Mattei's, be if they weren't a marvel for all to see. And as you've got skylarks in there, sing, my little one, now's your chance. And I straightened up, let my hands down my sides, and as I held my scarlet dress from waving in the wind, I sang all the songs which I knew, and most of all those which I didn't know, but Mummy and Anastas listened to me rapturously for hours. When I finished my throat had softened and the fear had gone somewhere once and for all.

Bethlehem carefully looks into her face. Only you out of all the Finas and Nebesnas don't have blue eyes. You haven't inherited their eyes, you've inherited their look.

She looks at her eyes in the mirror. Her irises are colourful as skylarks' eggs. Slightly narrowed, with visible tension, questing. Open wide, without any defence, observant. Lighthouse keeper, Ilya, her non-existent grandfather, recognised her by her expression, she's sure. Expression in the expression, life in the life. A secret in the secret. Folk who continue in time, unconsciously become one and the same. Our one unsuspected life exists and if we look for it, we'll uncover its full truth. I am Fina-Nebesna-Fina-Nebesna, also I am before them and they are me. But I am also Antula, Bethlehem and Marguda, because a person can continue to harbour in herself not only her nearest blood relations but also those who are fated to share their lives.

My daughter Nebesna didn't speak a word after that July morning. I remember in the summer of 1947, all the sunrises happened to be especially bright and the brightest was Antula's. On one such bright dawn, but a month later, Nebesna spoke at last, came out of shock, she rocked herself in her particular way and began to intone one and the same thing days and nights after that dawn: *I see it tomorrow and yesterday…one and the same thought like a torment like a callousness like a rusty nail driven in the heart what am I Nebesna without Antula…half of night and day one face of the moon the left eye without the right sorrow without joy tears without laughter the shadow without the sun…Half a soul….I'm missing Antula as though they've separated my half she was a woman and because of me the female in me quietens down hides somewhere…and it can't just be without a reason…without Antula, because of Antula, after Antula…At either end of one and the same street of one and the same life of one and the same death we two with Antula are two halves of one common soul between us like a sacrificial lamb little Fina stands but God accepted Antula's self-sacrifice so this sunrise be remembered as long as we live…* That's how my daughter talked in 1947 at the end of the summer, lit up by that dawn and I wrote ungrammatically with a purple pencil, I licked it, I was trying to leave on the page a trace of Nebesna and Antula and also of myself. Well maybe our words will be necessary for somebody in some other times. Does anyone know what exactly is good to bequeath to the lives of folk who are following…

…One day she set out along the traces of the one-time narrow gauge railway. Here the rails cut off, there they appeared through the grass. She jumped from sleeper to sleeper. She listened to the quiet of the forest. Her own breathing had strengthened, she heard it herself, as if she wasn't breathing, but the forest was. Her nostrils opened and closed in a new rhythm. Surely such had been the smells of scorched thyme and damp foliage then too, when Nebesna had travelled on Ilya's train to the sea.

As soon as she crossed the mountain, she sensed the smell of the distant sea. It changed her very breathing. In the air salt crystal sparkled, the smell of iodine and the horizons pulled back. The little town bleached and its houses were clustered, as if the seagulls had gathered to watch the lazy swell of the water, before plunging in.

She asked two or three sun burnt holiday makers about the onetime café, they hesitatingly pointed her towards an old Greek house close to the port. A dark green fig tree in front. The trunk was as twisted as a ship rope. A beat up sign over the shutters: C… FE…Tasty malebi, sherbet, ice lemonade…a padlock on the boarded up door. Her hands in her pockets, clenched into fists. The unlit cigarette in one corner of her mouth, manlike. The tattooed rose on her shoulder twitched, its leaves have surely wilted in the heat. She stood and looked at the sign. Close by the noise of the sea was triumphant, time cannot touch it. Over the sign, salt spray and seagull shit. She dropped the cigarette, stamped it out with her heel, and then bent down to pick it up and when she threw it into the nearby bin, she saw the man. Hunched over the ground, with his onetime café apron round his waist, he looked like a dwarf. With drooping white moustache, and a sad beaklike nose, with wrinkles in his face like a cobweb. He took a large old fashioned key out of his apron pocket and tried to find the padlock. As she watched him it seemed to her that the key was bigger than him. That this was a very special key. The old man at last found the padlock, because he let out a satisfied sigh. And he pulled hard, the door opened creakingly and the man smiled proudly, just as if with ease he'd opened none other than the door of time itself.

Inside it was chilly. The floorboards creaked under their feet. Over the old fashioned counter were shelves, and on them green glass bottles. Onetime lemonade bottles with marbles in their necks, narrow glasses, Greek clay jugs with painted amber grapes and blue peacocks, a ceramic candle stick, with a red candle, half burnt…She sat at the window in front of a narrow wooden table and the old man came straight away. He waved a striped rag once or twice for form's sake, and the ends barely touched the table. To the question as to what the café offered, the man silently pointed to the foot of the counter, there one on top of the other were stacked yellow crates of lemonade and beer. I have Coca-Cola for special guests. In the fridge, he nodded conspiratorially. And there was a fridge. And a television, fixed high up over the counter, the man switched it on for her benefit. She ordered a cold Astika beer. As she waited for him to pour it from the bottle into a tall glass, she looked through the window. She saw the new lighthouse and the old one too, and old man Ilya's cottage, perched on the high cliff. It seemed she could see him too. He sat unmoving, staring at the waves.

The beer was ice cold, the glass immediately sweated. The woman had been limp all over from exhaustion and the heat, now she let herself go completely in the cool of this place. It was if she'd stay here forever, where the world stopped at the threshold of the old Greek house…Allied forces occupied the second most important town…we're showing you the footage from the spot where the action took place early in the morning, today, the seventeenth of July two thousand and…She started to ask for the TV to be switched off, but from the corner of her eye she caught the stare of enormous childish eyes, filling the screen. She turned. Now they were showing an army patrol. Dressed in camouflage. Masks on their faces. Machine guns aimed at something. They were searching a poor neighbourhood. In some faraway town. The camera zoomed

206

in. Searched. Revealed. The skeleton of a house, a white curtain instead of a door, blowing in the wind. A man comes out in front, hands raised. He's dressed head to toe in a long white shirt, a black beard reaches to the middle of his muscular chest. After him a woman. Hands raised. After her two boys, fifteen years old, also with raised hands. In the end the curtain swells and tangles a weak body, which can scarcely stand: trembling like a duck in a net, like a dragonfly in the crusader spider's web, get a move on, move, one soldier makes an eloquent gesture with his machine gun and he emerges, his arms are thin, bare to the elbows, because the wide sleeves of his robe have slipped back – his arms are lifted high. The eyes are frightened to death, the movements are servile, the steps are hurried and obsequious. The shoulders are hunched, the head is sunk into them. That's what little Fina was like, standing in the way of the snorting bull, which flew towards her and flapped its fateful wings. Again the eyes of the child, a look, frightened to death, and at the same time obsequious....

She turned her back. She moved the glass with the undrunk beer further away. She paid and left. In a little while she turned one last time and saw the old man. He was trying to close the door but now the big key couldn't lock it. The Café owner shook his head and waved his arm half-heartedly. He left the door unlocked and walked away. He walked deep in thought, eyes down, turning the key with his index finger, thrust into the big brass key ring...

If now from the nothing or perhaps from the something of beyond, Marguda turns up, I'll ask her to kindle her fire, we'll scatter the embers in a circle and we'll rush into it. To shriek, to forget, to survive the pain, to survive life, which we share on this earth with billions of folk, without even having the chance to look them in the eyes at least once.

Marguda prepared the embers of her fire towards the Feast of the Assumption in August 1947. She pulled by hand cut logs from her yard, dragged them and piled them in the church yard. She stacked them, she calculated. Her black headscarf had slipped low over her eyes.

When the fire flared up, it could be seen from all corners of the village, because the church had been built on the highest point. Frightened folk rushed there, carrying buckets of water to put it out. They saw. Marguda was wading barefoot in the embers. She cried out, waved her arms in black sleeves, as though a human sized raven had landed here from some unknown sky. It waved its wings, rolled its eyes and screamed in a human voice. People let their buckets drop, silently formed a circle round Marguda and her fire. Ah, Ah, Ah, her moans were like the cawing of a bird.

A week before Antula had left this world. Seven days from when Marguda had not been able to shed a tear, nor close her eyes, nor to find her voice. Something urged her to run to Mavrud's house, to enter uninvited and to find little Fina there. She didn't know what exactly she wanted to do with her, but understood, that the urge which cut her off at the legs and stopped the pulse of her heart was not good. Not good at all. This urge was terrifying, it ate at her. Her insides became ever emptier, the restlessness of the feeling melted her flesh and dug out a hole like a dry well. She felt the urge to start raking earth and stones, sand and straw, and whatever else came to hand to fill the hole. To stuff it to the bottom, so it didn't gape so deathly empty. And clear dawns continued to break every day. The world is one and the same from its creation. Nights however are impenetrable. And now the fire lit up in red just such an evening, dark as Marguda's soul. Marguda wove the coals, sparks flew and rose to the sky.

The people continued to be silent, only the little children squealed happily and ran in the circle. Suddenly Marguda stopped. Her arms fell as though broken. She stood amid the still burning embers and clearly didn't know what else to do. She stepped out to leave at last and right in front of her is little Fina, right in front of her. She stands motionless right in front to the very fire,

208

her eyes are shining from the glow of the embers. The damaged eye doesn't move, the lashes on the other one quiver. The woman squats down, catches the child by her shoulders, harshly silent. The little one doesn't move, just her eyes grow even larger. A single tear rolls down Fina's face, and drips into the fire. Marguda manages to hear the quiet hiss of the embers where the tear has fallen. Her hands slip over the sharp shoulder blades, wrapping the narrow little back and it trembles under her hands. The child suddenly leans her head on her shoulder, the woman squints. She lifts one of her hands with effort, lays it on the little one's smooth hair, plaited in two and tries to stroke it, from her wrist down it weighs like a stone and she can't move. She makes an effort and at last her fingers come to life and begin to stroke the hair, the childish sharp shoulders, the back…That's when something happens that no-one expects; however unimaginable, impossible it is, but because it happens before their very eyes, there's nothing left for them but to take in this moment and to remember it, for as long as they live, because in human life such things are not coincidental.

Fina took a step and entered the fire, her bare feet began to stamp alongside Marguda's, ow, ow, ow, their moans reached them, a ladder of fiery sparks rose to the sky and wrapped the little one, so she disappeared from view for a second, ow, ow, ow, it curled, a thin fiery whirlwind, a hot light, a glowing pain in front of the eyes of the whole world; a pain of light, impossible, tender, not childish…

Marguda came to, she stopped amid the embers, after that she grabbed the child in her arms and carried her running out of the fire.

I, Nebesna, share with you, Nebesna: our common fate is the golden eyed wolf cub.

I understood, the world outside is no bigger than the world inside. Time in the inner room is no slower than outside time. The times are not set up as we try to live them. The present is a border as thin as a hair between what's been lived and what's forthcoming, and over this thread we leave our fate to hang like a spider and weave. More and more often I pose the question, as I live between four walls, am I certain who is defending what: does the room guard me or do I defend the inner room from timelessness, if it's one and the other at the same time, that's really my life.

The cripple took off his cloak. He just swept it off with his shoulders and it fell at his feet like a thin shadow. See me, said the man. As much as it is possible for you, see me. His unnatural form. His stumps openly hanging by his sides. Long legs, shortened arms. Out of proportion. Unique. He's stopped seeking secrets. The secret of creation. The secret of life. The secret of death. The secret of the Milky Way and all other roads. Nebesna's secret. To weasel your way into the insides of the secrets is a cursed activity. Surely it's harsh there. As frank as blinding. In the end, unacceptable. One naked secret. The secret is the most solitary thing. See me, the man repeated, here it is my pitiful secret. Share it with me. If you turn away, there's no harm done. Nebesna touches the edges of the stumps with the tips of her fingers. Rough. They are rough, aren't they, the man repeated her thought aloud, you shouldn't be scared. I-I-I can touch you with eyes…My hands, your eyes, says Nebesna, They're enough…her half open eyelids she sees a little white. His sad arms with hanging sleeves. Their handicaps. Because other people are not like this, they pass as handicapped. If it was the other way round? If everyone had arms without hands, eyes half seeing turned towards the sky. And then someone quite by chance born with hands with five fingers on each, would be handicapped. It turns out that the handicap is to be different. Only because I'm different am I defective. It isn't going to happen. I don't accept it. You're beautiful, your hair's like the moon. The light in your eyes, they're b-b-beautiful…I touch your forehead with my fingers. I catch high thoughts, your hair is soft and bashful…your skin exudes r-r-radiance…So touch it, touch it with what's left of your hands. Teach your arms to remember their fingers.

210

The two of them lived together. They were mostly silent, just sometimes they shared their thoughts aloud. Most often they tried to explain what they thought life was. And death. And time. According to the man, who was the son of a farmer, time moves like a grater on a threshing floor, and it grates out lives. Everything stays under the sharp edged flints, it's just as if it's grain, and the straw, the bristles and chaff are people's actions, and also thoughts and feelings of the living, their sins and dreams, their loves and hatreds… The flints of time are sharp, Nebesna, and they have no mercy for anything or anybody. Because only this way, ruthlessly, do we get pure grain for milling. For the milling of following lives…But according to Nebesna, pain was the muscle of life, she's known it a long time, but has shared it with no-one, because she was not sure about one thing. It sometimes seemed to her that it could be the other way round. Life could be the muscle of pain.

The cripple's stumps gradually attained a new sensitivity. Through the ten years living with Nebesna day by day, night by night, his arms remembered their fingers. The memory of his missing members had retained touching, effort, caresses, pains, the tops of brushes, the paint palette… One evening, as they sat in the inner room, each with their silence, the man moaned quietly. A thorn, a thorn's driven into my thumb. I'm picking violets and crocuses in a low bush, for you…After a period of silence he added: the skin on the outside of your breast is as smooth as a violet.

On one autumn day ten years after the start of their living together, uniformed men arrived and gathered the population in the church yard. They'd changed some times, thought up by humans. The new human time had decided that there be no churches. As a lesson, because like stupid children they'd believed in a made up heavenly force, the villagers had to watch what was about to happen in silence. Just this. A young blondish boy from the newcomers went into the church. He was carrying a bucket full of paint. They heard how he ran up the inner stairs, how he whistled a piercing folk song. When he squeezed through the trapdoor, he stood boldly on the roof like a living monument to the new time. He put down the bucket, holding between his feet, put his hands on his waist, and stayed like this, looking, crazily whistling, stayed and didn't take his eyes off the painted bell tower. It was unbelievably beautiful. An unknown Greek had left his hands, his soul over it in its ringing. The bell tower was blue, brighter than the clearest sky. Angels with milky cloaks and trumpets in their hands bring the news. People stood with outstretched hands await, waving palm fronds. The boy stood with his hands at his waist as though struck dumb, they had to shout to him from below. He didn't heart them, he stretched out his hands too. They whistled to him.

He came to. He dipped in the bucket and began to cover the wall of the bell with gloss paint. When he came down he hurried to slip into the jeep in which they'd come. We've closed God down. We've exchanged God. That's what one of the newcomers said, short and crafty, with a handsome face with a grey mousy scar on his right cheek. Grinning ear to ear, he took out a large padlock and locked the church.

The outsiders left and folk dispersed in silence. Only from their yards did they lift their eyes to the bell tower and surreptitiously crossed themselves. The bell turned red, as though they'd tied a red scarf round it, bought in some spring fair. The breeze rocked the bronze clapper and the bell tolled encouragingly.

And with the lightest breeze, the bell rang, and when it blew strongly, and when it swirled up, the ring became so much stronger than ever before. Clear, solemn, mighty unstopping ring. And one day those outsiders came back. They gathered the population in the church yard. This time they drove Marguda, the fire dancer, to the front. They banned her from setting a fire on holy church holidays, they banned church holidays entirely: to dance on the fire is the devil's work. She looked at them gloomily: if you believe in the devil, then you admit there's God. The blondish boy was left to whistle down below. They forced Mavrud to climb up on the roof. You, they said, talked in proverbs, God got you by the balls. Let's see now. If you don't do it, we'll rip out your tongue

Mavrud climbed on the roof. In his hands he was holding a lever. He stood to his whole height and closed his eyes tight. The light caught behind the lids grew pink and suddenly in the light came the vision from the inner room. The woman and the child with tar black curls, the bowl with fresh milk and the snake which sowed drops of poison. And the man with the mousy scar is there. He gave him old rusty shears and told him he'll pull out her silver tongue three times…And Mavrud opened his eyes and said out loud to the bell, forgive me. He pulled out the clapper and he threw it into the back yard of the church.

After that he came down, he bent down into the weeds and vomited, as though he'd drunk too much poisoned rakia.

The cripple touches the edges of his stumps

His touches are gentle, careful. Very slowly drawn out. He strokes, rethinks, establishes in his memory. He sat on the church roof, hugging the bell as much as he could. The sensitivity of his arms has returned sufficiently to feel the softness of the angel feathers beneath the layers of gloss paint. He feels from time to time the prickle of palm leaves. He wipes his new hands, satisfied. He sets to work. The brush falls continually from his arms, the paint spills on the tiles.

With Mavrud they broke the padlock in a dark hour. He shouldered the clapper of the dumbed bell and got it on to the roof. He fastened it anew. The young one set to painting the scene of the entry into Jerusalem. They kept silent. No-one must know. The light of coming dawn was just about adequate. The most important thing is to get the heavenly colour. And also the fiery prayer of the stretched out hands. And more, the joy at the tips of the fingers which are touching heaven…The first day he painted the back of the bell tower, so as not to be seen from the village, the second day he finished the job in front. Just the moment when the sun came out and the golden trumpets in the angels' hands shone. He sat and looked. It didn't look like anything. Not a hint of the previous. Over the blue he'd painted curly clouds, supposed to be angel's faces. In their fists bobbins instead of trumpets. The lifted hands were like logs with fat chopped fingers, looking like dogs' paws. Only the palm fronds were reminiscent of some plant. Mavrud saw the broken expression on the young man's face and patted him on the shoulder: and clouds are heaven, aren't they.

Before slipping down the stairs, the air cannot hold out, they pull the rope and swing it. The bell tolls, waking the village.

They enter straight away, they don't ask permission. One of them in a cloak that drags on the ground. That same one with the little grey scar on his cheek. They find the cripple in the inner room. He's sitting beside Nebesna, the pair are listening to the deer scratching in the wall. They say that it was you. They saw you. He shows them his stumps. With these hands? They leave.

Again they forced Mavrud to take the clapper out of the bell. Again he had to paint over the freshly painted entry of the Messiah into Jerusalem. This time, they spruced up the church with a black tape. They left a heavier padlock and just in case ordered the Polish watchman to guard the church from trespassers.

The pair found another way to reach the bell. From the back a young poplar tree had hung over the apex of the roof, and the church wasn't very tall. The cripple climbed first. He held on to the trunk with amazing strength. Mavrud climbed with more effort. Up there they sat to meet the light, listening to the Pole's snoring. And if he sees us, he won't have seen us. It turns out he's my cousin.

And they set to work. This time the hands of the welcoming folk came out more successfully. The clouds no longer looked like sheep's heads, but as washed out pale nimbus. What icons I painted once, I painted icons for half the churches in Bulgaria, my hands remember each stroke.

Descent was easier for Mavrud. The cripple had problems and as he waited for him, the old man sat on the grass. Someone put his hand on his shoulder. The Pole. I'll still have to see you one day, you do understand. I think tomorrow I'll be ill. Well even yesterday I got ill, that night a breeze blew up towards the river and I caught a chill, and even now I'm lying in bed at home. I'll have to lie down a few more days. When I come back I don't want anyone wandering about. And bread is as important as the church, you agree, don't you.

The bell duly lost its tongue again. The third time, they smothered its walls with dark brown paint. Again they forced Mavrud to pull out the tongue. He took it out with the lever and threw the bronze clapper over his shoulder and turned to see how they lifted it from the ground and loaded it into a jeep. Big deal, we'll make you something more coppery, even silver.

In just a week, white angels again landed on high, and blew their clear trumpets. For the last time, said Mavrud. I know this. We did what we could do. He pulled the rope gently, to hear the ring of the new clapper. He smiled.

He slipped down first. When at long last the cripple got down with his scuffed stumps, a low voice from the shadow of the church rooted them to the spot.

And they didn't come home, the pair of them, not that day, nor that month not that year. The crippled husband of Nebesna didn't return at all.

The night is frosted in the white moonlight. Everybody's asleep. The houses are quiet, it's as if folk have abandoned them. Only the door to Marguda's house creaks open. Ten years after Antula's death, Marguda is still wearing a black scarf. In these years she hasn't shed a tear, her eyes have dried up and the woman is trying to keep her eyelids from blinking, because every blink brings pain to her dried up orbs.

At one of the windows a sleepy Bethlehem stands, she sweeps back her cinnamon coloured hair from her face and jerks her head in puzzlement, what's up with you Grannie, this time in the morning. Marguda signals impatiently for the girl to go back to bed and she obediently retires. The old woman stands still a long time, at last she sighs and turns her head towards the church. The bell tower cannot be seen. The bells clapper was removed a long time ago, but a slight ringing tone is carried from time to time, so quiet, that it's as if it doesn't come from there but from the little bell of a distant snowdrop. Marguda makes a deep sign of the cross towards heaven and sets to work.

Folk are awoken by the sun, they set about their work and they see: in the church yard, embers are glowing, Marguda's shuffling about in it with bare feet. People gather around her.

Marguda doesn't look at them. She just grunts and waves the silvered icon of Saints Constantine and Elena. She lifts it towards heaven. As they're standing there, one by one, they start to enter the fire with her. They take off their shoes and enter. And no fear of the fire, no pain, no blisters on their feet. They step on coals with their heels, they extinguish the heat of the embers, they turn them to cinders. Not for the first time the force grips them en masse. Evil force, you can't slip away from it, it pushes you in the back, drives you into the fire. In the fire they realize that this power that plagues them isn't from God. It can't be from God, this thing, which rips the heart straight out of the chest like a piece of meat. Evil force, evil. However, no-one can stop it, and it shakes folk in recent years at the beginning of June. And this time it's not forgotten them. Help, Lord and you, Saint Constantine, they prayed silently and jumped crazily and grunted, save us from Her…

Marguda settles to one side and rests her chin on her arm folded on her knee. She's sitting and watching how Bethlehem and little Fina, shoulder to shoulder, are walking towards her, from the opposite end of the street and the wind is blowing their hair and they mesh, her granddaughter's brown curls with the golden locks of Mavrud's granddaughter; the pair are laughing, they shout something to her from afar, they glow in the clear morning, as if Antula and Nebesna are walking down the street towards her and as

216

she sees how much they've grown up and are close to each other, her heart relaxes. Grannie, it's so easy, don't make a fire and That one won't have where to push you, he just won't, says Bethlehem, now up close and looking at her with laughing eyes. Marguda feels something pricking her eyes under their lids, scratching, cutting into her eyes, it's unbearable, the pain is like red hot nails and at last bloody tears run down Marguda's dried up face.

Bethlehem looks at her grandmother in wonder, but then realizes, with nimble fingers she lifts the eyelids and with the tip of her warm flexible tongue she licks the eyeballs one after the other, and two black coals fall from her eyelids, and roll on the old woman's lap and she brushes them to the ground.

Anastas, at last I sat in front of the computer.

My heart beat is ringing, as always, when I feel the proximity of writing. Even my teeth chatter from excitement, my eyelids stiffen and my sight mists over, as though a spider has woven its cobweb over my eyes. As if I've set to counting its circles and that the most important thing is not to miss a single circle, nor thread of the silver web of the time which belongs to me and my writing. Do you remember the cave with the crusader spiders and that creature with the blue wings and the crazy yearning in its hairs, eyes full of light. What was it Anastas, I'm even asking now. I continue to see horror, mixed with the blessing of intuition before death, blessing and horror intermixed, just like life and death. I feel the same way about life and death now, sitting in front of the computer. If anyone apart from you understands that, they'll tease me death. Today's writing isn't so old fashioned, it's not about life or death. The sort of writing from which you're left without breath, is thought of as abandoned in time. I don't think that any writing can abandon its time. I'm completely convinced that the times really do pass by, but who can say which time precedes the others. It's true my writing is solitary, without doubt it's the language of all the Finas and Nebesnas, of Antula and Marguda, of Bethlehem and Vassilaki, of Ilya and our crippled grandfather, of our father Mattei and of course above all my own. At times when my writing swings and times rush urgently, it seems to me, that I can express this language and that which is before and after the words and what can normally not be expressed. Then I'm completely sure that my stock of words increases as many times, as there are people, who carry on living.

You know what, something suddenly occurs to me which I'll share: that creature, bright blue, there inside the web of the crusader spider, isn't this our unexpressed. It's got transparent blue wings and blinding eyes. Sometimes it's stunned by its own impulse to free itself from the nets of time and when this happens and freedom beckons, it doesn't know how to use it. In the first moment it even forgets it has wings.

Anastas, I get more and more confused in my desire to tell you about my words. They resemble too much that skylark singing, which stuffed my vocal cords when I was a child, do you remember how they strained and throbbed and it was scary and sweet to feel their pulsing. My whole throat is now full of the unspoken, with what has not been expressed by me or so many others. Such unforeseen turbulence, so much craziness, emptiness, abundance, freedom and fear of freedom, so many human things whirl up in me, until I prepare to sit and at last begin to await the first sentence which will lead out the rest. Our life is not at all without gifts, I now realise, because it's a life within lives, life is so many lives and my words rush to narrate them…

Bethlehem looks long into my eyes, before speaking: Anastasia, you haven't organized this book of yours very much. In fact you don't organize it at all. I mean to say, you leave it to write itself, just as our lives live us, folk on this earth. Although, what do I know about writing books…

I gratefully stick my cheek to the old woman's forehead. After that I look her in the eyes as well, I want to tell you, that I'd like you to call me Nebesna…

~ *EPILOGUE* ~

She left the computer in the inner room, switched on. She quickly put on her old cotton dress. It was a bit awkward on the shoulders, but that didn't bother her. She knew Antula once had a similar one. She wondered how exactly the first Fina, Mavrud's wife, would have defined the colour; she should have named with this word the unusual scarlet, which folds the summer glare into its very core. Poppy. She rummaged in the old chest, took out a white scarf, so wispy, that it felt like cobweb. She covered her hair and went out.

At the end of the street, close to Antula's house, she met Vassilaki. I'm going round from house to house and asking folk if they remember the heavenly letters from the storm. They walked together to the end of the village, not a word between them. And then they saw her.

She's sitting by the fence of the last house, leaning on her stick, her head shaking barely perceptibly. The sun lights her up strangely from four sides, in spite of now setting out westwards and the little old woman shines all over, as if she has no flesh. She looks like a doll with her huge empty eyes, the wrinkles on her face seen from afar are like a delicate embroidery, sewn with gilded thread. Old Vassilaki stops stunned and nudges Nebesna. She finds the strength to cough, open her mouth to speak and suddenly realises that she doesn't know her name. You'll get sunstroke, Hey. The old woman signals them to come closer, she looks Nebesna right in the eye for some time, and she's ready to swear that the old woman's irises are like weakened suns, they resemble two other eyes so much. Close up, the wrinkles around them are suddenly malicious, as if some unknown sadist has carved them, but the eyes are gentle with their quiet and golden and defenceless emptiness, as though they've turned towards other worlds. I've remembered she tells them, I've remembered the heavenly letters.

Vassilaki trembles too, he furtively makes the sign of the cross. Nebesna waits silent. The old woman leans forward, she wipes the dust from her legs and begins to write with the tip of her stick. With an uncertain, trembling hand, she draws two letters: I don't know what they mean, that's how I saw them, that's how I remember them.

Vassilaki supported his chin in his hand, so it didn't jerk too much and said in a reedy, frightened voice: these are Greek letters, they're Alpha and Omega, Nebesna.

The old woman winked at Nebesna surreptitiously with her golden eye. Vassilaki, comically hopping, rushed towards the village and said something to himself in a thin crackling voice. The young woman waited a while, smiling, then walked to the river.

There was no way of escaping the thorn, it drove its point into her bare sole and Nebesna sat on the tuft of bluish grass. She'd had the foresight to bring a needle, she'd stuck it in the lapel of the dress, she sat Turkish style, turned up her foot and she spat on the blackened spot. Just like a surgeon, she'd not forgotten how to extract a thorn.

And this time she consciously lengthened her solitary walk under heat charred sky. However it wasn't as before. She walked slowly, stepped carefully. She felt burdened. Not by the years. Could be from the words, so many words gathered recently. They'd returned into her womb, they were somewhere there, inside. She wouldn't have been surprised if her tummy began to grow just like Bethlehem's.

She sat on the shore and for a long time watched how the river ran. Her gaze ran on with the water, it separated from her eyes and set into the current. It sank to the bottom, it rose to the surface, it took itself to the very mouth and stayed there a long time. There where the fresh and salt water mixed, paths joined up. Close to that place was her birthplace, her father Mattei's house. Dolphins were leaping in the blue space of the sea. Their stomachs looked like snowdrifts, their long beaks dipped and showered streams of shining water, their bodies dived and arced. Still more dolphins were swimming there, a whole school. The she-dolphin with the purple spot also swam up.

Just then the fishing launches turned up. Nebesna tried to come out of her paralysis, to open her mouth and scream, to warn the dolphins, but her voice would not come. One of the launches released the metal floats and they gently rocked their thin nets. The fishermen lined up one next to the other and aimed through the sights of their carbines. But before the first shot could be fired something happened, which drew Nebesna's attention. A white boat appeared, the woman read its blue name Mattei the Dolphin, her heart turned and thumped in her chest. The man in the boat got up and lifted his hands against the guns. At the same time with the first shot his body described a perfect arc and he flew into the boiling abyss amongst the floats.

And there he was Mattei the Dolphin in the bloody wild water. There something unimaginable happened. The dolphins shrieked, their babies squeaked, their powerful bodies thrashed, bashed into the floats, one after the other they went belly up and before sinking, the animals rocked heavily on the surface. The fishermen caught hold of them with hooks: stabbing through the skin, stabbing deep and they lifted the bodies with a crane. Mattei was still alive, he plunged and again came to the top. He found his she-dolphin with the purple spot; only that she was wounded. At that same moment she gave birth, didn't manage to escape and isolate herself. The man tried to protect her wounded belly, he plugged the hook gash under her spot with his hand, his fist sank into her. Surely she'd unhitched herself on her own. The baby dolphins came out of her womb, one after another and squeaked. Mattei left the female and embraced one baby dolphin, and then the water all around began to boil from new firing and Mattei, hugging the little dolphin, began to sink; a delicate skein of foam ringed in red over their bodies. Nebesna's gaze descended under the water before them, to meet them. Bottom feeding fish shot like colourful darts, radiating light through miniature openings. Wondrous plants waved, grains scattered from sand tunnels, dug by the snaky bodies of invisible animals; just their movements, rapid and meandering, lifting sand and folding it, and the feeling of something not right, hidden, unavoidable suddenly overcame Nebesna, in spite of the beauty around her. She was left with less and less air to breathe, in spite of it being just her gaze down there; as she sat up on the bank, her rib cage began to blow up, convulsions jerked her chest muscles and the woman opened her mouth like a fish on dry land. But suddenly she calmed down. It began to occur to her that she was lying in a big warm womb. What's the big deal, she wondered, isn't this the sea, the big water, the womb of life…In the next moment she saw the bodies of her father Mattei and the baby dolphin slip down and lie at the bottom, the little one's beak was pressing against the man's cheek, his hand was clasping the waist of the animal and they stayed like this, lying next to one another in the woman's gaze. How they'd passed through the net, she didn't know. Perhaps the heavy bodies of the dead animals inside had pulled it downwards. It must have been like this because other bodies of dead little dead dolphins were slipping out from below, lying around motionless, with beaks outstretched and eyes open forever. Forever in the sea deep, in the womb of the world. With them was the other new-born. Nebesna's gaze circled the bodies, stopped over the face of Mattei the Dolphin. The unfamiliar face, not seen, but close and familial. And he would be forever with eyes open. What else she tried to tell him, what else really, when the choice is in us from birth.

She almost managed to unglue her eyelids and tried to recover herself, but she didn't succeed. Her heart was thumping in her chest, it lifted her ribs. Her sight was sinking again. The thought crossed her mind: to reach the bottom means acquiring a new painful experience, a lot more real than that which you get ready made on the surface. At that moment she heard the voice of Maria-Fina: your father didn't choose death, quite the other way around; the choice really was in him from birth, and I'm happy that you've understood this business on your own, Nebesna. Weeks after that day, the sea cast up tens of dead dolphins, their bodies lay on the sand, swollen up, with gunshot wounds in their heads or stomachs, and in the middle lay our Dolphin, hugging a little new-born in his arm…That game which you played as children, you and Anastas, you called it freedom, it's lined up against the great un-freedom of our human lives, whether we accept it as a concept, as providence, as fate, as whatever; but against it we still have something, which preserves us from the horror of being helpless, that's our little human choice, my child: ravelled up in the nets of our fate, we can find a gap and slip out for one fateful second; and in that second be free as much as a whole eternity…At the same moment she saw her mother, standing at the highest point of the poppy field, her stomach swelling her thin dress, steep and rounded at the same time, her hair tousled by the wind and her one wide open eye, had taken in the sun's rays, it shone weakly, while her other eye was dark and hidden under its thick butterfly lid. Her mother spoke strangely as never before. She spoke of life and death. Soon I'll give birth to you and Anastas, in Mattei the Dolphin's boat, I'll bear you in a little sea; up to now; till then you cry for your father, because I couldn't do this, neither in the day which you now are dreaming of, nor whenever; you cry from pain and happiness, future girl… The voice was very close, the words were spoken in her very ear and Nebesna straightaway began to cry, the tears poured from under her squeezed eyelids and rolled down her cheeks.

Maria Fina put her hand on her shoulder, look everyone is here, before life and in life, in death and after death, everyone is together. Nebesna wiped her wet face with her hand and looked and was left amazed. White lightning flashed, blinding and soundless. The sky turned white all over, because the lightning stayed there a long time, a lot longer than that split second, when a lightning fork splits the sky and disappears almost simultaneously. She stayed staring at her and felt how she filled her with a feeling of great calm and fulfilment. Under her ribs a precious spot unfurled, from that, bliss suffused every corner of her body, as if a small sun shone inside her and loosed its rays through the vascular branches of her body. In one second she saw: in the heart of the lightning all of them were standing, with lengthened transparent bodies, with silvery faces and phosphorescent craniums. After a while they smoothly descended and stopped on the opposite bank: Mavrud and Fina with the dove grey eyes, their daughter Nebesna and her golden eyed wolf cub, Marguda and Antula, dressed in a mauve dress, in her hands she held a green apple; There too the cripple and Vito the Italian, even the creation of her own imagination, the red fox, squatted by their side and watched motionless; on the opposite bank were Bethlehem and Vassilaki and Anastas has come. They stood one against the others on both banks and watched how the water flowed. This is time, she tried to tell them, water is time. Her voice did not come, but it looked as if they understood her, because suddenly, she heard the words of her grandmother Nebesna: you're mistaken, granddaughter, the two banks of time, just them; think a little and you'll understand, that I'm right. Water comes from the sky and the sky is a river without banks. The others nodded their heads silently, signalling agreement. But even so where does water come from, from below, or from above, isn't it from…from the ice packs on the earth, from…are you just thinking of the water itself, or something else, she posed the next confused question and they started to smile, again everyone was smiling at her.

She tried to imagine a river with no banks. Vertigo made her reel. Suddenly she realised that she'd posed her most naïve question. She smiled in thanks and she woke up with a smile.

On starting, she bent, she picked a round white stone and put it in her pocket. Most unexpectedly she'd thought of the girl in the seaside park, of her glasses and her heavenly look, monstrously magnified by the thick lenses. There was no way that they wouldn't meet again. Their paths had crossed and this was no coincidence. Burgas is not such a big town, scarcely three hundred thousand. She would find her, no way not to find her in one of the kindergartens, or simply on the street, or in the shady path in the park. Probably with that Chrissie, who'd killed the pregnant snail, they'd be friends again. She's surely forgiven or hopefully forgotten: then she'd remembered painfully, she'd learned everything too early – birth, killing, death, grave. She hoped she'd forgotten. And hopefully through those thick lenses she'd know her this time too. Because Nebesna was sure, that on this summer day on the sea shore, the two had looked and fatefully recognised one another.

As she walked to Mavrud's house, and from time to time put her hand in her pocket, and touched the smooth white stone, she suddenly saw: back leaning on the same fence as before, the little old woman was watching her with glowing eyes wide open. Nebesna stopped and shut her eyes, it was as if she was looking into the pupils of the sun or straight into the heart of the lightning.

January 2004

April 2006

Burgas

CONTENTS

PROLOGUE
*In Which All the Heroes in This Novel Speak to the Reader
for the First Time about Themselves, Their Lives, Their Dreams,
Their Disasters, Their Bright Dawns and Their Dark Abysses.* 5

PART 1 13

PART 2
*In Which in One Place it Rains, and in Another Place
Quite Close By, the Sun Shines. There Where It's Damp,
Saturated by the Rain, the World is Intoxicatingly Transformed,
and in the Sunny Place by the Green Bench, Dusky Things Come
to Pass, as a Result of Which One Woman, Fallen into a Trance,
Feels Light Years from her Being.* 51

PART 3
*In Which the Woman with the Rose Tattoo on her Shoulder
Remembers What She Knows about the Inner Room, also about
the Solitude in That Room as a Choice and as a Way to Strengthen
Inner Activity, and Vassilaki and Bethlehem Will Continue with
Their Memories so that Everyone Can Untangle the Ball of their
Shared Life and Stretch the Thread Like a Path Through Time* 71

PART 4
*In Which it Becomes Clear that Time Lives in People, and not
the Other Way Around, at least in the Immediate Moment that
Bethlehem and Her Guest Feel Things in This Way, and more so, in
that the Old Woman Unexpectedly Grows Younger as She Begins
to Talk Like Antula and her Excitement Completely Resembles
that Inner Strengthening Work of the Mind from which are Born*

226

*Imagination, Sudden Long Visions and Strange Experiences,
Created by one Strong Thought, Passing Unstoppably Through
Times, from Person to Person.*..........................123

*A Short Interval in which They'll Gather
the Strength to Continue Further*..........................139

PART 6

*In which Everyone Recounts their Life Through One Another,
and their Memories Catch up with Each Other, add to Each Other
or Right Out Contradict Each Other. But This does not Hinder
the Common Story Line, Because to Return Time is the Same
as to Read the Bible Back to Front, or Mixed up, and Still Get
the Meaning, if the Meaning of Life is Anything Which can be
Got at All.*..........................151

PART 7

*In which Some Folk Share their Solitude, so as to Give Their
Common Loneliness Another Name, Apart from that, Antula's
Sunrise will Grow and Light up Lives, Nebesna will Drink Milk from
the Ceramic Cup with the Golden Snakes, Mavrud will Tear out the
Silver Tongue Three Times, and Beneath the Green Apple Someone
will Come*..........................186

EPILOGUE..........................219

About Christopher Buxton

I am a novelist and translator, happy to acknowledge my passionate affair with Bulgaria, which began with my three year stint as a teacher there from 1977. I have been writing Bulgarian orientated fiction since 2006 and have had 4 works published by Bulgarian publishers. So far, 7 of my books are published in English:

Far from the Danube
Prudence and the Red Baron
Svetlana is Dead
Radoslava and the Viking Prince
The Devil's Notebook
Surge
The Bossy Princess and the Seven Scallywags (for children)

My translation of **Rumen Balabanov**'s *Ragiad* was published by *Dalkey Press* "in *The Best European Fiction 2013* and I edited the English translation of **Alec Popo**v's *Mission London* (*Istros Books*, 2014).

My translation of *East of Eden* by **Izabela Shopova** was published by *Inkwater Press* in 2015. My translation of *Nikola Filipov's "Bulgarians around London: Where they go, what they do and should I care?"* is published by *Author Press* in 2014.

My translation of extracts from **Milen Ruskov**'s masterpiece, *The Heights* was published by *Missing Slate Magazine* and was used in the awards ceremony for **the European Writer of the Year**, which was awarded to Milen this year. I also translated the screen play for the upcoming film production.

I am currently preparing to translate **Alec Popov**'s latest work - the tragi-comic *Palaveevi Sisters*.

I am a regular guest at the **Dimcho Debelyanov Festival** in Koprivchitza, where I read my translations of that poet.

For further detail about me and my work, please log on to **www.christopherbuxton.com**.